*This one's for A.
Always and forever my hero.*

About the Author

Rowan Eira writes romance and fantasy stories with happily ever afters (for characters who deserve such things). Her debut series, **Birch Lake Romance**, features bookish heroines who find love amid the stunning world that only exists in northern Minnesota… and gives a few subtle glimpses into the rich world of her upcoming romantasy series.

When Rowan isn't writing, she's probably out wandering the forests or fighting off mosquitos in the garden, in a desperate attempt to prove that she has a green thumb, after all.

Stay up to date on Rowan's work—and connect with her on social media: https://rowaneira.com/links/

Winter Getaway

A Birch Lake Romance
Book 1

Rowan Eira

Rowanberry Nook, LLC

This book is a work of fiction. Names, characters, places, and incidents are the product of the author's imagination or are used fictitiously. Any resemblance to actual events, locales, or persons, living or dead, is coincidental.

Copyright © 2024 by Rowanberry Nook LLC
Cover image designed by Rowan Eira

The scanning, uploading, and distribution of this book without permission is a theft of the author's intellectual property. If you would like permission to use material from the book (other than for review purposes) please contact the author directly.

Thank you for your support of the author's rights.

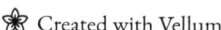 Created with Vellum

Chapter 1

Rune

I used to love Mondays.

To me, they always signified a fresh start. A new opportunity. A wide open door.

Turns out, that only holds true when you're young and naïvely unaware of what it's like to have a job. Specifically: a really shitty job.

Pardon my language, but there's no better way to describe it.

Outside, the skies are a heavy gray. Sleet pelts down, freezing the streets and sidewalks of Chicago as I hurry to work. My shoes aren't meant for this kind of weather. They're already soaking wet. I can't stop shivering, wishing I could walk into one of the warm bakeries along the way. The rich, intoxicating smell of fresh baked pastries and coffee is like a taunt. I'm already late and I don't want to jeopardize whatever end of the year bonus has been set aside for me by my irritating boss Craig. Freaking Craig.

It's only three weeks until Christmas, but here in Chicago there's no real snow to speak of. No Christmas-y holiday vibes. Just those sad piles of dirty slush here and there, the rest of the streets and sidewalks are the same depressing shades of gray and brown that they always are.

You'd think that the office would be a relief after trudging sixteen blocks through the sleet, but no—the glass doors are a facade at best. They're clean, like always, with crisp white lettering that announces this as the business site of Timson & March, a boutique marketing agency. The lobby is clean and minimal, giving off really nice vibes—along with Tim, the friendly receptionist. But the moment I walk upstairs into the offices, the temperature drops to a balmy 62 degrees. Upper management is thrifty like that. To stave off the chill, my coworkers and I thrift our way through winter with second hand sweaters and electric blankets. None of us makes enough to do more than thrift.

Granted, my coworkers—the ones who sit nearest me—are the reason why I don't *hate* hate working at Timson & March. Most of us are a bookish, creative sort. We dreamed of being writers or artists, but settled for writing ad copy and designing website pages.

"Rune, how much do you have left on the Icicle ads?" Meghan's head pops over the gray cubicle wall behind my computer.

I click open the tab and check what I've accomplished so far. Not much. "I'll have it done today."

"You said that yesterday."

"Yes, but today I mean it."

Meghan looks around and drops her voice. "How much farther did you get on your illustrations?"

"I'm almost done with another one," I reply in an equally hushed voice. Ok, so maybe I get paid to design ads, but in my dream life, I create illustrations for fantasy novels. I have been working on some for my favorite fantasy romance series and can't help it if an idea strikes me when I'm sitting in my cubicle. I have to sketch it out. Sometimes, like yesterday, the idea just keeps going. The next thing you know, two hours have gone by and I expanded my color palette and blocked out three separate scenes.

"That's spectacular. When will they be done?"

"When I finish."

"You've been saying that for almost six months," she points out.

This is true. As it turns out, my 40-hour-a-week job is more like 80 hours when you include the amount of time it takes to recover from the stress of it all. Stress that comes in the form of tight deadlines, an ever-changing list of responsibilities, and a salary that doesn't quite cover the monthly bills. Thank goodness the company believes in quarterly bonuses. Even if they only barely make up the gap between what I'm getting paid and what it takes to live in the big city.

"Here, I'll show you a sneak peek." I whip out my phone and show her some of the work-in-progress screenshots that I took. "The nose on the main dude is wrong. I can't figure out how to fix it."

"Whoah, these are actually incredible." She sounds a little surprised. "Are you going to sell them as prints? I would totally buy them. These are way better than the fan art I've seen floating around."

"I want to! I was thinking of finding out if I could get them officially licensed and then open an online shop."

"That would be super cool, maybe even your ticket out of here?"

I shrug one shoulder and slide my phone back into my pocket. It's a nice sentiment, but I'm not sure that hobby illustrators selling fan art typically earn enough to quit their 9 to 5s. At the very best, I'm hoping to earn enough to buy a new car in the next year or so. Or at least get new tires for my existing one, which is in a sad state.

Add that to my long list of things to buy if I save up enough money...and that's a big if.

I moved to Chicago four years ago to be closer to my boyfriend, Sebastian, who's from the area. We made our relationship official during graduation week of college. In a deluge of cheap beer, shots, and nostalgia, we realized we were destined to be together forever.

Sebastian also took a job in Chicago. Albeit at a travel agency, with the unfortunate result that he's very rarely here. When he's traveling, which is most of the time, he's too busy to do more than send a quick text or two. The last time we had sex was nine months ago. It was pretty okay, even if it wasn't mind-blowing. He promised to hang out at Christmas, if he doesn't get booked for a last-minute trip.

Is it the most romantic of relationships? No. But we're doing good. He's making the big bucks to save up for our future. And I should be grateful for his hard work, since obviously I'm not pulling my own weight in that particular area. But—it does get lonely. I have a pretty spectacular roommate, but she's not Sebastian.

"Craig alert," Naomi hisses, two cubicles down.

We all whip back into our chairs and click furiously at our computers. Paul even sets down his coffee so that he can type with both hands.

We've learned the hard way: if you don't look supremely occupied when Craig walks by, bad things happen.

Things like—

"Hey guys, check your emails. I put a quick huddle in five."

There's a collective cringe within the office. Nothing with Craig is ever quick.

I like my job here at Timson & March, I really do. In the four years that I've worked here, I've moved up from design intern to graphic designer. If I can get just one more promotion, I'll get the raise I need to actually start making a dent in those college loans.

I was more confident before Craig signed on. With a strong background in sales, Craig managed to schmooze his way into a director's position. This despite the fact that he clearly lacks some key skills...like how to actually lead a team. Maybe the content department wasn't terribly efficient before Craig came on board, but it's definitely gotten worse with every impulsive, poorly-thought-through decision he makes.

Lately, he's been promising to increase company profit margins through "strategic initiatives." It's vague enough to sound ominous.

Meghan and I have our theories, all of them bad. Paul's theories are even worse. Management promised to announce the changes a month ago, but "logistics" have held things up. It feels like working with a thundercloud over your head. Thank goodness we have our bonuses to look forward to. Not to mention the few days of vacation in the holiday week between Christmas and New Year.

We're silent as we file into the meeting room, where Craig is already chatting with Diana, the stunning blonde junior marketer. Their backs are turned to the rest of us as we huddle into the meeting room. Diana giggles and trails a perfectly manicured finger down Craig's shoulder. A little intimate for the setting, if you ask me.

"Are they sleeping together?" Meghan murmurs.

If they aren't, it certainly looks like they will be soon.

Craig begins with a pep talk (or so he calls it), which is really just an unnecessary recap of insignificant memos.

"As you know, we're restructuring our strategies a bit and establishing new metrics that can be used to gauge the effectiveness of both our internal culture and the effect it has on our overarching growth potential..."

I've already lost interest. Craig rarely has real announcements to deliver to the team. Instead, he likes to read lengthy memos and deliver corporate catchphrases. It's annoying. It eats up the time that could be so much better catching up on emails or drinking coffee or sleeping in.

He's been working here for six months now. It's scary how quickly his madness has become "the new normal" for our office.

A small gasp from Meghan jolts me back into the present moment.

"We've had to rearrange the budget to ensure loyal employees receive the growth opportunities they need to thrive in their career," Craig is saying, "So let's take a moment to congratulate Diana for her outstanding great contributions to the company and well-earned promotion to Senior Project Manager."

A dumfounded silence meets the announcement. Diana is many things, but she is certainly not Senior Project Manager material.

But Craig isn't finished. "To make way for exciting opportunities like this, we have the unfortunate need to dissolve other positions. Those who will be parting ways with the company will have their employment terminated effective immediately, with three weeks of severance and a letter recognizing their contributions to the company."

I bite back an incredulous laugh. Three weeks is nothing. Three weeks takes us to Christmas. I can't believe they're firing one of us so that Diana, of all people, can get a promotion.

"Who's being let go?" Paul asks aloud for all of us.

"Well, not too many, don't worry. Diana and I are working on finalizing the list today. I'll connect with each of you as we decide.

And actually, Rune, would you mind coming into my office for a minute?"

All eyes turn to me.

I think I'm going to be sick. I don't dare look around, don't dare see the expressions on my coworkers' faces. Heat rises to my face as I follow Craig across the hall to his office. He makes a point of sitting behind his huge fake mahogany desk, the leather chair squeaking as he gets comfortable.

"Have a seat, Rune," says Diana from behind me, as if she's the one managing the meeting. I ignore her and remain standing, staring at Craig.

"As you know by now, we're doing a restructuring exercise and reallocating our budget to ensure each of our employees is give the utmost tools to succeed personally and professionally. Unfortunately, this means we must also part ways with some of our valuable talent. Rune, we're grateful for your hard work. We wish that we didn't have to have hard conversations like this. But times are challenging and we're committed to doing what it takes to ensure the company can continue to grow and thrive."

A thousand questions fly through my mind. Who's going to design the ads if I leave? What about letting go of the people who are dragging you down? What about terminating the jobs that are a fucking joke? What about parting ways with the employees who only exist to make the rest of us work harder? (Like Diana, for one.)

I wish I was brave enough to voice these thoughts. But it wouldn't make any different because this is Craig. He hardly listens on a good day.

"If you could just sign this paperwork acknowledging your termination of contract, we can get you your check and you'll be all set to start your next venture," says Diana, smiling like she's doing me a fucking favor.

"That's...it?" My voice trembles. "Why me?"

Craig shakes his head with a smile that's probably meant to be friendly. "Don't look at it as getting fired, Rune. We're simply restructuring the team. New skills can be taught, but what we're really looking at is culture fit."

I am too dumbfounded to say anything more. To do anything besides sign the paper and stand around awkwardly as they print out my final paycheck. Then I get my purse, my coat, and the silly thriving aloe plant that I used to think was a symbol of how I would thrive no matter where I was planted. I think about logging off my computer and shutting it down to save on electricity. Then I see someone else has already done that. Also, they can probably afford to pay for the extra electricity, since they now have my entire salary to work with.

"Well, goodbye," I say to no one. My voice sounds very far away, like my head is underwater. No one seems to know if they should make eye contact or give me space to be miserable.

"We'll keep in touch," Paul says, clearing his throat.

I know I'll only cry if I stay to talk, so I just nod and hurry away.

Even Tim at the front desk merely winces at me as I walk by. I don't know how he knows that I've been canned. Possibly because someone told him. Or maybe because tears are now streaming down my face and I'm leaving the office with a cephalopodic plant cradled in my arms and he's put two and two together.

"Have a nice day," he calls after me, almost desperately. I don't answer. I head out into the downpour of freezing sleet.

Chapter 2

Rune

I don't believe in using liquor to drown my problems, but there is a time and a place for everything. The moment I get back to my apartment, I pour myself a shot glass of whiskey and down it in a single gulp.

"What are you doing home so early?"

I nearly jump out of my skin as my roommate Danielle emerges from her bedroom, still wearing pajamas. "I didn't know you were back."

"The conference ended early, so I came back late last night." She squints and pours herself a cup of coffee from our battered little coffee maker before settling on the oversized armchair. "What's going on? Why are you drinking already and without me?"

"I got fired." Saying the words out loud is unreal.

Danielle's eyes widen. "Because you did something...wrong?" Her voice drops to a whisper on the last word.

I shake my head. "There were a lot of meaningless catchphrases about restructuring and budgets, but—I think it's because I made the wrong enemy." Diana and I have never been friends. I've had to correct her work too many times.

It's a testament to the many stories I've shared over the past two years that Danielle knows exactly what I'm talking about.

"Diana is a bitch," she seethes. "Did they at least give you a good severance?"

"Three weeks. And no quarterly bonus."

"That should be illegal. You could renegotiate. Or threaten a lawsuit for discrimination."

"Discrimination? I don't think…no, it wouldn't get me anywhere." I struggle with confrontation on the best of days. I am definitely not starting now. Is it pathetic that I feel like it's just better to cut my losses than try to fight for a low-paying job with a boss I can't stand?

Danielle looks as if she might argue, but remains silent as we each take another drink.

"This hasn't exactly been your ideal role," she says finally. "Maybe this is an answer to your manifesting."

"What manifesting?"

"You haven't been manifesting?" She looks appalled, in *a no wonder this happened* way.

"Diana's clearly been manifesting. I got fired, she gets a raise." I glower at my empty glass, thinking of her stupid finger trailing down Craig's sleeve. Annoyed, I exchange my glass for a cup of coffee and throw myself down on the lumpy sofa.

"Aren't you glad you don't have to deal with her anymore?" Danielle tries again from a different angle.

"I suppose."

"You can find a better job."

"If there are any."

"You'll have more time to finish those illustrations and start that side gig you've been talking about."

"Yeah, for sure." I force a little smile. I have no energy to be optimistic about this. Not right now.

Listlessly, I pick up my phone. There are a few unanswered texts from my coworkers, all varying degrees of *I can't believe they did this to you* and *Are you ok?* I tap out a couple of responses with smiley faces and thumbs-up emojis.

I should probably text my sister, Jules. I share absolutely everything with her, despite the fact that we live across the country from each other. But she'll probably want me to take action immediately, when all I want to do is disassociate. So…maybe later. I'm about to set my phone back down when I recall Sebastian, my long distance boyfriend.

He might be half a world away, but he's always been someone I can count on when I'm in need. When I broke up with my sophomore year boyfriend, he was the one who sat with me, listened as I sobbed about my broken heart, and then made sure I had a wingman every time I went out.

My spirits perk up just a little as I realize that Sebastian is the one I need to talk to. He'll know what to say to make me feel less awful. I tap out a quick text.

> Me: Are you still in Paris?

Not a minute later, the phone lights up.

> Sebastian: Mais oui, ma cherie. Pourquoi demandez-vous?

. . .

I don't know the first thing about French. I show the phone to Danielle, who snorts and translates it for me.

"You should tell him that *tu* is more appropriate in this scenario. And that he forgot the acute accent over the *e*."

I ignore her and type a response.

> Me: Do you have time for a call?

> Sebastian: It's getting a little late here. What's up?

> Me: I lost my job today.

The speech bubble pops up and disappears several times. I stare at it, oddly comforted. It's nice to know that someone is thinking about me, trying to find the right words to say to make me feel better. Then my screen lights up, revealing a shirtless Sebastian, the light from the phone illuminating his face against a shadowy background. His head is resting against what looks to be a headboard. He looks very mussed. I must have caught him falling asleep. It's nearly one-thirty in the afternoon here, I don't know what time that makes it in Paris.

"Hey, you ok babe?" he asks. There's a muffled something in the background and Sebastian covers the phone for just a moment before reappearing. "Tell me what happened."

I tell him the abbreviated version: the company is making cuts and apparently I was one of them. I don't bother mentioning Diana, since I haven't told him about her before now. Our conversations have been so few and far between lately, it seemed ridiculous to waste time on work drama. Sebastian asks about severance and is appropriately upset at my answer.

"I'm really sorry, Rune. You're talented. You'll manage to find something," he says, which is a nice sentiment.

"When are you coming back?" I ask. "I wish you were here. I always feel better when you're around." Which is true, even if Danielle is silently gagging at me. She does not share my fondness for Sebastian on any level.

An unmistakably feminine voice murmurs something in the background of the call. Danielle must hear it too, because she sits a little more upright and looks intently at my phone. There's a blur next to Sebastian, followed by a slender hand that emerges to rest on his shoulder.

"Is there—is someone there with you?" I glance up at Danielle, whose brows are raised.

Sebastian clears his throat. "Rune, I just wanted to make sure you're doing ok. Is there someone with you right now? Is Danielle there?"

"I—Sebastian, who is in bed with you?"

"Please answer my question," he says, sounding actually irritated. "Is Danielle there?"

"Yes," I say, dazed. All I can do is stare at that hand resting on his bare shoulder.

"Good. Do you need money for a plane ticket to see your parents?"

"What—no. Absolutely not." Like hell would I ever share any of this with my parents. He should know that. "Sebastian, are we —" I really don't know how to voice this question, considering the fact that someone else is currently with him in bed. A woman, from the looks of it. I try again, "—is that?"

"Rune, I'm glad to hear you're doing ok," he cuts me off abruptly. "I'm sorry about your job. Is there anything I can do to help you right now?"

"I just wanted to hear a friendly voice. That's all." My voice quavers a little at the end. I don't know what to do. He's hiding someone. It looks like a woman. Why is he hiding a woman from me?

"It's fine. Let me know if there's anything I can do to support you during this time. Goodnight, Rune." Before I can reply or ask any more questions, the call cuts out. Dazed, I set my phone down on the coffee table.

Danielle looks at me with an expression like she's just seen a ghost. Or a spider.

Her phone buzzes, but she only glances at it for a moment before flipping it face down on the table next to mine. It's something in her expression that makes me lunge forward to flip her phone back up. The notification bubble is still there. A text from Sebastian.

"Think you should read that?" I ask, my voice hoarse.

She shakes her head, but does it anyway.

> Sebastian: Hey, Rune just texted that she lost her job, wanted to make sure you're with her.

Fuming, I text him back on my phone.

> Me: Why didn't you tell me.

> Sebastian: About what?

> Me: The FEMALE in bed with you?

> Sebastian: We haven't seen each other since July. I assumed we were on the same page.

> Me: ASSUMED?

> Sebastian: We can talk about it later. This is obviously not the right time. Don't say anything to my parents. She's a client.

"He's sleeping with someone. In fucking Paris." My hands are shaking so badly that I drop my phone onto the carpeted floor. "What did I forget to manifest here?" I stare at Danielle, waiting for an impossible answer.

She looks like she wants to cry. She isn't great at confrontation, either.

"He's an asshole," she says finally.

Is he? I wonder. *Or am I just naïve?*

I look around, dazed, at this shitty, expensive apartment. I came here to build a life, a future, with Sebastian. Sure, we might have hit a rough patch, but who doesn't after four years? The last time I saw him we went out for pizza. And the time before that we were laying naked together in bed. How was I supposed to know when he stopped looking forward to the next time with me? Has he been sleeping with other people all along? Suddenly, all those weeks where he barely responded to my texts take on an entirely new meaning.

I am a fool and now the walls of my little life are crumbling around me.

"He's a *fucking* idiot and not worth your time," Danielle says, watching me nervously.

"I came here because of him." My voice sounds far away, even to my own ears. "I was working towards a future with him."

And what a shitty future that's turned out to be.

Sebastian has been earning twice as much as me since we graduated. He's traveled the world many times over. And what have I done? I'm jobless, soon-to-be-homeless, and apparently emphatically single. The fact that this apartment alone eats up most of my monthly paycheck, which means I have barely enough for next month. And then what? What if I can't find a job and all that money is just...gone? Four years and absolutely nothing to show for it.

Danielle comes to sit by me on the couch, wrapping her arms around me as tears course silently down my cheeks.

"What can I do to help?" she asks.

I just shake my head. The thought of Sebastian—of us—has kept me motivated all these years. If I only stuck with it long enough, I thought for sure I'd get the ring, the husband, the house.

And now I'm just supposed to...what?

I have less than two months before my money runs out. In that time, I either need to land a new job or find a new place to live. Someplace free.

Do I have parents? Yes. However, I refuse to tell them what's happened, let alone ask them for free room and board while I figure out the next step. I'm sure they care, in their own way. They just have a really weird way of showing their love and concern. It usually looks something like a stinging critique followed by several misguided ideas, each one more irrational than the next.

I could ask my sister Jules...but that, too, reeks of failure. She's off living her own life in Portland right now as an executive assistant. If I can, I want to figure this out on my own. I want to prove to myself that I'm capable of doing what it takes to stay independent.

"I'll find something else," I tell Danielle, rubbing my tear-blurred eyes. "I won't leave you with all the rent."

"That is literally the last thing on my mind. Besides, I've been thinking that with the lease up for renewal next month, maybe it wouldn't be a bad idea to look elsewhere. There are lots of other places out that are in much better condition than this one."

"Like where?" Pretty sure this is one of the cheapest places out there, and it's falling apart.

"Brian's house."

Brian is Danielle's boyfriend, who she's been dating since August. He's a snappy, high-earning entrepreneur who just bought a fancy house a few miles away. With cash, if the man is to be believed.

"Did you talk about it with him?"

She nods, looking a little guilty. "A couple weeks ago. But I didn't want to tell you."

Now I feel even worse. They've been dating for less than a year and are already talking about moving in together. That's one stage Sebastian and I never got to, even after four years together. "Do you want to move in with him?"

"Yes," she admits. "But I won't if it puts you in a bad situation."

I put my coffee down. What I should do is give her my blessing. Smile and congratulate her on having landed a boyfriend who wants to move onto the next step in their relationship. But I can't seem to get the words out. The best I can do is a flat, "That sounds sensible."

"We don't have to. I swear it's not that big of a deal," she says hurriedly, which makes me feel even worse.

"It's fine. I approve. I think–I think I just need some air." I avoid eye contact with my roommate as I gather my phone and keys and put on my coat. "I'll be back in an hour or two. Talk then?"

I barely hear her quiet assent as I close the door behind me and take the three flights of stairs to the street. I feel like a villain. Danielle has a great job and a boyfriend who clearly wants to amp up their relationship. I don't want to hold her back from that. I should have said something nice, something supportive, but all I can think of is that hand on Sebastian's shoulder. I wonder if that girl is pretty, if she speaks French, if she's successful in life. I wonder if she's everything I'm not.

I pick up my pace as the light mist turns into all-out rain, heading towards one of the more upscale neighborhoods, filled with spacious, modern houses and a string of boutique shops. When I first moved to Chicago, I walked this street and dreamed about living in one of the houses—the blue cottage on the corner lot, to be precise. Despite the rain, I pause in front of the fence, looking at the white gazebo. It would be the perfect place to read books. To work on my illustrations. To dream.

I showed it to Sebastian once, hoping that he would also latch onto the vision, but he shrugged and insisted that high-rise apartments are far better. I didn't take it to heart; I was sure he'd come around eventually and set his sights on the blue cottage-style mansion, too.

Joke's on me, I guess.

The icy wind grows stronger and I turn back towards the shops that line the edge of the posh neighborhood. Every store on this block is unique, but there's one in particular that I'm drawn to: a three-story bookstore tucked into a narrow brick building.

The door is painted black with panes of glass on the top half and a fancy brass knob with etched leaves.

There's an ancient-looking carved sign hanging above the door:

Rowanberry Nook: Something for Every Reader

I step inside to warmth and the rich smell of espresso mingling with the iconic scent of book pages. Thousands upon thousands of books, packed into every nook and cranny in this building. It smells like heaven and looks like it, too.

In the front of the store, the shelves are filled with carefully curated limited editions and signed copies; farther back and on the second floor are the regular books, with used volumes taking up the entire third floor.

Usually I go straight upstairs, but today I linger near the front. Window shopping for beautiful books is nearly as cathartic as buying a large stack of gently used novels.

There's always something new to see here, but today is a special treat.

Right in the front, propped on a stand, is a signed, special edition volume of *A Tale of Crimson and Roses*, the first book in a fantasy romance series by R.E. Andersson. It's my absolute favorite book by my absolute favorite author. It also happens to be the book that I've been creating my illustrations for.

I wave my hands around to dry them off before carefully reaching for the book and turning it over reverently in my hands.

"How did you get this?" I ask Brett, the store owner, who has emerged from behind the counter to greet me.

"The author stopped by to drop off a few signed copies. You actually just missed it all."

Of course I did.

"Is R.E. Andersson from the area?"

"No idea." He shrugs. "Seemed a bit nosy to ask."

I leaf through the leather bound copy. The signature is the most precious part—R.E. Andersson actually held this in her hands—but the pages are also filled with delicate floral sketches surrounding each chapter number. There's also a bonus scene at the end featuring the main character and her love interest.

I have to have this.

I know I'm out of a job, but—I glance surreptitiously at the price. $125 isn't that much for a book, is it?

"Do you have any more copies?" I ask.

"Nope. Believe it or not, the other four sold while the author was still here. That's the last one I have."

Well, that decides it. I take the book to the counter, ignoring the little voice in my head that whispers frantically to put it back. Everything else has gone wrong today, I might as well treat myself to one nice thing.

"Off work early?" Brett asks conversationally as he rings up my book.

"Well…I got laid off." It's a testament to the power of shopping therapy that I don't burst into tears. At least I'm not distraught enough to break down completely and say something like— "I also learned my boyfriend has been cheating on me."

I cringe. On his side of the counter, Brett does as well.

"I'm sorry, I didn't mean to tell you that," I say.

"Wow, that really sucks. You, uh, want a coffee on the house?" He motions at the fancy espresso maker behind the counter.

"You don't have to give me a pity gift," I say, but I scan the handwritten menu.

"Please. We humans have to stick up for each other. What d'ya want—latte? Cappuccino?"

"A latte, please. And thanks." I slide onto a stool and stare at the author's signature on the inside cover of my book. It feels like a lifeline. R.E. Andersson is a goddess among authors, which basically makes this a relic. "It's not like the job was even that great, you know?"

"Jobs are jobs. It's nice to make a livable wage, but sometimes the cards don't always give you that."

"I guess."

"I wish I could offer you something, but I'm full staffed already." He hands me a steaming latte. It tastes like heaven after the piss poor coffee I've been drinking at work. Which I will not be drinking anymore.

"That's ok. I haven't really processed any of it yet. I should probably get started doing that." Therapy would not be remiss here, but I no longer have health insurance, so scratch that.

"A mental reset. Nice. You gonna eat, pray, love your way into a better life?"

"I wish," I sigh. My bank account definitely cannot support that kind of an endeavor.

"You got any family or relatives to visit? Sometimes a change of scenery is just what the doctor ordered. Helps you to see outside the box."

I'm about to decry the idea when a sudden thought snags in my mind: I actually do have relatives to visit. My aunt, who lives on a lake up in northern Minnesota. My sister Jules and I used to spend a month there every summer, back before our parents became snobs and cut ties with the rest of the family. Thanks to college and very little PTO, I haven't been to visit in years, despite a standing (and often repeated) invitation.

I whip out my phone and send a text to Aunt Mairi, asking if her favorite niece can come visit for a few days, maybe a week at most. The answer comes back almost immediately.

> Aunt Mairi: Obviously yes. I'm heading down to the Cities tomorrow. Will be back on Friday, but you come whenever. The door will be unlocked.

I blink back the sudden moisture gathering in my eyes. Another lifeline.

"Good news?" Brett says cautiously.

"Eat, pray, love," I reply, trying to sound cheerful. But it comes out a sniffle. "Looks like I landed a visit with my Minnesota aunt. She lives out in nature. Maybe I do need that."

"Atta girl," he says proudly.

I sit for a while chatting with Brett, surrounded by the warm comfort of the bookstore. I don't leave until a crowd of new customers comes in and steals his attention away from me. With a little wave, I leave the coziness of *Rowanberry Nook* behind me.

When I get back to the apartment and update Danielle on the turn of events, she's almost beside herself with relief.

"That book is totally worth the money," she affirms, touching it as reverently as I did. "Also, I talked to Brian when you were gone. He brought up the fact that there's basically a small apartment in the basement of his new house. If you want, you could have that to yourself. We don't have to commit yet, of course, I—I just wanted to let you know that it's an option."

"I like that idea," I say, even though I cringe at becoming such an obvious third wheel. But my real options are pretty limited. "How soon do you want an answer?"

"Go on your trip and maybe we can talk about it when you get back?"

"Ok," I say, relieved. I'm not in any state to make long-term decisions. After a long shower (in which I burst into tears again, recalling the utter embarrassment of being singled out at work as the first to go), I curl up in bed, too worn out to do anything except run my fingers along the cover of my new book. It feels like a good luck charm. Like a token of promise that somehow, somewhere in the future, things will get better.

Chapter 3

Rune

If I keep moving, I won't have time to break down inconsolable. If I keep moving, I'll find the proverbial other door that's supposed to open when the one in front of me closes.

That's what I keep telling myself as I hurry to pack my bags. Warm sweaters and wool socks, here we go.

My weather app tells me that winter in northern Minnesota is drastically different than winter here in Chicago. Like a solid forty degree difference, plus snow. Aunt Mairi insists she has extra snow gear for me to wear, should I want to spend time outside. And I do want that. I need the healing power of Nature in my life.

I have an idyllic idea forming in my mind of what I want this trip to be: quiet and grounding. I want to get back to the basics and shit like that. I've spent too much time in big cities and not enough time doing real human things.

And just in case I have energy to work on some new illustrations, I carefully pack my drawing tablet alongside *Crimson and Roses* in a little plastic bag alongside my travel pillow. Hopefully nothing will jostle it too badly.

Even though Aunt Mairi won't be home for two more days, I decide to make the drive up on Wednesday, departing long before sunrise. I am eager for a change of scenery...and Danielle has been hovering since I told her the news. It's making me feel nervous.

"Be safe, and text me when you get there," Danielle makes me promise, yawning against the early hour. The sun isn't even up yet, but I'd rather drive for a few dark hours in the morning instead of at night.

"You got it, mother hen." As is tradition, I flash my middle finger at her in lieu of a wave. She does the same to me. It feels almost normal.

Despite everything, the tiniest spark of excitement flickers somewhere deep in my soul as I merge onto the interstate. I haven't been outside of Chicago in forever, and I probably do need some perspective to help me through this.

My phone blares loudly through the bluetooth speaker on the seat next to me, providing a background score of nostalgic hits from high school days. Moments like this, it's a little easier to tell myself that that jobs come and go, that relationships aren't meant to last forever. I remind myself that men are stupid and so is Diana. But nothing can keep me from achieving what I want in life... whenever I discover what that is. For the next week, I'm going to put it all in my rearview mirror (figuratively and literally) and move on.

Is my new, positive mindset too good to last?

Of course it is.

Four hours into the drive, somewhere in Wisconsin, the oil light goes on in the dashboard. It's been doing that at increasingly frequent intervals over the past few months, which is probably a bad sign. I pull over at the next gas station to buy a quart of oil to top it off.

Might as well get some food for myself, while I'm at it. I

wander into the little pizza shop attached to the convenience store to get an early lunch. There aren't a lot of people here, excepting a trio of truckers who are loudly debating some conspiracy theory at the only clean table in the place. Guess I'll eat in my car.

While I wait for the tired worker to heat up my personal pan pizza, I pull out my phone and force myself to reply to the texts that have been piling up from my coworkers over the past few days....or ex-coworkers, I suppose.

> Naomi: Girl are you ok?
>
> Paul: Well, shit. Sorry.
>
> Meghan: FUCKING CRAIG
>
> Meghan: I know you're processing and shit but text me please? I'm worried about you.
>
> Paul: Can you text Megs back? She thinks you're dead or dying. Won't listen to reason.
>
> Paul: Srsly. Txt her back. I can't handle her angst.
>
> Paul: Wait, u are ok, right?
>
> Meghan: I'm going to call the police to do a wellness check on you...

The last text from Meghan was from this morning. Knowing her, she would definitely do it, too. My fingers tap out replies like it's my job.

> Reply to Meghan: I'm fine. Going to visit my aunt in Minnesota. Still in shock. Did anyone else get fired after I left?
>
> Reply to Paul: K I texted her. Was just thinking and busy, not dying. Thanks for the concern.
>
> Reply to Naomi: I'm doing ok. Thanks.

There. I feel a little guilty that it's taken me so long to reply, but I haven't exactly been in full possession of my mental faculties for the past couple of days. As I get back into my car, my phone lights up with another text.

> Danielle: Don't forget to watch the weather. Text me when you get there. I miss you already.

I open the weather app and scroll down until I can make sense of the giant cloud of red spanning the entire Midwest.

Well, shit.

Looks like we're in for a very intense winter storm.

The bald tires and worn brakes on my car are awful on a good day. In an actual snowstorm, I'm not sure I can keep the car on the road, let alone moving in the right direction.

But there's nowhere to go except onward. Maybe I can beat the snowstorm. The weather forecasters are rarely accurate, anyway. Grimly, I settle in for the journey. The clouds darken with every passing minute, but for the next three hours, the roads remain clear.

The moment I reach the Minnesota border, however, my luck fails me. Real flurries fall from the sky as I navigate the steep hills of Duluth. It's coming down so fast that I wonder if I should stop at one of the nearby hotels for the night. Probably...but it would take up an outrageous percentage of my final paycheck and I still have to make a payment for my college loans this month. And every month after for the next decade or two.

So I guess that means I keep driving. I'll just drive slow, I promise myself.

Half an hour later, the gentle flurries turn into a whirling white madness that makes it nearly impossible to see anything besides the faint glow of the tail lights of the vehicle in front of me. I count three cars that have gone into the ditch. The minutes creep by, then an hour, then two.

It's dark and the clock reads five; I would be at Aunt Mairi's house already if I was driving at a normal pace. But here I am, creeping along at 45 mph down a two-lane highway. My phone flickers in and out of service, leaving me no way of knowing how close I am to my actual destination.

Despite my maddeningly slow speed, I catch up to another vehicle that's driving along at a literal snail's pace. Unbelievable. I don't dare try to pass them. Not with the way the snow is piling up on this windy little road, and especially not with all these damn turns.

The road veers sharply to the right and the brake lights flash frantically in front of me. I watch, horrified, as the car goes into a dramatic fishtail.

I slam my own brakes on instinct, flipping the steering wheel to try to avoid colliding into the car in front of me as they wildly fluctuate from side to side on the road. I realize too late that I've over-corrected and my car spins sideways. It still won't be enough to avoid hitting the vehicle in front of me.

Shit, shit, shit.

Just before we collide, the car in front magically straightens out.

I do not.

With one last attempt to flip the steering wheel, my car spins in a complete circle and slides off the road into a a steep, snow-filled ditch with a hard stop and a gut-wrenching crunch at the bottom.

The other car vanishes into the snow as it continues on its journey.

Chapter 4
Rune

I'm stuck in a ditch and I might just die here.

It takes me a moment to locate my phone, but I finally find it wedged underneath my backpack.

There's not a single bar of service.

I have no idea where I am or how to get help. I don't dare keep the engine running for more than a minute or two at a time—the snow is so deep here that the carbon monoxide is a risk. Shivering, I pull two wool sweaters out of my bag and put them both on.

There's nothing but darkness and snow outside. Very terrifying, not at all cozy. Before I can talk myself out of it, I force myself to go outside to assess the situation outside and see what my chances are for being rescued.

The deep snow makes it difficult to open my car door, but eventually I manage...and immediately regret every part of this decision as I tumble into waist-deep snow that I have to basically swim through to reach the road. Still no cell service.

The silence is eerie: there's no sound of anything besides my own heavy breathing and the almost audible deluge of thick flakes. There are no cars passing by. No one to help.

What the hell am I supposed to do now?

Last I checked, the temperature was sitting around fifteen degrees. I might not be a native Minnesotan, but I do know that I will freeze if I stay out here in the open for much longer. I'm wearing leggings and low-top boots, neither of which protects me at all from the wind or the deep snow that I have to fight my way back through to get into my car.

I'm well and thoroughly stuck until someone decides to take their chances and stop to help.

The minutes tick by. Then an hour. No one has driven by in the entire time I've been here. I guess I was the last idiot to risk driving these roads. I'm paying for it now.

Maybe if I had matches I could gather sticks from the forest and...I don't know, build a fire?

Too bad I don't have matches.

Trying not to think about the fact that I'm alone and thoroughly lost, I curl up and pull my jacket over me. I have no choice but to wait this out and hope that someone comes to help.

I must fall asleep, because I'm jolted awake by a mittened hand pounding on the driver's side window, two inches from my face.

For a moment, panic takes over and I shriek, slamming down the lock on the door. The windows have frosted, but I can just make out a face with a gray beard on the other side of the frozen window. All my stranger danger instincts scream at me to keep the doors locked until they leave. But that's ridiculous: I'm stuck in a ditch.

I take a deep breath. Undo the lock. The moment I open the door, a blast of icy wind and snow slams into my face.

Standing in the midst of it is an old man, hunched against the wind, an old flannel cap pulled low on his forehead.

"Hey, you alright, kid?"

I force myself to take a deep breath. He's old. Non-threatening. I could outrun him if I had to. Maybe.

"Yeah, I'm stuck," I say, gesturing with my hand. Like it isn't horrifically obvious.

"Sure are. You got help coming, or—?"

"No, I'm really stuck. My phone doesn't have service. I haven't been able to reach anyone." I'm shivering so violently now, it's hard to form the words. "I've been sitting here for hours."

"There's service about a mile down the road, but you probably won't get anyone out here to pull you out until morning. You live around here?"

I shake my head. "Drove in from out of state to visit my aunt."

"Come on. Let's get you someplace warm where you can make your phone calls."

Thank fuck.

I grab my backpack with my toiletries and the bag with my pillow and book. The rest will have to stay in the car. I follow the old guy back through the deep snow. He's surprisingly nimble through the drifts, easily making it to where an expensive-looking SUV sits parked on the side of the road. Its headlights reflect against the bright white flakes of the snowstorm. It's a testament to how worked up I've become over this whole thing that I don't even think twice about getting into a car with a stranger, albeit an aged one, with no working cell phone for backup.

It's blessedly, mind-numbingly warm in his vehicle.

"Thank you so much for stopping," I say, feeling emotional. "I thought I'd have to wait until morning."

He gives a sympathetic grunt. "Not a lot of people out on the roads in this weather."

"I'm glad you were, Mr. —?" I let the question hang.

"Most people just call me Bob," he says.

"Rune," I say in reply. I clench my teeth to keep them from chattering as Bob puts it in gear and slowly wheels onto the snow-covered road. I don't know how he stays on the pavement at all, seeing as how it's all one endless layer of white.

"So you live around here?" I ask, to distract myself from the sudden fear of going into the ditch a second time.

"Eh?"

I repeat the question, only to be met with a "You'll have to speak louder, my hearing's not what it was."

"DO YOU LIVE AROUND HERE?" I half-scream the words, feeling like a fool. Thank goodness he can't see my flaming face.

"Sure do. Born fourteen miles east of here. Used to be a hospital there, back in the day."

"NICE," I shout. "YOU MUST NOT MIND THE COLD?"

He shrugs. "Makes for good ice fishing."

I suppose it does.

Despite the almost painful shivering, a heavy drowsiness starts to pull at me by the time Bob flips on his blinker and turns into a narrow driveway that's lined with thick, snow-clad spruce trees.

I don't know what kind of house I'm expecting to see. A modest mid-century home, perhaps. Or a rustic cabin like Aunt Mairi's. Certainly not the woodland mansion that comes into view as we round a curve in the driveway. My eyes widen at the log-and-stone masterpiece, its massive timbers decked out with a myriad of twinkling white Christmas lights. There's a truck, covered in snow, parked next to an exorbitant garage. That's real luxury, I decide. To have not one but two working vehicles. Vehicles that you can trust to stay on the road and not eat oil like a kid eating candy at a parade.

Bob pulls up to the steps near the front door. "Go on in and get warm. Key should be under the tall planter if the door's not unlocked. I'll be back, just gotta turn on my heat tape."

I don't know what heat tape is, but that's besides the point. I thank Bob profusely and scurry outside with my backpack. Halfway to the house, I realize that I should have asked if he has a wife or anyone else inside that I should be aware of, but he's already backing up. Whatever heat tape is, it must be farther down that lengthy driveway.

Might as well face the awkwardness of walking inside and possibly having to introduce myself to his wife on my own. It's definitely better than staying out in this cold a moment longer. I fumble for a moment at the door—which is locked—but quickly locate the key under the tall planter, just like Bob said.

Stepping into the house is like walking into another tax bracket entirely. The entryway opens to a massive open layout with log beams spanning the tall ceilings, floor-to-ceiling windows at the opposite end, and a stunning stone floor. It's absolutely incredible.

There's a large mirror hanging above the bench in the entryway that captures my attention as I walk past. I wince at my reflection: dark circles sit under my eyes and a chunk of wet hair has escaped the ponytail I put it in this morning. I look like a sad, slightly traumatized, escaped convict. I take a moment to attempt putting myself in order, but it's a lost cause. Good thing I'm not here to impress anyone.

"Hello?" I say awkwardly, announcing myself.

No answer.

"HELLO?" I shout, in case Bob has a wife who is also hard of hearing.

Still no response, so I take off my wet shoes and coat and make my way across the stone floor further into the house. I expect it to be cold because, well, stone, but the floor is warm and feels amazing on my feet.

I could live in a place like this.

Bob left the lights on, revealing a chef's kitchen with dark granite countertops, an island, and stainless-steel appliances. The refrigerator alone probably costs more than my car. Past the kitchen is a living room with an even taller ceiling and a crackling fire in the stone fireplace. I snatch up a fluffy white throw that's set artistically across the back of an armchair and wrap it around my shoulders as I sidle up to the heat of the fireplace. I shove my hands so close that I'm all but touching it. Finally—*finally*—it feels like I might have a chance of getting warm tonight.

The excitement of being in this beautiful house has me feeling more awake. Everything here is so clean. Orderly, like a house that no one actually lives in. Bob must be an absolute neat freak...either that or he's rarely here. I recall that this is a popular area for vacationers looking to escape the city. Maybe Bob's just come up north for a holiday getaway, like I am.

A sudden sharp sound of a door closing upstairs jolts me out of my reflections. Shit, there is someone else in this house. Footsteps softly pad down the stairs and I open my mouth to say something—anything—to let the person know that I'm here, when a man rounds the corner at the bottom of the stairs and stops dead in his tracks.

A man.

Wearing nothing but a towel.

Chapter 5

Rune

For a long moment, the towel-clad man and I stare at each other, our eyes wide and shocked.

Slowly, two things become clear:

One: This may be the most awkward situation I've ever been in. I'm standing in the middle of a complete stranger's house, obviously intruding on the very personal routine of a grown man. One who's alarmingly good looking: dark hair, piercing blue eyes, and a chiseled body that I can see far, far too much of. I'm not even sure where to look with so much skin showing.

Two: Those. Abs.

"I'm sorry, can I help you?" The shock on his face has been replaced with a sort of bewilderment.

"Sorry, I—uh, Bob—I mean—" I stutter over my words and have to start again. "My car went into the ditch and Bob stopped by to help."

The man blinks. "...Bob?"

"Yeah." I realize Bob didn't tell me his last name, but I look around for a picture of him—surely there must be a picture of him in his own house. "Really old guy, hunting cap, nice SUV."

"Right." The man tightens the towel around his waist. He seems at a loss for words as he casts his gaze around the room as if Bob is hiding somewhere in the shadows. "So...pardon me for asking the obvious, but what are you doing in my house?"

It takes far too long for the question to register.

His house. *His*.

"Is this...not Bob's house?" My voice is barely a squeak.

"I'm afraid not."

Well...fuck.

I stare back at the man, silently pleading for him to follow up with something that will calm the onset of panic. Something like, *Just kidding, this is Bob's house*. But he doesn't. He just looks at me, brows knit with confusion and expectation.

"Bob dropped me off in the driveway and told me where the key was. Under the planter." I say the words slowly, pointing towards the back door.

"Did he say why he was dropping you off here?"

"Honestly, I didn't ask him. He knew where the key was. How could he have known that?" I demand. What if this man throws me out into the snow? What if he calls the police? What a nightmare. "I know he's a stranger, but he picked me up on the side of the road when my car went into the ditch. I swear I did say hello when I walked in, but you must not have heard because of the—er, shower." My face heats as my gaze drops from his still wet hair back down to those freaking abs.

The man rubs his forehead with his hand like he has a headache. That makes two of us. "Where is this Bob?"

"He left." I wince at the incredulous look on the man's face. It's so ridiculous. Why did the old man send me into a stranger's house? "He said he was going to turn on...heat tape?" I don't know what that even is.

"Right. Okay." The man gives a short laugh. "I don't have heat tape."

I lift my hands in a defeated shrug. I don't know what else to say besides, "I don't know. I'm so sorry. I'll leave now."

Slowly, regretfully, I unwrap myself from the fuzzy white blanket and put it back on the chair. No amount of explanation can change the fact that I'm currently trespassing like a criminal in a total stranger's luxury home. My face burns with utter humiliation, even though I'm fairly certain that none of this is remotely my fault—apart from putting my car into the ditch. I need to leave before I burst into tears in front of him like an absolute maniac, but also...I really don't want to put my wet shoes back on.

He holds out a hand to prevent me from walking past. "No, no —just wait."

Dear god no, I cannot handle more of this conversation. I stare at my hands, fighting against the moisture that's filling my eyes. It's a losing battle. Several tears escape before I can brush them away with the back of my hand.

I fully expect him to say something cutting, maybe lecture me on the foolishness of blindly trusting a stranger, but all he does is tighten the towel around his waist and extend his hand. "Finn."

"Rune." I shake it, sniffling.

His eyes widen. "Your hand is freezing."

"I've been sitting in the ditch for a while," I explain. Maybe he missed that part of my story.

He gives me an appraising look. "I assume you don't have any alternative means of transportation besides your car, which is currently in the ditch, and...Bob?"

"No," I whisper. A few more tears escape and the embarrassment is becoming intolerable. "I can go," I say. Freezing to death might actually be preferable to this level of humiliation.

Finn heaves a long sigh. "Then you can't leave. The temperature is dropping and the snow is only getting worse. The first course of action is to get you warm—" he hands the blanket back to me "—and then we can figure out the next step. Do you have any dry clothes to change into?"

"Kind of," I hedge. I only really grabbed my toiletries, which was dumb, now that I think about it.

Finn's brows rise as he takes in my soaking wet leggings. "I might have something you can wear while we throw your clothes into the dryer."

The something is a pair of Finn's sweatpants and one of his t-shirts. And maybe I'm overthinking this, but it seems a little intimate to put on a complete stranger's clothes. Especially when said stranger looks like *that*. I don't think any woman would be immune to wearing Finn's clothes.

"Take your time," he says, motioning towards the bathroom. "I'll start the kettle for some hot chocolate."

"Thanks, but dairy and I don't mix," I admit.

That pulls an unexpected smile out of him. "Me either," he says. "I mix it with oat milk."

He shuts the door behind him, and I'm left alone to stare at my reflection in the mirror. I look really, really bad. Worse, somehow, than I did when I first walked into his house.

Even though the bathtub looks like heaven to soak in, I change quickly into Finn's clothes. I have to roll up the legs several times to keep them from dragging on the floor, but my whole body sags with relief at the dry outfit and the heated stone floor beneath my feet.

By the time I return to the kitchen, Finn has two coffee mugs out, both filled with steaming hot chocolate. He's also changed out of his towel and into a pair of gray sweatpants and white t-shirt that does nothing to hide his sculpted body. I'm not sure it's any better than the towel he was wearing.

He glances at me and the barest hint of a spark catches in his blue eyes. "You wear those well."

A laugh escapes me. I look like a child playing dress up. "Thank you for loaning them to me."

"My pleasure. Here's your hot chocolate: completely dairy-free."

"Thank you so much." I wrap both hands immediately around the mug, letting the warmth seep into me.

He takes his own cup and goes to sit at a red armchair in the corner of the room. Awkwardly I follow, taking a seat at the chair just across.

"Do you live around here—sorry, your name again?" Finn asks, sipping on his hot cocoa.

"Rune," I supply. "And no. I was born in Minnesota, but I live in Illinois now."

"Long drive."

"You're telling me."

"So what brings you to Minnesota?"

"We-e-ll," I draw the word out, debating how much is appropriate to share with a complete stranger. It's probably best if I keep things superficial. He probably already thinks of me as an insane woman, there's no need to tell him my job and boy drama. "I came up to visit my aunt. I should probably have stopped in Duluth, but I just thought if I drove slow enough, I could make it."

"Hey, we've all been there," he says. I think he's just being nice until he adds, "I went into the ditch last winter. Hit a patch of black ice up near Ely."

"Did it damage your car?" I ask, remembering the screeching sound my engine made in the ditch.

"Nothing that a little trip to the mechanic couldn't fix." When he sees the look on my face, his slight smile fades. "Sometimes you escape unscathed. Just depends."

I look down at the hot chocolate in my hands. I'm going to have to ask this guy for a favor—to either let me stay the night or drive me to Aunt Mairi's. My face gets preemptively hot as I try to think of the best way to phrase it.

Before I can say anything, we're interrupted by the slam of the back door and a cheery, "Hey there, still up?"

We both turn.

And there's Bob. Covered in snow, tracking all of it into the house as he shuffles into the kitchen and plops a pack of beer and a bag of pretzels on the countertop.

"That's Bob," I mouth to Finn, who looks from me to Bob with a befuddled expression.

Bob doesn't seem to think any of this is strange. He picks up a newspaper from the edge of the counter and examines it before taking further notice of us. "Ah, you two have gotten acquainted. Finn, I've brought you a guest." He winks at me.

What the actual fuck.

"Don't mind your boots." Finn looks pointedly at the trail of snow and water that Bob's currently tracking across the floor.

Bob ignores the comment and pulls out a chair from the kitchen table. He sits down heavily. "Called Len while I was driving," he says conversationally, looking at me.

"Len?" I parrot.

"Owner of Len's Towing. Nice guy, lives in town."

"Can he—?" I don't know how to finish that sentence. Tow my car? Find it?

"Said he's got a few lined up before you. Could be tomorrow afternoon by the time he gets to yours."

Oh no. No, no, no. That is *so* not quick enough.

"Isn't there anyway he could get to it sooner?"

Bob gives a little huff of laughter. "In a rush?"

What a ridiculous question. "Yeah, actually. I'm supposed to be at my aunt's house, so I can—" I catch myself just in time. I was going to say, *so I can wallow in misery*.

Finn quirks a brow, noticing my awkward hesitation.

"It's first come, first serve with Len. Always been that way. He runs a fair business." Bob nods sagely. I don't know whether I should be grateful or annoyed. "Most folks are off the road by now anyway, not a good storm to be driving around in."

"So why are you out and about?" Finn asks.

"Had to bring you two something to drink. Boy, I tell ya, the all-wheel drive on these new vehicles is something."

"Make sure to tell that to Len when he has to pull your ass out of the ditch, too," Finn says dryly.

Bob just huffs another little chuckle and gives a pointed nod at Finn's cup of hot chocolate. "That hot chocolate?"

"It's got oat milk in it," Finn tells him.

Bob looks revolted. "Can't believe you kids drink that. In my day, we had real milk."

"Yeah, yeah. I'm just making sure there's enough real milk left over for old guys like you." The shitty grin Finn gives Bob—along with their easy bantering—suggests that maybe they do know each other. I notice Finn didn't ask Bob what he was doing in his house.

I clear my throat. They both turn to face me. The smile falls off Finn's face. He looks at me like I'm a particularly difficult puzzle that needs to be solved.

"So," I say, "I don't want to intrude, but—"

"You're not intruding." Bob cuts me off with a wave of the hand. "Finn here spends too much time alone. It'll be good for him to have company. Besides, we're not going to leave a kid to freeze in a ditch."

I'm not a child, I want to object, but I don't think that Bob really cares. I turn to Finn for help, unsure of where to go with this. But he's not looking at me anymore. He and Bob are currently immersed in a silent conversation.

"I could probably tow your car out," Finn says finally. "In the morning, or whenever the snow lightens up a bit."

"No, absolutely not. You don't have to—" I begin, but Bob cuts me off with a scoffing sound.

"Finn's got a winch on his truck. Should be able to get a tiny thing like your car out. He'll do a better job than Len, anyway. Just give a call in the morning when you two want to start. I'll swing by to help." He stands up and shuffles his way back across the house.

I just sort of assume that he's going to take off his shoes or coat, maybe tell me that he'll drop me off at a hotel for the night. Instead, I hear the back door open and shut.

Bob is gone. Again.

Chapter 6

Rune

This is getting ridiculous.

I look at Finn in a panic. "He's just going to leave me here?"

Finn gives a wry grin. "Looks that way."

"I can't—he can't—but *why*?" I bury my face in my hands. What did I do to deserve this? All of this—the job, the breakup, the car in the ditch. It's almost like I'm being punished for trying to turn my life around. "I am so sorry to intrude," I start apologizing again.

"This isn't your fault," he sighs heavily.

"I'm the one who drove into the ditch. I shouldn't be here." And here come the tears again. My hands are shaking so badly that I set my mug of hot chocolate down on the end table next to me to avoid spilling it.

"Hey, now," Finn says, his eyes darkening. "We'll figure this out. You said you came to visit an aunt? Have you been able to contact her, let her know you're okay?"

I shrug. "I didn't have cell service to let her know I wasn't.

She's not coming back from the Twin Cities until Friday. She just said to come whenever."

"Does anyone know where you are?"

"My roommate from Chicago knows I'm traveling. I haven't had cell service for hours and then my phone died."

I don't know why he seems so upset by that, but he blows out a long breath and looks out the window. It's totally dark outside but the thick flakes are still visible, still falling.

"Well, Rune, I do have something to apologize for. The man who brought you here is my great-uncle. I didn't know he was up north, he's usually in Iowa this time of year with my cousin."

His great uncle. I guess that's marginally better than being a complete stranger. Very marginally.

"So you do know him," I confirm carefully. "But you didn't think of him when I said the name *Bob* and *an old man*?"

Finn gives a rueful smile. "The family always calls him Uncle Fisher. Honestly, I forgot that he even goes by another name."

"He dropped me off at your house. Without even asking first."

"I'm aware," he replies, amusement lacing his voice.

I don't know why he's being so calm. "You can't possibly be okay with this. I could be a murderer. Or a thief. What if you'd come out of the shower and found your whole place trashed?"

"That would have been unfortunate. Has it been a while since you had something to eat?" Finn calmly breaks into my tirade.

"I'm fine," I lie. I ate two granola bars when I was sitting in the ditch. It's not like I couldn't survive till morning or whenever I'm able to get to Aunt Mairi's house.

"Well I'm hungry, so I hope you don't mind if I whip something up for us," he says smoothly. Noticing my shiver, he adds, "You can drink your hot chocolate by the fireplace. Might help you warm up faster."

I take his advice, if only because it will save me having to make conversation. There is nothing I can think of to say that will make this situation any less awkward.

Thank goodness for the fireplace. At least I can sit here in silence and attribute my burning face to the heat. I pull my phone charger out of my backpack and plug it in. It restarts to a deluge of texts from Danielle.

> Danielle: How's the drive going?
>
> Danielle: Did you make it?
>
> Danielle: Just tried calling. Did your phone die? You ok?
>
> Danielle: Trying not to be paranoid here, but please call me back as soon as you get this. The snowstorm is all over the news, please say you made it safe.

It's nine o'clock now—over five hours since her first text. Guiltily, I try to think of the best way to respond.

> Me: Made it up north. Lost service a while back, just got it now.

She's obviously been watching her phone, because she texts back immediately.

> Danielle: Omg thank god. How's your aunt's house?

I hesitate, fingers dancing just above the screen. This misadventure is something that will likely be great in the retelling…but in the middle of it? Not so much. Still, I don't want to lie to her.

> Me: Not quite there. Had a little bit of car trouble. Some old guy helped me out but it's too snowy to drive any further.

> Danielle: What kind of car trouble…

> Me: The ditch :/

> Danielle: Where the fuck are you, Rune???!!

I send her a dropped pin with my location.

> Me: If you don't hear from me by ten tomorrow morning, this is the last place I was seen.

> Danielle: Tell me you're joking. Who is there? Are you safe?

> Me: Probably safe. I'll text you tomorrow.

> Danielle: Please don't die.

I wince a little at the flood of angry and shocked emojis that follow in a subsequent text, along with a few snowflakes and police cars thrown in. It's enough to make me paranoid about my safety. Maybe I should text Aunt Mairi, too? But no, I don't want to bother her. I'll be fine.

Still, Danielle's warning sticks with me uncomfortably. Maybe I should be more concerned, sitting in a house alone with a complete stranger. It's just hard to summon the right amount of fear when I think about how much better this is than sitting in that ditch. *That's how they get you*, says the voice that's read about too many serial killers.

Except Finn didn't look like he was in on the plot at all. He looked like he'd just walked in on a stranger in his house and was trying his very best to figure out what to do about it.

He also looks like a Greek god, which is a very dangerous thing to notice. I'm on this trip to ground myself in reality, to discover what's next in life. I can't allow myself to be swept up into a distracting crush with a stranger.

"I have some food ready, if you want any," Finn calls from the kitchen, breaking into my thoughts.

What I want is to fall asleep for a year. To wake up and realize this has all been a nightmare. But I'm also starving. I force myself to get up and face Finn as if I'm a normal, mentally stable house guest and not the slightly hysterical intruder that I actually am.

What would a normal person say, I wonder, surveying the very attractive charcuterie board that Finn has curated on the island countertop. It's filled with multiple varieties of cheese, cold cuts, vegetables, crackers, hummus, and a few grapes.

"Impressive," I say.

"Dig in." He picks out a slice of cucumber for himself. "Would you like something else to drink? Uncle Fisher—uh, Bob—

brought some beer." He winces at the cheap six pack. "Otherwise I have water or some Chianti?"

"Chianti sounds nice." Because it's classy and alcoholic.

He pours a glass for each of us. "Cheers."

We tap wine glasses politely. Can I down a glass of wine in two seconds? Yes. But I force myself to drink slowly, sipping like the kind of fancy person I imagine Finn must be used to hanging out with, watching as Finn makes little sandwiches out of the crackers, cheese, and meat. I try to chew quietly in the silence that stretches between us. It's difficult. I really want to shove it all into my mouth. I'm so freaking hungry.

"So," Finn says after a while. "I think it's safe to say that Uncle Fisher has abandoned us and the snowstorm is likely to last till tomorrow morning."

"Yes," I reply.

"In which case, I suppose I'll have to extend an invitation for you to stay the night."

I flinch at his words. He's been forced into this situation, and even though I know this wasn't my intention, I feel horrible. "I really am sorry. I would never have—"

"You're lucky that Uncle Fisher brought you here," Finn says firmly, cutting me off. "It could have been hours before anyone else found you. There's no need to apologize for anything."

With nothing else to say, I make my formal acceptance speech. "Thank you for the offer. I accept."

We go back to eating, easily polishing off all but a few crumbles of goat cheese. By the time the food is gone, I'm half asleep and can't focus on a single thing that Finn's saying. I can't stop the yawn that threatens to crack my jaw.

"So, sleeping arrangements," he says. "I have a second bedroom, but the bed is awful. You can definitely sleep in my room and I'll take the couch, if that works?"

That jolts me awake. Wearing Finn's clothes is already making me feel things I should not be feeling. I don't think I can handle sleeping in his bed, too. "Actually, I wouldn't mind sleeping on the couch," I say. "It would be nice to sleep near the fireplace."

"That works, too."

He pulls together a pile of blankets and starts making a bed on the couch. A patchwork quilt folded in half as a base, followed by a fluffy down comforter and another soft throw folded at one end.

"Just in case," he tells me.

I have my own pillow, but he brings another one, anyway. It looks more comfortable than my own bed at home.

Finn gives a satisfied nod at his work. "Just like when I was a kid staying at my grandma's house." There's a light in his eyes, the hint of a smile that causes a weird little flutter in my stomach. *Stop it, Rune.*

"And you sure you're ok with me being here tonight?" I confirm.

"I'm not worried that you're a serial killer, Rune," he teases.

"Okay, but you don't think it's ridiculous or indecent?" I ask, trying—and failing—to stifle a yawn. Those aren't the words I mean to say, but my exhausted brain can't think of the right ones.

His eyes meet mine, looking somewhat abashed. "I'm sorry, I didn't think to ask whether you were comfortable staying the night here. If you're not, I can call a neighbor, and—"

"No, no, that's fine." If I'm worried about bothering the man, forcing him to find me new accommodations seems like it would be worse. "I just feel bad about the inconvenience of it all. And—and didn't know if you had a girlfriend or something who might be upset." After I say that last bit, I realize it sounds like I'm fishing for information, which I'm not. Much.

If he notices, he doesn't let on. "No one will be offended that

I'm playing the hero. Just try to refrain from murdering or thieving and I'm sure it will be fine."

Spoken with the true confidence of a man who believes he has nothing to fear.

I settle into the makeshift bed. It will be fine, I tell myself.

It's only for one night.

Chapter 7

Finn

I don't know whether to laugh or curse at Uncle Fisher and his rationale. Who finds a young woman in a ditch and drops her off, unannounced, at a guy's house? The girl is lucky that I'm not some creep. This could be a really bad situation—a deadly one. As it is, she's safe here, looking disconcertingly adorable in my clothes, which are a few sizes too big.

I don't know what it says about me that my first thought upon walking into the living room and seeing a total stranger standing there was not, *What the hell are you doing in my house?* For the first few shocked moments, all I could think about was how pale and scared she looked. Like a baby deer who's been discovered and doesn't know if it should run or remain still. It unsettled something deep within me.

I'm still unsettled.

I should have asked what kind of food she liked for breakfast. Or told her to help herself to the food in the refrigerator if she wakes up hungry.

This is why I don't like having house guests, especially ones that stay the night. It requires planning. Consideration. And far more emotional energy than I care to expend.

Definitely not the night I was hoping for.

All I wanted after a long day of work was to shower and shut off my brain with some cold pizza and beer. Instead, I'm tiptoeing around my own house, cleaning up the remnants of our late-night snack. Rune is asleep on the couch, hugging that fluffy white blanket like it's a stuffed animal. Even asleep, she looks exhausted and nervous. I hope she didn't catch a chill, sitting in the ditch for so long. As soon as the thought registers, I push it away with a shudder. I'm not a worrying type of guy. And I don't intend to start now, just because my routine has been shaken up by an intruder, no matter how captivating those big eyes are.

I check the locks one more time, making sure to bring the spare key inside. I don't need any other uninvited guests coming in when Rune's sleeping alone in the living room.

Since there's very little chance of me falling asleep at the moment, I go into my office upstairs and turn on the desk lamp.

I've had a difficult time writing these past months, with almost all of my efforts turning out flat and uninspired. I've rewritten scenes from my novel repeatedly, with no success.

Tonight, I'm gong to try something different. Flipping open my laptop, I open a blank document, my fingers flying as I try to capture the vibrant image in my mind that Rune's unexpected appearance conjured up. There was enough emotion in my house to power an entire novel, which is *so* atypical.

It takes a surprising amount of time before the words begin to slow from my fingertips. I lean back and scan through what I've written, my heart beating a bit faster than usual.

This is...good stuff. Far better than anything I've been able to come up with lately.

Eventually, it will all be taken apart and woven into the rich tapestry of inspiration that will ultimately become the final novel in my series.

The one that I haven't written yet.

The one I'm afraid to write.

It's one thing to write a book, thinking that a few hundred strangers will read it, maybe a few thousand, at most. But to sell over a million copies, to have my face recognized by complete strangers—I'm not sure how I feel about it.

Actually, I do: it's terrifying.

Especially when the fanbase seems to have taken on a life of its own. There are fan theories on top of fan theories, each crazier than the next. All of them mess with my head, with the original vision I had for this series. I cut myself off from social media, but the damage has been done: my creativity is paralyzed.

Whenever I try to write, all I can think of are the thousands of fans who are bound to be disappointed by whatever I come up with. My ideas for the finale are nothing like theirs. I keep hoping that if I just take a little more time to plan it out, to think through the details, then it will be okay. I'll somehow do my readers justice.

Instead, the longer I procrastinate, the more I realize that Liz Gilbert's theory about muses rings true.

I'm kind of scared mine has abandoned me completely.

The worry makes me feel heavy, but—I glance through my writing from tonight again. There's a glimmer of inspiration, a thread that connects to an idea I had about a subplot. I jot down a couple notes about a new twist, which would free up a character for a bigger role in the third beat, which I've intentionally left blank until this point.

Before I know it, it's nearing midnight.

But I have something. Something that I can work with. I push away from the desk. It's late and I still have a trip to pack for. Speaking of—I glance through my inbox, double checking that the reservations are in order for my upcoming trip. Plane ticket, hotel, transport—check. All meetings added to my calendar app, check. And a growing sense of dread just thinking about it.

I don't mind traveling. It's the coordination and planning that exhausts me. Especially when I remember that I'll have to spend some time assisting my unexpected guest with the retrieval of her vehicle tomorrow. I feel a new twinge of concern when I remember how cold her hands were.

I turn up the thermostat a couple degrees.

I think she'll be warm enough. I gave her the warmest blanket, the one that usually covers my own bed. But, just in case—I get one more from the hall closet and lay it across the arm of the couch, easy to see if she wakes up cold in the middle of the night.

And then I try not to think about the brown-eyed mystery girl on my couch, trying to clear my mind so that I can fall asleep. Slowly, eventually, it works.

Chapter 8

Rune

I wake up to the rich, intoxicating smell of coffee.

For a moment, I think I'm back at my own apartment. I always set the timer on my coffee pot at night so that it turns itself on a half hour before I'm supposed to leave for work. Which means I need to get up now, or risk being late. Reluctantly, I open my eyes...and am fully disoriented when I see a massive stone fireplace and floor-to-ceiling windows.

I blink, confused. Then I notice the white blanket tangled up next to me on the couch and it all comes back.

I don't have a job. I don't have a boyfriend. At the moment, I don't even have my car.

This is not a great situation to be in.

I brace for the panic to strike, but it never does. I'm lulled into a sense of contentment by the gentle warmth of the fireplace, the incredible view. It's hard to freak out when you feel warm and cozy and the daylight is shining through the windows. The snow must have stopped falling sometime in the night, and a perfect winter wonderland now meets my eyes.

No longer sleepy, I kick the blankets off and walk over to the windows to get my first real glimpse of the landscape: snow-clad pine trees, birds flocking around a feeder, and a frozen lake with a distant horizon. It's wildly magical.

Screw Sebastian and his stupid trip to Paris, I think suddenly. This is so much nicer.

"You're awake."

I turn at the sound of Finn's voice, sounding a little soft and raspy from sleep. He's sitting at the counter in the kitchen, an open book and coffee mug in front of him.

Some audacious butterflies come to life in my stomach. I thought he was stunning last night. It's nothing to the tousled hair look he has this morning, still wearing the same white t-shirt and gray sweatpants. Objectively speaking, Finn is physically very attractive.

"Want some coffee?" he asks.

"Yes, please."

"Do you take sugar? Oat milk? I don't have any fancy creamers, I'm afraid."

"Just black, thanks."

He stands and stretches his muscled arms over his head. The movement gives me the slightest glimpse of his chiseled abs. "How was the couch?"

"Excellent," I assure him, trying not to notice the sliver of skin at his waist. I don't need to be reminded about his stomach muscles. "Warm and cozy. I highly recommend it."

"Some of my best naps have been taken on that couch."

"I believe it. Thanks." I accept the coffee and breathe it in deeply. With a nod towards the book that he just set aside, I add, "Don't let me disturb you."

"The great thing about books is that they'll still be there when you get back to them."

I'm not normally the kind of person who enjoys conversation

early in the morning, but— "Thanks again for letting me stay here last night. Your house is really beautiful."

"My pleasure. Nice to get my annual good deed out of the way," he jokes, moving into the living room and settling into an armchair.

My mouth twitches with a smile at that. "Happy to be of service."

"So Rune, my mysterious visitor. How do you like this snowy paradise that you've ventured into?"

"Oh you know. Started out a little rough, but it's growing on me."

"Yeah, it does that." The grin he flashes me makes my stomach flip.

No, Rune. Bad. You're supposed to be in mourning over your last relationship.

On the edge of the little table, Finn's phone starts buzzing and he glances at the screen. "Sorry, I need to take this."

While Finn takes his phone conversation into another room, I sip on my coffee near the windows. It's idyllic here. Very calming. I'd like to know what kind of a job allows you to live like this. I hope it's not the medical field, because I failed biology twice.

Too bad that wasn't the only thing I failed at in life, as my parents tend to remind me. *Don't forget to put extra effort into this opportunity*, my mom likes to tell me. *It comes a little harder for you than it does most other people.*

Thanks, Mom.

Her complete lack of faith in me is very probably one of the reasons that I stuck with my not-dream-job for as long as I did. I am often convinced that I've peaked in life and it's all going to go downhill from here.

I have to remind myself that my mother can only ruin my day if I let her. Which includes now, I suppose. Here I am, standing in a veritable mansion with the most beautiful view—and a drop-dead gorgeous host who's been far more gracious than is warranted—and I'm resurrecting my mom's haunting commentary. Nice, Rune.

"Sorry about that," Finn says when he returns. "Work called."

And what is it you said you did for work? I want to ask. But my confidence fails me. Maybe it's too nosy to ask about his work.

"So," he says, rubbing his hands, "what do you think about rescuing your car?"

❄

An hour later, we're both sweating and panting, shoveling nearly two feet of snow out of the way to clear a trail to my car.

"We're getting close. You can pop back into the truck any time you need to warm up." Finn leans on the handle of his shovel for a quick breather.

"And miss this opportunity to show off my exceptional shoveling skills? Never." It's an obvious attempt at humor. My muscles are decent enough, but this snow is hard to handle. It keeps slipping off my shovel at the most inopportune moments, forcing me to work twice as hard to get my side of the car cleared. "Couldn't do it without your jacket, though," I add. I'm completely dressed in Finn's clothes at this point, including a jacket of his that I borrowed to stay warm.

"Don't start thieving my things now," he deadpans.

Eventually, we clear enough of a path for Finn to hook up the winch and slowly, carefully, drag my car back onto the road. He spends a few minutes helping me clean the packed snow out of the wheel wells and looking underneath for—I'm not really sure what. Engine stuff. I checked Aunt Mairi's address this morning and discovered it's only about six miles away. Six miles in the opposite direction. I guess I missed the turn in the snowstorm. That's embarrassing.

"I guess we did it!" I say brightly to Finn. Everything is really looking up.

"Well, sort of."

"What do you mean?" I ask, cringing internally at the cautious tone. Please *god*, I cannot handle anything more at this point. I am hanging on by one tiny thread of lingering optimism.

"The undercarriage is a bit roughed up and you're leaking oil something bad."

"Bad as in…?"

"It may need some repairs."

I don't like the look on his face. I can barely afford to fill up the tank with gas, let alone substantial repairs. In no scenario does this sound like something my bank account can withstand. "Think it will be a cheap fix?" I try to hide my desperation.

The way Finn scrunches up his eyes and takes a long look at my beat up rig tells me that no, this will absolutely not be a cheap fix.

"Well, thanks for letting me know," I force myself to say with as much positivity as I can muster, hoping I sound wealthy and unconcerned. It's embarrassing to be poor when you're around rich people. "I'll have to take it into the shop when I get home."

"I'm not sure your car will last five miles, let alone long enough to get you home."

I gape at him. "So I'm just stuck here? On the side of the road?" That doesn't sound safe. Fucking hell, I'm going to have to dish out money for a tow truck, after all.

"I bet we can get it to my house," Finn says with a level of confidence that may or may not be fabricated. "My neighbor Charlie is a mechanic. As long as Charlie has the parts and some spare time, it might be drivable by this weekend."

I should tell him no, I'll call a tow truck. But...my sad bank account forbids me. Thanks to skimping on my car insurance, I haven't had roadside assistance for years.

"Would it be too much of a bother?" I hedge.

"We're only a little over a mile from my house. I bet we can do it."

I start to believe him...until I turn the key and hear the engine squeal like a banshee. Panicked, I shut it back off again.

Finn takes one look at my face and opens the door.

"Let me try. You can follow in my truck."

I should argue. I don't.

By some miracle, the car makes it back to Finn's in one piece. While Finn makes a call to his mechanic friend, I change back into my own clothes.

"Good news," he announces. "Charlie says the parts we need should come tomorrow, maybe Saturday. So I guess figure on getting your car back in working order on Monday or Tuesday?"

My eyes widen. "That long?" I realize I sound whiny, so I hasten to back track. "Totally fine. Great. I just thought—well, it doesn't matter."

"What did you think?"

"I don't know," I mumble. "I was just picturing it to be like an hour or two for a fix."

Finn gives a short laugh. "An hour or two is changing tires."

"I'm not a mechanic!" I say defensively. "I don't know, maybe it's something you can like, put duct tape on for a temporary fix."

"Duct tape, huh?" Finn shakes his head, but there's a smirk twisting up the corner of his mouth. "We don't do half-assed patch fixes here. Only quality work."

"Right. I wouldn't have expected anything less."

"I did call the body shop in town just to make sure, but they have to put in an order, too." He sounds apologetic.

"No, it's fine, really—I just—that's a really long time for my car to take up space in your driveway."

He pours himself another coffee from the carafe. "It's not a bother at all. Hope that's not going to screw up your vacation plans?"

"I wasn't planning on doing much," I deflect, since my vacation is definitely screwed up beyond repair. "Probably catch up on the family gossip and play a million rounds of solitaire on my phone...and uh, probably beg some stranger for a ride over to Aunt Mairi's house." My face reddens a little. Obviously Finn is the one who will have to drive me there.

"Mairi...Olson?" He sounds surprised.

"Do you know her? She lives on the other side of the lake."

"Yeah, I know her. Your aunt, huh?"

"Ever since I can remember."

"Alright. What say we go grab some lunch and then I'll take you over there?"

❄

Danielle: Status update? You're alive, right?

Me: Yep. Good news: car's out of the ditch. Bad news: it needs repairs.

Danielle: That's 0% good news, 100% bad news. What happens now? Does your insurance cover it?

Me: No idea. Hopefully it won't be too big of a deal. Finn's got a neighbor who can fix it.

Danielle: Finn Sigurdson? The guy whose home you stayed in last night?

. . .

She's really done her sleuthing.

> Me: I don't know if I should be impressed or worried that you know his last name.

> Danielle: Please. This is all public tax information.

I'll take her word for it.

I slide my phone back into my pocket as I gather my things, feeling only a little awkward when Finn holds the door open for me to climb in. That's something Sebastian used to do when we went on fancy dates to restaurants where we could only really afford a drink or two. I guess we won't be doing that anymore. Correction: *I* won't be doing that anymore. Sebastian probably will. Probably with that Paris girl, too.

"You doing ok?" Finn breaks into my thoughts.

"Just thinking," I reply quickly. Maybe too quickly, based on how his brows rise.

When Finn's attention is fixed on navigating the freshly plowed roads, I take the opportunity to really take him in, distracting myself from thoughts of my ex.

Finn has a strong profile: a chiseled face with high cheekbones and dark brows set over piercing blue eyes. There are the tiniest wrinkles at the corners of his eyes that lend warmth to the otherwise serious expression on his face. A few dark curls escape from beneath the red knit beanie, making him look something of a lumberjack, especially when paired with the dark green wool hunting coat. A coat that somehow still manages to show off his strong shoulders and fit body. Combine all that with the bit of stubble on his jaw—just enough to look rugged, but not long enough to be abrasive if you're making out—and Finn is one good-looking man.

It's objectively true, and I can acknowledge it, even if I know better than to go jumping straight from a four-year relationship into batting my lashes at a relative stranger. Even if those lips of Finn's look like they'd be an absolute delight to kiss.

"So," I say casually, trying to distract my own wayward thoughts, "where are we headed?"

"To the great city of Birch Lake, Minnesota." He glances over at me. "And by great city, I mean a couple bars, a coffee shop, a gas station, and a newspaper office."

"Wow, a newspaper?"

"We take the town gossip very seriously."

"Naturally." I snort and turn my head to watch the landscape go by; an endless parade of thick spruce and balsam, coated in a healthy layer of white stuff. We pass a plow truck coming from the opposite direction, widening the road so that the shoulder is once again visible. "So, have you lived here all your life?"

"What makes you say that?"

I shrug. "This seems like that sort of place. Small towns kind of keep to themselves, don't they?"

"Do they?"

"You tell me. I'm just making up stereotypes over here."

He chuckles. "I was born in Duluth and lived there until about fifth grade when my great aunt passed away and left a bit of money for my dad. That's when they moved up here to live on the lake."

"Nice," I say, before catching myself. "I mean, not nice about your great aunt. Really sorry to hear that."

His mouth turns up into a smile, revealing the faintest hint of a dimple. "I didn't like her."

The thick forest opens up now to a brightly painted sign that reads *Welcome to Birch Lake*. I remember this place vividly from my summer visits years ago. Surprisingly, not much has changed apart from a serious lack of traffic. We seem to be the only ones driving through town, although there are a few cars parked along the street. An older man shovels out the walkway leading to the post office, his breath like smoke in the cold. Finn parks in front of Pike Bar & Grill, which turns out to be a very northwoods-y establishment. Whoever runs this place must be obsessed with logs: log walls, log tables and stools, log bar. Hopefully the chef has the same passion for good food as the designer of this place does for log.

The waitress, a woman who looks like she might be in her midsixties, briskly approaches us the moment we settle into a tall table near the bar.

"What can I do for you?" The waitress pulls a tiny notebook out of her apron pocket, watching us expectantly from over the top of her glasses.

"I'll have the red ale on tap." Finn taps on the drink menu item.

"Great choice. And for you, hon?" She peers at me over her thin-rimmed glasses.

"Same, please. And a water."

"That I can do." She gives a brisk nod and moves to the next patrons, leaving Finn and I to stare at each other across the small table. I cast around for something to say, but my mind comes up blank. I make a show of looking around, like the odd pieces of nature art hanging on the walls are worth every piece of my attention. They're actually cool, even if they don't hold a candle to the looks of the man sitting across from me.

"Have you ever been to Minnesota in the winter before?" Finn asks politely.

It's the kind of question you ask when you have nothing real to talk about, but I latch onto it anyway. "No I haven't. I used to come up to visit my aunt and cousins in the summers, though, back in the day."

"Sounds fun."

"Definitely."

"Hopefully our Minnesota winter will be on par with your summer experience."

"I'm sure it will." I don't mention that the winter weather is the least of my concerns.

Once our drinks arrive, we toast to mechanics and Uncle Fisher-slash-Bob. I begin to relax a little, thanks to Finn's easy demeanor. I'm sure I've screwed up his entire day, but he makes it feel less like I'm trespassing on someone's valuable time and more like I'm hanging out with a friend who enjoys my company and doesn't mind that my car is currently taking up space in his driveway while it awaits repairs.

"So tell me about life in the big city," Finn says, leaning his elbows on the table. "What do you do there for fun?"

"I mostly work," I admit, regretting that I don't have a cool hobby to brag about. Then a mental image of Diana's smug smile flashes to the forefront of my mind, making me wince. "At least, up until very recently."

Finn catches my expression. "Are we celebrating this change or drinking to the downfall of your enemies?"

I bark out a laugh at his phrasing, but it's the *we* that snags my attention and sparks a little warmth in my sad, cold soul. *We* makes me feel a little less alone. "The latter."

"May they regret their decisions," he says solemnly, reaching to tap his almost-empty beer glass against mine.

"I won't bore you with the story, but it was kind of recent. One day I was fully employed, hoping for a promotion. The next, I was singled out as the one person to get the axe." The few subsequent texts I sent to my former coworkers confirmed that I was, indeed, the only one who got fired. Apparently that's all the company needed to free up enough funds to give Diana her raise.

"I'm really sorry," Finn says.

"It's fine. It just means a new opportunity is around the corner, right?" I put on my optimistic smile, the one that's easy to hide behind, especially when we're both momentarily distracted from the waitress' reappearance with two large burgers and a basket full of fries.

"I'd definitely agree with the opportunity part," Finn says, "but don't gloss over the shittiness on my account. Life sucks sometimes."

"It really does. The worst part is that it wasn't even that good of a job: it barely paid the bills and my boss was a nightmare. I should have put more effort into finding a new gig somewhere, but I was hung up on the fact that I *wanted* to make it work. I thought that everything would brighten up if I put enough time and effort into it."

"That sounds like something a therapist would tear apart," Finn comments.

"Probably. I might be cured of that mentality, since I learned that it doesn't work with boyfriends, either," I comment, before realizing that Finn does not want my sob story flung at him while he's trying to enjoy a good burger. "I'm so sorry, I didn't mean to dump that on you. It's just top of mind and spilling over, you know?" Embarrassed, I break eye contact with Finn and focus on my fries. They're delicious.

"You can spill it if you want. I don't mind."

I shovel a bite into my mouth to buy time to think. I think he's just being polite, because why the fuck would he actually want to hear more? But part of me is so tired, so desperate for comfort and sympathy that I find myself sharing more.

"It all happened on Monday and I haven't really processed any of it," I try to explain. "I called my boyfriend to talk to him about getting fired, but it turns out he wasn't interested in being my boyfriend anymore." I probably don't have to expand on the part where I caught him in the act. That detail can be buried deep.

"So anyway, it can only get better, right?" I smile brightly at him.

Finn opens his mouth, then closes it with a frown. He must not share that sentiment. Technically, I don't believe it either. Things can always get worse until the day you die. Even then, my more religious friends would say that death doesn't always stop the downward spiral.

"Better days are always ahead," he says finally, "but that doesn't mean you don't deserve them now. If I'm being completely honest, I'm in awe of how you're handling all of this—the job, the ex, the car..."

"On the outside I can smile. Inside, I'm still screaming," I say wryly.

We both fall silent and I immerse myself in my meal. It's perfect American fare: flavorful and far too greasy. Comfort food, really.

"That looks absolutely disgusting," Finn comments when he notices me dipping my fries in a mixture of ketchup and mayonnaise.

"Don't knock it till you try it. The balance of flavors is—" I twirl my fingers, trying to think of the right word.

"Unbalanced?" Finn supplies with a grin. "I'll stick with ketchup only, thanks. You want anything else?"

When I shake my head, Finn motions for the waitress, who

brings the bill over. I reach for it, but he swipes it up before I catch a glimpse of the amount due.

"My treat," he says firmly, when I open my mouth to protest.

My bank account celebrates.

"Thanks."

"Seriously, no problem. I'm glad the snowstorm brought you in so I don't have to eat alone. Or worse, flirt with the bartenders."

"Wouldn't that be awful." I can't help laughing. The bartenders today are twice our age. But maybe Finn is into older women. I know nothing about him.

There's another flutter in my stomach when the corner of his mouth tilts up and he casts a wink in my direction. If it wasn't for the strange circumstances of our meeting, I'd probably be plotting a way to hang out longer. Maybe it's for the best: my heart's been battered enough without adding a vacation fling to the mix.

So when Finn opens the door for me and gives me a smile with the faintest hint of a dimple, I tuck away my feelings and shove my heart into a little locked box where it belongs.

Chapter 9

Finn

"This next driveway should be it," Rune says, reading the little red fire number signs posted on the side of the road.

Mairi's driveway hasn't been plowed recently; there's at least a foot and a half of snow piled up.

"I'm not sure I can make it through that," I tell Rune, eyeing the snowbank left by the plow at the end of the driveway.

"I can walk. The driveway isn't that long." Rune's tone is confident, belying the little furrow between her brows as she takes in the sheer volume of snow. "Auntie left detailed instructions on how to use her snowblower. I'll have this cleaned up in no time."

That pulls a sharp, incredulous laugh out of me. It would take me at least two hours to clear the driveway. She'll be lucky if she's finished by the time it gets dark.

"Can't think of a better way to spend an afternoon, right?" Rune looks at me for encouragement.

"Sure," I agree, to humor her. There's a reason I pay someone else to plow my driveway. The guy who does it is semi-retired and comes before dawn. By the time I came downstairs this morning, my own driveway was completely cleared off, leaving me free to spend my day working on other things…like helping Rune with her car and going out for a late lunch. Which, strangely enough, I enjoyed.

Despite the fact that she's now reached her destination—and I have a pile of work waiting for me at home—I find myself asking, "Do you want any help with the snow removal?"

She opens her mouth, looking as surprised as I feel about my offer. For a moment, I think she's going to say yes. Then she seems to catch herself. "I'll be fine."

I ignore the slight twinge of disappointment. I don't doubt that she'll manage, and yet—I take another look at that snow drift. "That's a sore back waiting to happen."

"Please," she scoffs. "Didn't you see my skills in the ditch? I'm a master snow person."

"A master, huh?" Not exactly the word I would have used.

"Usually I don't like to brag about it, but yes." She can't wholly hide the smile that's fighting the corners of her mouth. She's well aware of how bad her shoveling technique is. She has to be. I shake my head, but the spark of humor in those dark eyes has me wholly entranced. Like I've been all day, if I'm being honest. From the moment she woke up, eyes as bright as a kid at Christmas and dressed in my clothes, I haven't been able to look away. She's enchanting in a way I would not expect possible from someone to be when they've been through hell and back so recently.

Sweet, charming, and intriguing.

Her ex-boyfriend is a fucking idiot to have let her go.

"Here, give me your phone," I say, holding out my hand. I type my number in as a contact and send myself a quick text so I have hers. "Let me know if you change your mind and want some extra help. Or if you need anything at all."

Rune murmurs her assent. Our fingers brush when I hand her

phone back to her. The touch sends shivers up my arm, and I'm suddenly all too aware of our proximity, that we're alone together. *Say something clever,* my brain murmurs from a distance. *Bring that smile back.* But I can't. Her breath catches slightly and my eyes flick to her lips. I wonder if they're as soft as they look. I wonder what they taste like. I force my gaze back up to those brown eyes staring back at me.

I clear my throat and break the connection while Rune fumbles for her mittens. For fuck's sake, I hardly know her and she just broke up with someone. That should make her off limits.

"Well, thanks again," she says, throwing her backpack and duffel bag over her shoulder as she climbs out of my truck. She immediately sinks up to her knees in snow.

She has that same look on her face that she had this morning when she was struggling with the snow shovel in the ditch: half self-deprecating humor, the other half pure determination. I'm not going to lie...it's fucking adorable. When she looks back almost defiantly after making it across the big drift, I give her a thumbs up.

"You change your mind yet?" I call out through the open window.

To my surprise and delight, she merely pulls one hand out of a mitten and gives me the middle finger. "I don't give up easily," she shouts back.

That much is obvious.

I linger until she makes it to the house. Then, with no further excuse to stay, I drive off.

❄

It's nearly three o'clock by the time I'm back home. Despite the fact that I'm now crunched for time, I can't quite bring myself to regret spending the day helping Rune.

After all, I don't need to pack much, I reason; I have a full closet of clothes at my house in Chicago—but I do need to review a shitload of paperwork. Not the fun kind, either. This is legalese with nuances so small that I soon have a headache from parsing it out.

I make myself a coffee and settle into the chair in my office. With a sigh, I start working through the documents alongside the latest series of emails from my lawyer. Definitely the part of the job that I'm not fond of, which is why I have every intention of having this wrapped up before the holidays hit. I'm obviously not the only one with this mindset: it was absurdly easy to get people on board to meet on a weekend.

The blue sky fades into a bright red sunset outside an hour later, and I'm still working on the papers. Success looks so fun on the outside…but in reality, it's kind of a nightmare.

I wonder how Rune's getting on with her snow removal. I'm beginning to wish I'd stayed to help her out. It would have been far more fun than this legal shit. An odd thought for me to have, since I've never been a *fun* kind of person. The artistic and serious one, yes. But fun?—never. People and commotion make my head hurt. Which is why it's so odd that I'm still thinking of Rune.

As if in response to my thoughts, my phone lights up. A text from the woman herself. I open it to find a somewhat blurred selfie of her giving a thumbs up against the back drop of a cleared driveway, followed by another text:

Rune: "Finn the Hero"

I grin, despite myself.

That's what I'd labeled my contact in her phone.

Right before I felt the inexplicable urge to kiss her. I run a hand through my hair, offset by everything that's happened in the past twenty-four hours. For fuck's sake, I'm being ridiculous. She's little more than a stranger, freshly dumped by an asshole of an ex. And yet—I get up, restless. I probably just need to eat something. Then I can wrangle my mind back to work instead of thinking about whether I'll see her again or whether she might want to see me again.

Because if I'm being honest, I wouldn't mind an opportunity to test that spark between us, to see whether it would survive a real date, a longer visit.

Downstairs, I tidy up the makeshift bed I'd made for Rune. It feels like folding up the few vibrant moments of an otherwise grayscale year. When I shake out the last blanket, something tumbles to the floor. A phone charger, overlooked when Rune packed her things to leave.

I turn it over in my hands, considering. Chargers are a dime a dozen, but this one might have more intrinsic value. It's an opportunity (fine, an excuse) to see her again. I shoot off a quick text before resolutely walking away from both my phone and the charger. I have other things to do tonight rather than stare at a blank screen, waiting for her to reply.

With Rune's determination fresh in my mind, I sit down at my desk to write. The words don't flow as easily as they did last night, but I refuse to stop until I reach my quota. It's depressing how little I do accomplish by the time eleven o'clock rolls around and I have to quit several hundred words short of what I should have written.

I can try to catch up on the flight tomorrow, but—this isn't the first time I've missed my word count goals. At this rate, it will take a solid two years to finish any kind of a draft, let alone have a polished novel ready for the press.

I lean my forehead on my hand, weary and dreading this task that used to come so easily.

Chapter 10

Rune

My bladder wakes me up before sunrise, but it's a solid ten minutes before I have the energy to get up and do anything about it. I crashed on Aunt Mairi's couch last night, a handful of minutes after I came in from clearing the driveway of snow last night. It was back-breaking work; exercise that I'm unused to.

I called Aunt Mairi yesterday, letting her know that I'd arrived (it seemed superfluous to tell her about my mishap over the phone). She promised she'd be here sometime this morning, and I am so excited to see her.

In the meantime, I'm sore, tired, and ridiculously hungry. There's a cupboard of snack food and some eggs in the fridge that Aunt Mairi said were free for the taking. Her coffee canister is empty, so I heat some water for tea. I should have thought to pick up some groceries of my own, but I've been just a tad bit distracted. First by my own series of unfortunate events and then —Finn.

I still can't get over how he went above and beyond for a complete stranger that he'll likely never see again. I wonder where you find more men like him—who live in a beautiful home and look like *that*?

Is it bad that I find a veritable stranger so attractive this soon after breaking up with my boyfriend of over four years. Am I fickle? Is this what they call a rebound? Should I be concerned? I swear, I was two seconds from making a complete fool of myself yesterday afternoon when he dropped me off. Alarm bells were going off in my head, but I couldn't make myself look away from those beautiful blue eyes. Did I hurry my ass out of there the moment I realized I was waiting for a make-out session?

Yes...but what if I hadn't?

I plop a tea bag into the steaming water and think back to the intensity of his eyes. My hormones were so triggered that all I could think of was *doing* things with him. I'm sure that would not have gone over well, since I'd just spilled the whole sob story about Sebastian over lunch. I probably shouldn't have told him all of that. Sebastian said I needed to learn how to filter my words around other people. Which is offensive, but probably true.

While my teabag steeps, I distract myself from further thoughts of my ex with some harmless snooping in the living room.

There's a whole wall dedicated to books—mainly ancient philosophy like Aristotle and Boethius—but also a collection of Kierkegaard and some scattered names that I'm unfamiliar with. If I recall correctly, Aunt Mairi used to be a professor of philosophy, but she gave it up because her colleagues were, in her words, "unable to extricate their heads from their own asses." So she came up here, leaving her career behind in order to pursue something simpler. I move onto the next shelf to find it mostly filled with romcoms, followed by two more shelves of nature guides and homesteading how-to's.

Auntie's house isn't as massive or impressively decorated as

Finn's, but it's cozy and well-lived in. There's even a spinning wheel in the corner and several baskets of yarn set around the living room. Everything here feels simple, homemade, and wholesome—exactly what I'm looking for in life.

Wrapped up in a quilt, drinking my tea, I check my phone and find a text from Finn. Ignoring the surge in my heart, which means absolutely nothing, I open the message to find a photo of his coffee cup on the table, along with a question:

> Finn the Hero: Miss this?

Is he...flirting with me? My heart gives a little thump as I imagine Finn texting me in those gray sweatpants he was wearing.

> Me: Will have to make do with tea...no coffee here :/

Despite the early hour, he texts back almost immediately.

> Finn the Hero: ...I meant the charger.

I squint at the picture. Oh. Right. I see that now. I must have left it there by accident. That's embarrassing. I'm just a little train wreck where Finn is concerned.

> Me: Consider it my gift to you for your hospitality.

Finn the Hero: Do you want any?

> Me: ....?

Finn the Hero: Coffee. Want me to bring some over?

My fingers do a little dance over the phone screen. I might be in Minnesota for some inner peace, but it wouldn't *hurt* to see the guy again, would it?

> Me: So tempting...

Finn the Hero: Just say the word ☕

> Me: If it's not too much trouble.

Finn the Hero: Be there in 15.

I have fifteen minutes to get decent. I race to brush my teeth and wrangle my sleep-tangled hair into some semblance of order. By the time Finn arrives with a large thermos of coffee and a box of cookies, I've found a loose button-up shirt to wear over my sleep tank and I look more or less ready to receive visitors.

"I come bearing gifts. Coffee, cookies, and—this." He pulls my charger out of his jacket pocket and dangles it in front of me.

"It was a gift. A thank-you for letting a stranger stay the night." I lift my hands, mock offended. Damn, that coffee smells good.

"Your company was a gift in and of itself."

"Stop it. I'm blushing." I pull a coffee mug from the cupboard. Because I'm polite, I ask, "Did you want to keep me company and have another cup, or are you...on a schedule?"

"I have time," he says with a smile that reveals the slightest hint of a dimple on one side.

"Great." More than great. In the few hours that I haven't seen him, I've mis-remembered how stunning the man is. Dark, wavy-slightly-curly hair. Clear blue eyes. A perfectly chiseled nose. I wish there were more men like this five hundred miles closer to where I live. But I guess that's how I felt when Sebastian and I started dating, too: he could do no wrong in my eyes.

"You slept on the couch?" Finn looks into the living room at the pillow and blankets still strewn about.

"It was near the fireplace." I hurry to scoop up the blankets, trying to make it look like I'm not a complete pig, and motion for Finn to sit down. Every muscle in my back and neck objects to the movement.

"A little sore, huh?" He gives a knowing look.

"Only a tiny bit. Hardly at all." I shrug, feigning nonchalance, but even that hurts like a motherfucker.

"Really. No tight shoulders or pinched nerves?" He pauses. Then, "Well then, guess I don't need to offer my back massage skills. I don't like to brag or anything, but I'm not too bad at working out knots."

I waver between pride and the fact that a strikingly attractive man just offered me a back massage. Who am I to say no to that? "As long as you're offering..."

He flexes his hands and I sit on the floor in front of where he's seated on the couch.

There are such things as non-romantic massages, like the kind you get at a spa or the kind your roommate gives you when you won't stop begging. When Finn's warm, strong hands start working my painful shoulders, it's about as anti-romantic as it gets. It fucking *hurts*.

"Shit," he mutters, "your muscles are rock hard."

"You're telling me." My eyes tear up a little. It takes a ridiculous amount of focus to breathe normally and not flinch away from the pain. "You sure this is going to help?"

"I think so? I think they also say drinking a lot of water and taking a bath in epsom salts is supposed to help."

"Sure. I'll try all of that." *Ouch.*

Slowly, patiently, he works out the knots. The minutes tick by. My shoulders drop lower, the pain lessens, and my brain begins to clear. I am increasingly aware that Finn's hands are all over me. Also, I'm not wearing a bra, which he's probably realized, if he's paying attention. *God, those hands.*

Pain has officially faded into pleasure at this point and I never want this massage to end. Maybe I should, though. There's warmth pooling in places that his hands are nowhere near.

When his fingers brush against the skin of my neck, gooseflesh scatters across my body. *Shit.* He freezes for the briefest of moments, then brushes the exact same spot once more.

"Thanks for that, it feels so much better already," I blurt out, embarrassed by how badly I want those hands to keep wandering. I shouldn't have let this go on so long. He's being nice and I'm a perv.

I expect Finn to take my words as an opening to end the

massage. Instead, his hands slide to my shoulders and he leans forward until his lips are almost brushing my ear. "You deserve it, you know. You did an exceptional job with all that snow."

I cough out a laugh and turn my head enough to see the corner of his eyes crinkle with humor, but there's something else, too. Something that a wild, untamed part of me hopes I'm not making up.

"Finn—" I don't know what I'm going to say. Something suitably flirtatious and maybe mildly risqué to make it clear that I am interested in doing something with him. Preferably physical, although if he wants to profess his undying love first, I'll accept that.

"Yeah?"

Before I can get the right words out, a vehicle sounds in the driveway, followed by the slamming of a car door.

From Finn's vantage point, he can see straight out the window. "Looks like your aunt may be here. And possibly some of her offspring."

Well, there goes that. Disappointment must be written all over my face because Finn chuckles and tweaks my chin lightly. "Better go say hello, huh?"

Is it weird that I've invited someone into my aunt's house without permission? Or that he's the one who goes directly to open the door while I dash into the bathroom to put a bra on, under my clothes. It takes me all of half a minute, but by the time I'm fully clothed, Aunt Mairi is at the door—along with my two cousins, Ella and Courtney, their arms full of luggage and shopping bags. I didn't realize they were going to be here, too. It feels like Christmas already.

"FINNY!" Cousin Ella screams, dropping her bags and throwing her arms around Finn's neck.

Um, okay?

"Finny-Finn!" Aunt Mairi smiles. "How nice of you to clear the driveway."

"Why are you even here?" Courtney, my older cousin, asks.

"Be nice, Courtney." Finn seems nonplussed. "I've been having coffee with your cousin. Who, incidentally, is the one who cleared your driveway."

Comically, their eyes snap over to me, standing in the kitchen. I give a little wave. "Hi."

Ella squeals. "You sneaky little kitten, where's your car?"

"At Finn's," I say. It sounds suggestive of other things, so I quickly add, "I had some car trouble. He was nice enough to help out."

"Finn loves to help out," Courtney says drily.

I get the urge to defend him, but Finn only laughs and says, "Pretty sure you still owe me for the last time I helped out." Which is brave of him. The last time I taunted Courtney, she decapitated one of my dolls and put its head on a tiny wooden stake in the garden.

"Come here," says Aunt Mairi and wraps me in the warmest, most Aunt-Mairi-like hug there is. She's soft and warm and smells like cinnamon and nutmeg. Tears prick at the corners of my eyes. I cannot even imagine how she and my mother are related. My mother is like ice, cold and calculating, while Auntie's warm and genuine as the summer sun. "Car trouble?" she asks, looking from me to Finn, who nods.

"I went into the ditch," I admit. "And then—something else is wrong with the car."

"Just an oil leak, maybe some tie rods," Finn says. "Figured Charlie could have a go at it, since the shops are pretty booked out."

A look passes over Auntie's face for the briefest of moments, so quick that it's gone before I can identify what it is. "You're such a sweetie, Finny-Finn. Are we talking days or weeks to fix?"

"Should be done by early next week," he replies easily.

I try to look knowledgeable, as if that's the answer I would have given had she asked me instead of Finn. Because of course he was here to talk about my car. Not to work me into a frenzy with those talented hands.

"Don't let us distract you two from your visit," Auntie says. "Come on, girls, let's finish unloading the car before you start pestering Finn too much."

"As if," sniffs Courtney.

"One time I drooled all over Finn's pillow," Ella smirks, winking at me.

I don't know what expression is on my face, but it's enough for Finn to bother explaining that it was at a New Year's party a couple years ago.

Right.

Of course the moment between Finn and I has vanished. He offers a few polite suggestions for good food in the area while my aunt and cousins finish unloading their suitcases from the car, and then everyone is settled onto the couch and chairs, alternately voicing excitement about my visit and teasing Finn about some inside joke or another. I didn't realize they knew each other this well. I'm not sure what to think about this. It feels a little like going to your secret fort and discovering that the entire city likes to hang out there in their spare time.

"I didn't know you were coming up north," I say to my cousins.

"Of course not, because you didn't even ask," Ella replies, rolling her eyes.

"I thought it might be a nice surprise. Although we can always send them back where they came from if it stops being fun." Aunt Mairi gives Ella a look.

I adore my cousins, but there's a sick thud in my stomach when Ella throws herself down next to Finn on the couch and puts her feet on his lap with a playful request to warm them up.

Is it petty that I secretly want Finn to give her a disgusted look and ask her to please keep her feet to herself (and maybe come sit by me on the loveseat, for good measure)? Maybe. Instead, he gives her a good-humored smile and tickles—*tickles*—the bottom of her feet until she shrieks and removes them.

I force myself to watch, to fight the stupid sinking feeling in my stomach. What did I expect? I've only known the man for a day. He has a real life and real friends. I'm the one being dumb, building up a little romance in my mind where none exists.

The chances of him being actually interested in someone like me is close to nil. I'm quiet and reserved with an odd penchant for over-sharing; he's charming and at ease. I should be thankful that my cousins' arrival saved me from making a stupid assumption, from saying something embarrassing in that moment when his hands were resting on my shoulders. I should be relieved, but a quiet part of me wishes I was the one bold enough to put my feet on his lap and daring him to do something about it.

"You staying for brunch, Finn? You're welcome to." Aunt Mairi glances at the clock.

"No, I should be going. Just stopped by to update Rune on her car and give her the keys to the house."

"The—I'm sorry, what?" I blink confusedly as he holds out a lone key hanging from a leather fob.

"I have to head out of town for a few days. Figured I'd give you this in case you need to pop in and warm up when you're checking on your car, since my former hiding place has been compromised. Charlie has your number, so expect a text if there's an update."

The words register in slow motion and I get another pathetic, sick jolt in my stomach. I sort of assumed that Finn would be around during my visit and we could…I don't know, hang out?

"Rune's a klepto. You better give it to me instead," Ella's words break into my mini self-pity session. She's batting her eyelashes at him like a fool.

"What—no, I'm not." My face heats.

"You stole my purple hair bow when we were in fourth grade," Ella points out. "And had the audacity to wear it to Grandma's funeral."

Aunt Mairi snorts. "But rather than ask for it back like a human being, Ella decided to scream like a banshee. It was god-awful and I had to leave my own mother's funeral early."

Finn grins, dropping the key into my hand. "Good thing I don't have any purple hair bows to tempt you," he says with a wink.

"Can I come with and can we use your hot tub?" Ella asks.

Finn just shakes his head at her with an accompanying eye roll. To the rest of us, he gives a little wave and says, "Don't have too much fun. Nice to see you all."

And then he just—leaves. No hug. No special look. Not even a flirtatious smile to acknowledge our special time together.

It's outrageous.

"I didn't know you and Finny were friends. How do you know each other?" Ella wants to know.

"We don't and we aren't," I say, annoyed at myself and my stupid untethered heart. "His uncle stopped to help me out of the ditch and roped Finn into towing my car out."

There: simple. No need to explain anything further, especially not the part where I stayed at his house for the night. It's such an insignificant detail, after all.

"You went into the ditch?" Aunt Mairi repeats, looking concerned.

"It wasn't too bad," I lie.

"Boring," declares Ella. "Let's talk about our plans…how long are you staying with us, again?"

"I, uh, I'm not exactly sure. I won't overstay my welcome," I promise, looking at Aunt Mairi, who just smiles.

"You stay as long as you want," she says.

"I was thinking maybe a week? Head back next Friday?"

"Got some PTO that you have to use up?" Courtney asks.

I stiffen a little, then realize I should just rip off the bandage. "I'm sort of in between jobs right now."

I've been so scared of telling anyone about my current state of unemployment. Whenever I start thinking about it for too long, I feel dizzy and short of breath. And then, it's really embarrassing. How do you manage to get fired from a lower level job that you're actually rather good at? (Answer: you don't play office politics as well as the new girl with long blond hair and a charismatic personality.)

But, as with Finn, I face no judgment here. The moment the words register, a pity party of the very best kind ensues. Aunt Mairi makes a breakfast pizza while Courtney, Ella, and I curl up under the same blanket on the couch where the entire story tumbles out. Craig, Diana, Sebastian—all of it.

"Sounds like you should have left that place ages ago," Courtney says, garnishing her cold honesty with loyalty.

"Have you had revenge sex with anyone to serve Sebastian right? Is that what you and Finn were up to?" Ella asks eagerly.

"What—no."

"He'd be a good person for it. He's rich, successful, and really hot."

"Ella, he's a human being," I shoot back, even though everything she says is one hundred percent true.

"Doesn't mean he wouldn't be up for it, if you asked." She shrugs indifferently. "This is Finny we're talking about."

"I'm not sure Finny would appreciate that characterization," Aunt Mairi calls from the kitchen. I'm not sure *I* appreciate that characterization. Does Finn flirt with a lot of girls? *Probably. You're not that special, Rune*, a whispered voice tells me. A voice that is as reasonable as it is cruel.

"Ok, but how do you know him?" I ask, shifting the topic. "Our paths only inadvertently crossed. I didn't realize he was an acquaintance of yours."

"Acquaintance? What are we, British?" Courtney scoffs.

"We went to school together. He's two grades above Courtney," Ella explains. "The bus route was awful, so Mom used to pay him to pick us up and bring us to school when he got his license."

"Did you guys ever date?"

"Why do you care to ask?" Courtney gives me a look.

"Just curious, considering Ella's comments about him being hot and insinuating that revenge sex with him would be… adequate," I finish lamely.

Ella gives a sly smile. "I wouldn't say no if he was up for it."

"Ella!" Aunt Mairi scolds from the kitchen. "He's basically your brother."

"He is not!" she objects. "We're unrelated and he's single. At least I think he is. It wouldn't be totally appropriate." Turning to me, she adds, "The real problem is that he's either a recluse at his house or gone traveling."

Great. Another traveler.

"The real problem is that you're usually involved with

someone else," Courtney says dryly with a pointed look at Ella. "And also that Finn is not interested in you and never has been."

I've never been so grateful for Courtney's blunt comments. Probably time to change the subject. "Ok so everyone's relationship status aside, what's on the agenda during my visit?"

"I'm glad you asked," says Ella, producing a notebook. "I've made a whole list."

Chapter 11

Finn

"You all here, Finn?" Amber, my lawyer, leans her elbows on the table in the small corporate office kitchen.

"Absolutely," I say, looking up from my phone. A complete lie: I'm well and thoroughly distracted. "Why did we think this was a good idea?"

Her eyes narrow. "*You* thought this was a good idea. You said, and I quote: *Because it's a great opportunity to expand my audience and get a fat paycheck in the process.*"

A smart answer.

A reasonable answer.

One that I still agree with. Except— "The longer this drags out, the less convinced I am that it's worth the effort."

"What if we added another zero to the negotiations?" she asks, half-serious, brushing some crumbs off the table, into her hand. She's got a casual-yet-experienced look about her: a plain white fitted t-shirt and taupe blazer paired with dark skinny jeans and running shoes.

Amber has the unique ability to walk in the room and make you immediately feel comfortable, maybe even a little unfiltered.

But the moment negotiations begin, no one else stands a chance. She's fearless and precise in her communication and doesn't let shit slide by. She demands—and gives—respect. I really like having her in my court.

"Wouldn't be the worst idea we've had." Money is not my primary motivator, but I'm running short on inspiration for this project.

Seeing your book come to life in the form of a TV series is incredible. At least, that's what they make you think. So far, this whole endeavor just feels cursed. It's a never-ending series of meetings, negotiations, and re-negotiations as key players come and go in a seemingly endless cycle. We lost the original creative director a while back due to scheduling conflicts. Then there were casting difficulties that stretched on for months. The scriptwriters turned out an incredible product...but it made so many wild departures from key plot points that I felt obliged to ask for a revision. I felt like a dick. They were so proud of what they'd done. And honestly, it was really great and would have made a fantastic series, but it wasn't my story.

What was once a very promising project is now—well, it's been wearing on me. This is not what I'm cut out for. Honestly, I think even Amber is beginning to question the sanity of working with me on this. She's a brilliant negotiator, one of the best I've ever come across. But I'm losing enthusiasm, which makes it a lot harder for her.

I think I've come to the decision that I'd rather just make my money writing. It's what I do best. The fact that I have full control over the finished product is also pretty damn nice. My core readers are happy and I bet I could make them even happier with an exclusive edition, once I get the final book written.

If I get the final book written.

It's been a solid three months of not being able to produce

anything worth reading. That's a veritable lifetime for a prolific writer. I should be midway through a book draft, but all I have are half-finished ideas and a whole notebook full of blank pages. And then those three inspired pages from earlier this week.

I check my phone again. There's no missed call, no text. I haven't heard from Rune since I left her at her aunt's house four days ago. Which reminds me...I send off a quick message to Charlie, asking how the car repair is going.

Charlie: Just finished up.

Me: What's the bill?

Charlie: $1250 for parts & labor.

Charlie does great work and charges a fair price, and I wouldn't be surprised if that amount includes a friends and family discount. Rune's finances are none of my business, but she did just get laid off from work. Even if she has the money, it's an unplanned expense. I didn't miss the nervous tone in her voice when she asked about repairs.

I frown and tap out another few texts to Charlie, along with a money transfer to bring that amount down a little before Rune gets the bill. The snowstorm girl deserves a break.

I look up and see Amber staring at me, a strange expression on her face.

"Seriously, Finn, you good?"

"I'm fine."

Her eyes narrow like she absolutely does not believe me. But she doesn't push. We spent the past two days hashing out the details of our agenda. She knows where I'm willing to compromise and where the line is that can't be crossed. Obviously, Amber could handle this whole negotiation on her own, but it looks better when I'm physically present. Even if my mind keeps trying to escape the stark environment of boardroom negotiations and wander back to Minnesota, where a certain semi-stranger is currently enjoying a winter vacation.

I wonder how she likes the cold.

I wonder if she's having fun.

I wonder if she'll still be around when I return.

"*Finn.*"

Amber's irritated voice cuts into my thoughts. Her lunch dishes are cleared from the table. I didn't realize she had finished eating. From the way she's glaring at me, she's probably been done for a while.

"Fine, let's get this over with," I mutter, sliding my phone into my pocket.

Fortunately, the afternoon meetings go a bit better than the morning ones. For one, they're actually interesting. I am engaged enough to receive Amber's nod of approval when we wrap up the last one, a little after six.

"You heading back home or sticking around the Windy City for a while?" she asks, slipping her laptop into her backpack.

"My flight leaves at eight tomorrow morning. Figure I'll head back to the house and make it an early night." I hold the door open for Amber as she flips her backpack onto her shoulders.

"Do you even know what an early night is?" she lifts a skeptical brow.

I ignore that comment. My best writing has always been done late at night. Old habits are hard to break, even when I'm not actively writing.

"You need a woman in your life."

"A woman, huh?"

"Or a man. Whatever floats your boat these days."

I make a noncommittal sound. "I'll consider your opinion," I tell her, because it seems like she's expects me to say something.

Amber rolls her eyes. "Convincing."

"You seem very invested in my welfare."

She gives me a look. "I've seen more than my share of burnout over the years. Health problems, mental breakdowns—it's not pretty. You're a brilliant, prolific author, but there's more to life than that. Like going out for drinks with old friends. Speaking of which, you sure you don't want to come with me? Laurie and Colin are both out and about tonight."

"I'm sure. Thanks for the invite, though." Once upon a time I would have said yes. But my social energy meter is running on low. Nothing sounds more hellish after a full day of meetings than heading to a noisy bar full of people.

"Your loss. Until next time, Mr. Sigurdson."

We shake hands and I'm officially free. I feel like a kid on summer break. A tired, mildly cranky kid. It's a relief when my cab pulls up to the driveway of my Chicago house and I'm surrounded, at last, by silence.

I order some Korean food on the delivery app and am freshly showered by the time it arrives. Usually I would flip open my laptop, maybe do some editing over dinner, but—Amber's words are fresh on my mind. Maybe I do work too much. Maybe I've burned myself out and that's why my creativity has vanished. Writing and telling stories are the highlight of my life. I can't *not* do it. It's all the other stuff that feels like work: the marketing, the contracts, the constant barrage of emails, and now this TV series. I suppose I could delegate more, but I prefer to be involved in that side of the business, too. Even if it gives me a headache.

I mindlessly surf the TV channels before settling on a documentary about ancient civilizations.

Would it be better to take a real break from writing, instead of forcing myself to fight the mental fatigue on a daily basis? I haven't been out on the ski trails yet this winter, and Uncle Fisher claims the walleyes have been biting for the ice fishermen.

Unbidden, my mind flicks back to my great uncle's latest antic: dropping Rune off at my house without a single word of warning. I still can't shake the girl from my mind, from her big, doe-like eyes to the way her entire face lit up when she took in the view. How her body felt when I worked on those tight muscles. Her little gasp of breath when I touched that spot on her neck.

I set aside my empty takeaway container and reflect on what my next move should be. Solitude has always been my preference, but maybe I'll text her when I get home tomorrow. Just a quick check in to see how she likes her car...and maybe ask if she wants to grab some drinks before she heads out of town. Nothing big. Just a friendly visit; a bookend to wrap up the little adventure that she brought to my doorstep.

Satisfied with that plan, I settle in and try to focus on the mysteries of ages past.

Chapter 12

Rune

The thing I love about my cousins is that even after years of seeing very little of each other, it's almost effortless to pick up right where we left off. They take cousin time very seriously and are fully committed to ensuring that my time here is filled from morning to night. That having been said, Ella's list of activities is madness.

We shop every thrift, antique, and boutique store within a fifty mile radius and work our asses off cross-country skiing across the lake. Courtney joins us for the skiing treks, but otherwise stays at Aunt Mairi's, studying for the bar exam that she's supposed to take next month. Her dedication to her career is inspiring, if not mildly triggering.

Under her influence, I spent all day yesterday sending out applications for various jobs in Chicago. Unfortunately, all but one application received Out of Office replies. I doubt I'll hear back until mid-January at the soonest. But stress will get me nowhere, or so Aunt Mairi tells me. Which is why I've embraced Ella's exhausting social schedule for the past four days. It's nicer to think about used sweaters and coffee shops than whatever else is going on in my life these days.

That's why we're here, hanging out at Up North Coffee in adorable little Birch Lake, Minnesota while we wait for our daily lattes.

My car is parked on the curb just outside, already covered in a fresh dusting of the snow that's accumulated since we walked inside. I picked it up yesterday and was pleasantly surprised at how well it drives. Charlie the mechanic, who turned out to be a woman in her early thirties, not the old guy I was picturing, gave me a bill for ninety-two dollars. She assured me that the money would cover everything, which makes me suspect that someone else has possibly paid the rest. I can't even get an oil change for that amount in Chicago. I suspect Aunt Mairi. It could also have been Finn, but I have to stop myself from going down that thought path. Despite my slight obsession over him, he remains a stranger. He also hasn't texted me at all since he left on his trip. I can take a hint.

"The thing about thrift stores," Ella says, raising her voice to compete with the buzz of the espresso machine, "is that you don't have to sacrifice quality for budget."

"Stop preaching to the choir." I scored a beautiful rose-colored winter coat at a thrift store on Saturday for $6. It's filled with down and has kept me warm even as the temps drop into the single digits.

I'm just finishing up my latte when an older lady shuffles over. She's wearing a black wool coat, with short curled gray hair peeping out from under a felt hat.

"Good morning, Mrs. Mustonen," Ella says with a smile.

"Hello, Ella, how have you been?" The woman pulls a chair out from the table next to us and sits down, settling in for a chat.

Ella seems to know everyone, no matter where we are. I merely observe while the two chat about mutual acquaintances and some slight gossip ("Did you see that Jennifer's house sold? A family from Michigan bought it..."). I wonder what it's like to have roots this deep in an area, where you are intimately familiar with the rich, faceted history of the people and places you encounter on a daily basis. I've never had that and I wonder if I'm missing out. When, the conversation wanes a little, Mrs. Mustonen produces a flyer from her large black leather purse.

"If you girls are looking for something to do this week, we need volunteers to help with the fundraiser for the senior living center."

"I thought that was cancelled?" Ella says.

"For lack of volunteers." Mrs. Mustonen levels her a look. "The committee figured a little recruiting would help."

"What do you need?"

"The Smiths stepped up to MC, but we're still looking for help with setting up the room tomorrow and with serving during the fundraiser."

Ella's looking at me, waiting for me to say something. Like I'm the one planning our schedule.

"I'm leaving Friday," I point out.

You got something pressing that you need to hurry back for?" Ella asks with just a touch of sarcasm. She's well aware that my timeline is my own. To the old lady she says, "Put us down to help with the set up. Two energetic young women. And put us all down for dinner tickets on Saturday."

Because I'm Midwest polite through and through, I do not argue until Mrs. Mustonen is out of earshot. When she is, I glare at my cousin. "I'm going to overstay my welcome."

"Oh please, is that even possible?"

"Did we clear this with your mom? You know, the one whose house we're staying in?"

A crazy question, apparently, based on the way Ella's eyes roll back into her head. "She adores you and you can do no wrong. How could she not love this idea? Besides, she knows you're the reason I've stayed so long in the first place. If it was just Courtney, I'd have gone back to Duluth after the weekend."

As it turns out, Aunt Mairi does love the idea, even if she purses her lips at Ella. "Did you let Rune make this decision, or did you make it for her."

"She was basically begging me with those big brown eyes of hers: *Please let me stay longer,*" Ella says.

"I don't want to intrude," I add, feeling obliged to make the statement.

"You aren't," Aunt Mairi says firmly. "It's nice to have you around. It's too bad that Jules couldn't join us, like old times."

I note that she doesn't say anything about her own sister, my mother.

My parents effectively decided to raise Jules and I away from our grandmother and aunt, apart from a few scattered visits here and there. It was a veritable miracle when they decided to ship us to Minnesota for a week or two in the summer so they could go on an adults-only vacation. Jules and I didn't mind. We loved the cozy, laid-back lifestyle that Aunt Mairi crafted for her girls. We loved the way she listened, the way she allowed us to converse as if we were adults. She was the mother we wished we had.

"What is Jules up to, anyway?" Ella asks.

"She's still traveling the world, isn't she?" Courtney calls out from the living room, where she's surrounded by books, coffee, and a plate of snacks.

"She is. How's studying going?"

Courtney makes a grimace and gives a long stretch. "It's so good, really addicting, I highly recommend."

I snort a laugh at her wry sarcasm. "When is the bar exam?"

"End of February."

My brows fly up. "You're going to be at this for two *months*?" This is exactly the reason why I will probably never have a stable career. I don't have an ounce of the dedication that Courtney does.

"No, I'm studying in three sprints: two weeks of studying, followed by a half week of relaxing. Long enough to mentally reset, but not long enough to forget what I've memorized."

That's even more disciplined than I initially thought.

"Good for you, Courtney, make us all feel like degenerates," Ella says.

"Don't be annoying." Courtney rolls her eyes. "You're the only one who fits the term. Rune worked the same job for *years*."

"You've been sitting in a classroom for years," Ella shoots back. "I've actually contributed to society in that time."

"Keep telling yourself that."

I slowly back away from the sibling spat, into the relative safety of the kitchen.

"You sure you want to stay here longer?" Aunt Mairi mutters.

"I can probably survive till Sunday."

"You know you're welcome to spend the holidays with us."

Part of me wants to accept the invitation. I imagine Christmas being a warm, cozy affair with my aunt and cousins. At the same time, I don't know what normal holiday protocol is—my family certainly didn't have any when I was growing up—and I don't want to intrude. "I better get back home and figure out what's next," I say.

"Do what you need to, just know the offer stands."

If only I knew what I needed to do.

For now, I guess I'll just focus on the volunteer work that Ella signed us up for.

I've never volunteered for anything (apart from church events that my parents insisted we be a part of growing up), and I'm pleasantly surprised by the cheery camaraderie pervading the event. And it is definitely an event in and of itself: the entire retired community has turned out to help. Many came with cookies and coffee cake, so there's a table set up that's brimming with home baked goods. I'm pretty sure they actually do not need Ella and I, apart from the fact that we're younger and steadier on our feet.

Margaret, a woman with bright, twinkly eyes who appears to be somewhere in her late seventies, takes me by the arm and leads me to a tall ladder set up against the wall. There's a large pile of synthetic garland on the floor next to it.

"You look as if you have some balance left in you," she says.

"We'll find out," I say, clambering up the ladder to drape the fake pine garland over the doorway. It's tedious; the hooks are small, and I have to twist wire loops around the garland to get it to hang properly.

Meanwhile, Margaret untangles the garland, providing both direction and entertainment from below.

"Make that loop just a little lower, would you?" she instructs.

"Quit bossing the poor girl. It looks fine," another volunteer calls from nearby.

"Says the woman who can't tell a crow from a raven," Margaret retorts. Turning to me, she continues, "I found a crow last summer that had fallen from its nest. Fed it puppy chow and grasshoppers until it could fly."

"Really," I say, intrigued. This is wilderness living at a whole new level. I climb down the ladder and slide it over a few feet, before stepping back up to hang the next section of garland.

"Truly. It's smart as a whip, too: it's learned to say 'delivery' in its screechy crow voice to get me to open the door and visit with it. Took me a whole week to realize it was the crow talking and not the voices in my head."

I laugh at her self-deprecating humor.

"It's name is Delivery," she adds with a wink. "There's some law against keeping crows as pets. I keep telling him that, but he gets very grumpy when it's cold and I won't let him come into the house with me."

"Since when has legality stopped you, Marg?" The other volunteer pipes up.

"I'm always on the right side of the law, Joan." Margaret waves her hand and lowers her voice, as if telling a secret. "The real reason I don't let him in the house is because he would shit all over the place. I just talk about the law so his feelings aren't hurt."

"Crows don't have feelings." Joan rolls her eyes.

"I'll let you tell him that."

"I'm not going near that monster."

"He stole a doughnut from her once," Margaret says proudly. "Stole it right out of her hand and dunked it in her coffee before eating it."

Ella walks by, a large clear plastic box full of tableware in her hands. She catches my gaze and we grin at each other.

It's true, she mouths.

I bite back a laugh and focus on getting the rest of the garland strung up while Margaret remains distracted arguing with Joan.

By the time Ella and I bow out two hours later, the room is fully transformed.

"See, aren't you glad you volunteered?" Ella says happily when we're back in the car. "I miss those ladies. I used to see them at the quilting club once a month when I was in high school."

"Technically, you volunteered me," I point out. "But yes, I am glad."

"Kind of makes you want to move up north, doesn't it?" she says slyly.

"You don't even live here anymore."

"Duluth is basically here."

I give a noncommittal mumble. Truthfully, it would be nice to live some place like this: a forest far away from the big city. In Chicago, the view outside my apartment is just a sad, decrepit building. Every time I glance out the window, my stress levels drop lower. But—my friends are in Chicago. And I haven't seen any full-time jobs advertised here, even though I have been paying attention when we've been out and about.

"If you find a job that pays a living wage, let me know," I tell her.

"Okay, okay, fine. We'll look for something. What does Jules say about all of this?"

"I haven't told her yet."

"Seriously? I thought you two were like this." Ella holds up a pair of crossed fingers.

"We are," I say, which is fundamentally true, even if it feels a little bit like a lie at the moment. Thanks to our jobs—and my lack of disposable income—we've seen less and less of each other over the past couple of years. I don't want my big sister to feel like she has to bail me out. And she totally would. She'd drop everything just to help me, even though she has her own life to live, traveling the world as the assistant to some CEO. "Anyway, if you find something, let me know. But I want this vacation to *be* a vacation. I'll think about work after."

"Atta girl. So in the meantime, you up for another thrift store?" She tosses me a grin.

"Sure. I've got a couple fives left in my purse."

"Good, take a left here. The one I'm thinking of has an incredible selection of sweaters." Her eyes gleam with anticipation.

❄

Three sweaters and twelve dollars later, we make it back to Aunt Mairi's. Ella disappears for a nap, but the conversation we had about my sister has been living rent-free in my mind all afternoon. Have I made the wrong decision, keeping her in the dark? On the one hand, it's my life, but on the other...if our situations were swapped, I would want to know how she's doing. For that reason alone I pick up my phone with a resigned sigh and tap on my sister's contact before I change my mind.

It's a mere three seconds before she answers.

"Heyyyy, are you still alive?" A blurry face becomes visible on the screen, the background dark behind her, as if she's just woken up in bed. Which is surprising, since Portland time is two hours earlier than mine and I've never known my sister to go to bed this early.

"Heyyyy, are *you* still alive?" I squint at the pixelated image.

"Why are you so blurry? I thought Chicago has great service."

"I'm up in Minnesota at Aunt Mairi's."

"Oh, *nice*. I should meet up with you. I'm in Finland right now, which actually reminds me a lot of Minnesota. Same trees, same frigid temps"

"Finland? What the actual fuck. Since when?"

"Since I got here." Classic Jules, keeping her cards close. It must run in the family. "Did you finally get some PTO?"

I bite back my questions about her travels, even though I'm brimming with them. "I have a work conundrum."

"This sounds juicy, tell me more."

So I do. I tell Jules absolutely everything: work, Sebastian, and my series of misadventures, minus the part where I saw Finn in a towel. For some reason, that feels too personal to even share with my sister. I also skip the part where he's super attractive and probably single.

"So your shitty coworker Diana got a raise and you were kicked to the curb? Sounds like you shouldn't have put so much effort into fixing her work. It made her look too good," Jules says.

"Then the clients would have had to suffer. That's not fair."

"I mean, you definitely took the high road, but was it really your responsibility? Your boss is the one who made the call."

"Craig had no loyalty to our clients. He just wanted the numbers to keep go up magically every quarter, like we were some monstrous corporate company without an upper limit."

"Interesting. So basically you should have quit ages ago."

I don't respond to that. Hindsight is 20-20.

"You aren't telling mom and dad, are you?" Jules asks, one brow quirked.

"Of course not. That's why I called you."

On the screen, Jules smirks at my emphatic reply.

Our parents aren't the greatest at being parents. The most charitable thing I can say about them is that maybe they try. Maybe they've always tried. But it wasn't enough when Jules and I were younger, and it's certainly not enough now that we're adults. To tell my parents something like this is to invite them to share an opinion on a topic they know nothing about: their own children. Or how life really works. My mom would tell me I should just be happy with where I'm at. My dad would tell me that all my problems would be solved if I would stop being difficult and just get married so that a man can take care of my finances.

"Anyway, I don't know what to do." I sigh, laying back on the faded blue bedspread in the guest bedroom where I'm staying.

"I think you do. Get that resume out there and go for what you really want."

"So that's another problem: I don't know what I want."

"Put your big girl panties on and figure it out, Rune. I know you like to play it safe, but sometimes it's okay not to. You know that, right?"

"I guess."

Across the world, Jules scoffs at me. "Take those marketing and design skills and do something cool. Start that bookstore you've always wanted. The cool witchy one with herbal teas and art classes. What did you want to call it, again? Nature and Ink? Birches and Teas?"

"Something like that." I laugh a little under my breath. "I can't believe you remember."

"Someone's got to hold you accountable for pursuing your dreams. Hey, I have to catch an early train to Rovaniemi in the morning. I'll be back in the States in a couple weeks. How about I hunt you down then and we can spend some high quality sister time, yeah?"

"That sounds nice."

"Okay, cool. You need any money in the meantime?"

"Absolutely not."

She laughs. "Fine, whatever. Bye, crazy girl. Give Auntie a hug from me and don't let Ella be a bad influence."

"Obviously. Love you, too."

The room seems a little emptier when the phone goes silent. I miss my sister desperately. She's one of the few true anchors in my life.

A minute later, my phone pings with a notification: a five hundred dollar transfer to my account. The accompanying message:

> Jules: You can't tell me what to do.

I shake my head, both annoyed and grateful. I won't use her money. I *refuse* to use it, but that doesn't mean I'm not wildly thankful for the gesture. I take a picture of my middle finger and text it to Jules.

She responds quickly.

> Jules: I love you, too, little sis. Now go take some risks.

Chapter 13

Rune

The temps have been dropping steadily all week and by Thursday morning, my weather app tells me it's a balmy zero degrees outside—with a ten below windchill. Thank goodness for my new pink coat, which blocks both the wind and much of the chill.

Ella and I have one more morning of prep at the community center, which means that, before the sun has fully risen, I find myself bracing against frigid winds during the short walk from my parked car to the coffee shop.

"That wind sure wakes you up!" Ella laughs, shaking the snow out of her hair as we step into the rich coffee smell and warmth of Up North Coffee.

I just yawn. Seven-thirty is far too early to be out and about when you're on vacation—and no frigid wake-me-up wind will convince me otherwise.

The full tables here tell me I won't find much sympathy among the happy holiday shoppers of this town. They're cheerful, laughing with each other over cups of coffee and donuts. The only person who might relate is the sullen teenager who's glaring at his phone while his parents wordlessly dig into their bagels.

Actually, I take that back: the snippish barista behind the counter may be also be opposed to early mornings.

We find a seat near the fancy stone fireplace. I could totally fall asleep right here.

"Tell me when the caffeine hits." Ella flips out her phone to scroll through social media. She snaps a few artistic pictures of our lattes and posts them to her stories, with a giant neon *#cousintime* hashtag advertising my existence.

"Does anyone care whose coffee drink you're taking pictures of?" I lean back into the cushioned armchair, enjoying the ambient heat from the electric fireplace in the wall.

"Obviously. I'm a big deal in certain circles."

"Okay," I snort a laugh. I don't doubt it. My social butterfly of a cousin was prom queen in high school.

The breakfast crowd ebbs and flows. I'm mindlessly alternating between people watching and drinking my latte, when a toddler at the table next to us spills her hot chocolate all over the table—and Ella's bag on the floor next to it.

"Oh, shit!" Ella exclaims, then exchanges apologies with the mother over her child-inappropriate language and the state of her tote bag.

"I'll get some napkins," I volunteer, glad for an excuse to escape the awkwardness. As I take half a stack of napkins, I notice the cranky barista has suddenly become chipper, batting her lashes at the guy ordering. I guess all she needed was a little eye candy to make her morning. I absentmindedly lean to get a better look at his face when he turns towards me.

"Oh!" The stupid exclamation flies out of my mouth.

"Well hi, stranger." Finn's blue eyes crinkle at the corners and I swear it's suddenly fifty degrees warmer in here.

"You're back." *Duh, Rune.*

"I am, yes. You, uh, collecting those?"

"What?" I blink, then look down at the ridiculous amount of napkins in my hands. "There was a hot chocolate conundrum. I need to—" I motion towards where Ella is still chatting with the young mother.

"I'll come over in a moment." His mouth turns up in a smile.

"Cool. Great." *Stop talking, Rune.* I turn, willing myself to appear cool and detached, like I'm not totally melting at the realization that Finn is *here*. And that he remembered me.

Over the past few days, I've tried and failed to put him out of my mind. My imaginative subconscious has built him up and placed him in some sort of fairy realm along with his fancy house and 10/10 hotness. It's jarring to see him in a normal, everyday place. Extra jarring when I'm sure I look as tired as I feel.

"Sorry, I got distracted." I help Ella mop up the sticky remains of the hot chocolate.

"You should be," she says good-humoredly, shaking out her bag.

I force myself not to turn around. Not to stare at him again. Should I say something to Ella? Or pretend like I didn't encounter anyone when I got the napkins? My mind has gone blank. I don't even know what's normal anymore.

"Coffee hitting hard?" Ella asks, watching my fingers tap nervously against my cup.

"Maybe a little." I stare at the flames in the fireplace with determination. I'm definitely far more interested in the fake flames than anyone else who may or may not be here in this very building.

It seems like ages before Ella looks up from her phone and gives an excited wave. "Are my eyes to be believed?" she exclaims. "Is this truly Finny-Finn? Out at a coffee shop like a mere commoner?"

"Ha ha." Finn perches on the arm of my chair and I'm fully immersed in his pine-and-smoke smell. It takes a conscious effort not to lean and breathe him in. "So what have you two ladies been up to? Ella, I'm going to go ahead and assume you've been causing nothing but mischief. Did you get your car back in working order, Rune?"

"I did, thanks."

"Rune and I have been taking the northland by storm," Ella says. "See these boots I'm wearing? I got them for fifty cents at the Iron Ore Thrift Store. Cool, huh?" She stands up and twirls in a slow circle, modeling her brown snow boots, black leggings, and thick wool sweater.

"Yeah, they really make that hot chocolate stand out," I can't help teasing.

"Whatever, it didn't—oh shit, it did." She rubs at the brown splotch on the hem of her ivory sweater and sends an exasperated look at the door, where the mother and daughter have just exited the coffee shop. "Can you watch my drink? I'm going to see if I can get some of this off in the bathroom."

Finn gives her a mock salute before sliding into her freshly vacated chair.

"Thrift stores, huh?"

"Amongst other things."

"Like volunteering for the holiday bazaar?"

"How did you—?"

He lets out a soft laugh at my surprise. "People talk. Uncle Fisher was having coffee with some of his fishing buddies and one of them wouldn't stop bragging about recruiting 'Ella and her nice cousin from Chicago' to help."

"I try my best" I say, like it wasn't Ella who volunteered us in the first place. "How was your trip?"

His mouth twists. "It was ok. I enjoy traveling occasionally, but this one happened to be for work."

I nod sympathetically. "Traveling isn't all it's cracked up to be. Did I ever tell you about the last trip I went on? I ended up in a ditch."

He chokes on his coffee. "You don't say. How did that turn out?"

I shrug. "I got into a car with a stranger, who then tricked me into breaking into some dude's house."

"You did, didn't you," he says dryly.

"I'm still embarrassed, by the way."

"I would be too, if I were you." The corners of his mouth twitch into a smile that he can't fully hold back.

I don't have a comeback for that one, so I just smile and take another sip of my latte. I'm hyper aware of the way he's watching me. It's flattering, I think, but all I feel is a jumble of nerves. I'm typically the person who sits on the sidelines; I'm not sure what to do when the attention is fully on me. I cast around for something to break the silence. "Do you travel often for work?"

"More often than I'd like. I'd rather just stay home." He looks embarrassed to admit that, but if I had a house like Finn's, I wouldn't want to leave it, either.

"Home is nice," I agree.

"And what about you, Rune? Are you heading home soon or are you hanging out here in the northland for a while longer?"

"I was planning on going back to Chicago on Sunday."

He gives a nod of acknowledgement and goes back to drinking his coffee.

Why do you want to know, is what I really want to ask. I'm a little proud of myself when I hold that question back. I may be crushing on him, but Finn is clearly here for some polite conversation, nothing more. Mentally chastising myself for being ridiculous, I open my mouth to follow up with another inconsequential comment about the temperature outside when Ella returns in her customary whirlwind. She slides into the chair with me, half-sitting on my lap.

"Ouch," I complain.

"I can sit on Finn's lap, if you'd rather."

"You may not," he says calmly.

She wrinkles her nose at him. "Rude."

"Did you save the sweater?" I ask, changing the subject.

"It's a little better, see? Mom said it shouldn't stain. So, what are you up to for the holidays, Finn? Rune was supposed to head back to Chicago today, but she's caved to our pleading and decided to stay with us through the weekend."

"Great question. I was actually wondering if you two have plans for tonight?"

My heart ratchets up a few beats.

"Tell me what's up first, then I'll let you know if we're busy or not," Ella drawls.

"There's a formal-slash-informal gathering at the Lounge tonight with drinks and hors d'oeuvres."

"The Lounge? That's a classy place." Ella sounds suitably impressed.

"Yes, well, my parents are hosting," Finn says with a grimace. "They've surprised me with a visit and wanted to see as many old faces as possible. Figured I'd see if you guys and Mairi would want to come?"

"I don't remember your parents being particularly fond of me, but by all means, put us on the guest list. Do we get to get all fancied up and everything?" Ella's eyes are sparkling, delighted with the prospect of a fancy night out.

"There's no dress code. In fact, I—oh, thank you." Finn takes a bagel from the barista, who's emerged from behind the counter to personally deliver his order.

"So you were saying that your parents are in town, Finn?" She leans against the corner of a table, one lush hip out. I might look like a troll that just got dragged out of bed, but this girl's makeup is on point; her glossy brown hair is twisted into a perfect low, messy bun.

"They are, yes."

"Does your mom still read a lot? I remember she used to come to book club here years ago."

"Yeah, she likes her books."

"I remember she drove that silver SUV—what kind was it? Toyota? Subaru?"

"I think it was a GMC."

"Oh right. Do you have any fun plans while they're up north?"

I take a sip of my latte to hide my smile. The girl must have overheard his mention of the party. I would bet the last five dollar bill in my wallet that she's fishing for an invite. Finn is either oblivious or very good at evading the issue.

She gives a flirty little smile and leans close, but stops short when one of the other baristas gives a shout behind the counter.

"Emily! We need you!"

Finn looks up from his food and his eyes widen slightly at her nearness. "Uh, thanks for the bagel," he offers again, like maybe that's the reason she's got her cleavage on display for him.

"No problem. Say hi to your parents for me." With one last flutter of her lashes at Finn—while pointedly ignoring Ella and I—Emily the barista leaves.

Ella and I share a look.

"She was hitting on you," Ella points out the obvious to Finn.

"She was being nice." His cheeks are pink, which is entertaining. And also a little annoying.

"Oooookay," Ella says with an exaggerated eye roll.

"Anyway, I'd better get back to entertain my parents." He stands with a long stretch. "I'm glad I ran into you."

"Hard work, huh?" Ella looks sympathetic.

"You know Sherri and Pat," he replies dryly. "See you tonight?" The question is for both of us, but Finn is looking at me.

I nod. "As long as your parents don't mind a stranger showing up to their party?"

"The more the merrier. I'll see you then." He zips up his jacket and brushes a hand lightly against my shoulder in farewell as he walks by.

Ella looks at me, bemused.

"What?"

"Nothing," she says quickly. "You seem awake now. Ready to work?"

"I suppose so."

The community center is a chaos of old cardboard boxes filled with dusty bags of streamers, balloons, and white plastic tablecloths.

"The garland looks nice enough, but this will make it look like a kid's birthday party," I mutter, holding up a sparkly red roll of streamer paper.

"Just wait," Ella promises. "This stuff can be so much cooler than you would ever imagine."

Sure enough, I watch as Ella turns the fragile red paper into a massive holiday bow, complete with curled ribbon ends.

"These can go onto the table ends—like so—and also up on the wall where the garland swoops up."

"Incredible."

Slowly, painstakingly, I try to follow along as she creates over a dozen more. Mine aren't nearly as beautiful as hers, but by the third iteration, they're passable enough to display.

It's lunch time before we even take a breath, but our hard work has paid off: the room is ready with white-clad tables, glass vase centerpieces with sprigs of pine and fairy lights; the paper streamer bows adding vibrant pops of color throughout.

Ella rubs her hands proudly together, surveying the work. "It will look even better when the tables are set and the lights are low."

I can imagine.

The volunteers seem swept up in the excitement of seeing all the hard work finally come together, and most of us barely take a lunch break, opting instead to put the boxes for decorations back in the basement, followed by a final sweep of the floors and a lighting test.

Ella shoos me out of the room for the last bit, extracting a promise that I'll wait in the entry and won't peek. "I want you to be surprised when you see it on Saturday," she insists.

"As long as it's quick," I warn, because the entry is cold.

"Five minutes tops," she promises.

Which is an absolute lie. I'm freezing my ass off by the time Ella is ready to leave.

"I think I'll be the one to judge whether it is, in fact, worth it," I grumble on the ride back to the house. My hands are still cold, despite holding them up against the heat register in the car for the past fifteen minutes.

"It will literally blow your mind."

"I'll literally tell you if that's true or not in two days," I mock. "But in the meantime—what I should expect for this shindig that we're supposed to go to tonight?"

"I can tell you it's fancy enough that you'll regret using the word 'shindig' to describe it. Finn's parents are high rollers," she explains. "Like, they only drink top shelf liquor and buy stuff from companies that donate to earth preservation charities. Good people, but—yeah, high rollers. I guarantee most of the guests will have those really ugly brand name purses and wear outfits that have been professionally tailored for them."

"Are there a lot of people like that around here?" I wonder. "This seems like more of a rustic-outdoorsy-naturalist area."

"Oh, they're definitely here. Tonight they'll be coming out of the woodwork. A lot of the rich people from the Cities like to buy second or third homes up in this area, especially those who grew up here or have some other ties to the area."

"Makes sense. If I had money, I would definitely spend a good chunk of it trying to get out of Chicago."

"I kind of liked Chicago when I visited."

"I mean, it's fine. Just because I haven't had a spectacular time there doesn't mean it's a terrible place. It's just that—" I search for the right words "—it's never really felt like home. Just a place to stay while I look for something more permanent. And I don't know where to find that anymore. Or even where to look."

I rub the fog off the cold window as we pull into the driveway. Aunt Mairi's outside chopping firewood. Despite the cold, she's dressed in nothing but a hoodie and jeans, her jacket cast off and laying on the hood of her car. With her hair pulled back into a braid, she looks far too young to be sixty-two.

"Well, you will not find all that tonight, that's for damn sure," Ella says emphatically. "You will, however, get to play classy lady and eat some fancy hors d'oeuvres. For *free*."

I bark out a laugh at the emphasis and meet her high-five. Free is good. Free is excellent. Especially when it comes at the invitation of a certain Finn Sigurdson.

Chapter 14

Finn

It takes all of my self control to walk away from Rune in the coffee shop without doing something crazy, like asking her out on the spot. Maybe I would have, if Ella hadn't been there, watching us like a hawk.

My head's all kinds of crazy over this girl. I had been en route to meet up with my parents when I recognized her car parked on the side of the road and figured a quick stop for coffee and breakfast was probably in order. Maybe say a quick friendly hello and be on my way. A true sentiment, but—there's nothing friendly about the way I felt when I saw her standing there. Blame my ego, but I swear those eyes lit up like a sunrise when she recognized me. It sent a jolt straight to my groin and made me think all sorts of wild thoughts. About the possibility of...I don't even know what. I shouldn't admit to anything. I hardly know the girl.

Besides, it's been years since I dated anyone seriously.

Dating makes me nervous. It resurfaces a lot of old insecurities, thanks in particular to the train wreck of a relationship that I had beginning in my junior year of college. My romantic interest was a cute English major named Amy, who gave off solid girl-next-door vibes and was as enthusiastic about getting naked together as I was. I've always been strongly introverted, but it really felt like we had something great going on between us: study sessions interspersed with sex. A lot of sex.

We dated for a year and a half, and I was starting to really think of a future with her.

I didn't realize anything was amiss in our relationship until I walked into the library one day and found her making out with a theater major. To make matters worse, she followed me out and explained in great detail all the shortcomings I had as a boyfriend that made her look elsewhere. And then she broke up with me. In the middle of the campus courtyard, surrounded by students who were mindlessly unaware that my heart and pride were being hacked apart with every word that tumbled out of Amy's mouth.

I spent the rest of my senior year alone in my dorm room, pouring my heart and soul into my writing. It wasn't great work, but it was the push I needed to start writing prolifically enough to make progress. It was also when I started to plot out the series of novels that would end up changing my life.

It's been nearly eight years, but the more I delve into my work, the less tempted I am to bring anyone in to upset the balance. I thrive on silence and solitude and no one has tempted me to go deeper than some short-term, highly physical relationships. For me, solitude and self-reliance are foundational pillars of my life and success. Which is maybe what Amber was getting at when she made those comments, now that I think about it.

But Rune—that girl makes me feel as if I'm missing something.

She has that look like she's thinking far more than she's willing to admit out loud. All I want to do is pry back the secrets behind those beautiful eyes.

I guess on the positive side, this new obsession gives me something else to focus on besides my struggles with work. Whatever brief inspiration I had last week seems to have disappeared. I set my alarm for five this morning, only to spend the next two hours forcing out words that seemed all wrong and staring into space in disgust at my ineptitude.

It's been that way since I got back from Chicago two days ago. All I can think about is the fact that I can't write anymore, that my career is apparently over, and—Rune. I've wondered if she's thought of me at all. It occurred to me that I should pull my head out of my ass and just text her, but I was afraid of coming off too strong. I've never thought of myself as an insecure person, but apparently I am.

I shouldn't care so much.

I'm overthinking everything about this. It will be good to see her tonight. Maybe I just need a real conversation with the girl to settle my thoughts. It's probably some latent caveman instinct that has me worried about the girl who came in with the snowstorm. Girl cold, need fire, etc.

It's not an emotion I'm familiar with, which intrigues me to no end, now. I might write about passion, but I've experienced very little of it in real life. Historically, the more solitary my lifestyle, the better my writing. But maybe that's no longer the case.

Maybe I just need a real life muse to get me back on track.

Chapter 15

Rune

"Just how fancy is this party?" I ask, watching mesmerized as Ella turns her long blond hair into a dreamy cascade of waves. My hair is straight and brown and even Ella gave up trying to get it to curl like hers.

"Fancy enough to make it clear that they're a few tax brackets above us," Courtney sniffs with displeasure. Although Aunt Mairi seems as excited about the party as Ella and I, Courtney straight up refused to go, insisting that nothing sounded worse than spending an evening rubbing elbows with a bunch of wanna-be socialites who've been drinking. Especially when she is planning to head out of town tomorrow morning to attend her friend's Christmas party.

"Is it too much cleavage, though?" I frown at the full-length mirror we've set up in the living room, holding my hand over the skin exposed by the plunging neckline. Although Ella falls under the "slender and willowy" category, we managed to find a black dress of hers with enough stretch to fit over my soft curves. It's snug but not obscene, according to Aunt Mairi.

"*Is it too much cleavage*," Ella mocks. "Rule number one: there can never be too much cleavage."

"Agree to disagree," I mumble, tugging at the neckline.

Aunt Mairi looks over from the kitchen, where she's steaming her outfit: a silver chiffon blouse and black skirt duo. "I think it looks nice. A little bit of sexy, but not too much. Maybe shorten your necklace just a bit?"

I adjust the silver chain with its little book pendant so that it rests just beneath my collar bone.

"Perfect."

I nod at my reflection, as if satisfied with my appearance. I'm not, but this is the best it's gonna get. Full of nervous energy, I force myself to sit down and open my fancy book. I've been so busy that I haven't made much progress on it, which is unusual. Even now, opening to my bookmark, I can't focus on the words.

"I can hear your thoughts from over here," Aunt Mairi murmurs.

"Do you think it's actually ok that I come with you guys?"

"I thought Finn invited you," she says, sounding surprised.

"He did, Mom." I don't have to look at Ella to know she's rolling her eyes. "He specifically stared at Rune with those pretty blue eyes of his and asked if he was going to see her tonight. And then he caressed her shoulder."

Shit, she's been paying more attention than I realized. Even Courtney is looking at me with a thoughtful expression and now I wish I hadn't said anything. I really, really hate being the object of someone else's speculation.

"He did not caress my shoulder. And maybe he was just being polite," I argue.

"If he didn't want you to come, he wouldn't have invited me in front of you, knowing that you're staying with us and would have nothing else to do," Ella insists.

"Men are not always perceptive." I shouldn't have to point that out.

"We're talking about Finn here. He's the epitome of perceptive."

"Regardless," Aunt Mairi breaks in calmly, "I think you'll be fine. This isn't a sit down event with placecards. People will be coming and going. I doubt we'll be the only ones who bring out-of-town relatives or friends tonight. Sherri and Pat's parties are somewhat famous."

"If I get kicked out for crashing the party, I'm going to blame you," I warn Ella, who's still smirking.

❄

The Lounge, where tonight's party is taking place, is as beautiful and classy as Ella claimed. More so, even.

It's an old brick building with massive floor to ceiling windows and minimalist-Scandi decor: all black matte metal and pale birch wood. The windows command an incredible view of the lake, or so they tell me; it's dark outside, so I can't actually see what's out there besides some snow. The lights are low as we enter; upbeat music wafts from the bar area around the corner. There's an enormous staircase leading to the hotel rooms that span the second and third floors. Around the lobby, groups of well-dressed people are conversing, drinks in hand.

It looks like a hopping place.

"Do you have a reservation?" The hostess peers at us from behind a tall counter.

"We're here for the Sigurdson party," Aunt Mairi replies.

"Ah." The hostess pulls out a sheet of paper. "Just add your names here."

I get another shiver of nervousness, but when I peer over Aunt

Mairi's shoulder, I see that she's simply written her own name along with the number 3.

"See?" Ella whispers as we hang our coats in the coatroom. "You're just a number. Could be you, could be Courtney. No one knows. Or cares."

Fine, then.

In a partially separate area, there's a table full of delicacies next to a very elaborate hot chocolate bar. Most of the women milling around are wearing either sleek black dresses or very extravagant holiday-ish fashion: a conglomerate of red plaid, gold sequins, and very high heels. The men take a more generic approach: tailored button-up shirts and black trousers or jeans.

I feel like I'm a child playing dress up amid a crowd of grownups, but it is kind of fun. It's been a long time since I had any occasion to get fancy and go out for an evening. I stick like a magnet to Auntie and Ella as they weave their way through the crowd.

"Mom, Rune needs a drink," Ella tugs on Aunt Mairi's sleeve, steering her toward the bar.

Auntie takes one look at me over her shoulder and agrees without a word.

"Why do I need a drink?" I demand, mildly peeved at being singled out.

"Because you look like a scared little mouse." Ella shoves a shot glass into my hand, filled with something bright and pink. "Shots first, then you can walk around with a proper drink like a classy lady."

"Cheers to a night out with two of my favorite girlies." Aunt Mairi taps her shot glass against each of ours before downing it quickly.

"Mom, you're so old. No one says girlies," Ella complains good-humoredly.

"That's what you think. Wait till you become a grownup," Auntie teases, booping Ella on the nose.

It's an adorable picture: Aunt Mairi, with her dark, silver-stranded hair drawn back into an elegant French twist, her face already flushed from the liquor and laughing, and Ella: blonde, but with the same sparkling brown eyes and mischievous smile. They're adorable, and I secretly wish I belonged to Auntie, instead of her sister.

Fortunately, I don't have time to brood over familial relationships. A hand lightly touches my waist and I turn to see Finn, dressed in a white shirt with blue buttons, the sleeves rolled up to his elbows.

"Hi." He looks down at me with a smile.

"Hi," I reply, feeling the heat rise to my cheeks and knowing there is nothing I can do about it.

"I was going to offer you a drink, but you've made a beeline and beat me to it."

"We just needed a quick warmup before our real drinks. Rune doesn't like crowds," Ella says unnecessarily.

"I'm introverted, not anti-social," I say quickly. "I've been known to frequent a club or two."

"That makes two of us." He gives me a wink before turning to the counter, waving down the bartender.

"What do you like?" he asks over his shoulder.

"A mojito, please," Ella says.

"Are you even old enough to drink?" Finn scoffs.

"Rude, Finn."

"How about you, Mairi?"

"A riesling, please. Thank you, Finny."

"Rune?"

"Brandy on the rocks."

"Preference on the kind?"

"I usually drink bottom shelf," I say honestly.

His eyes flash with humor and he orders something that is definitely not bottom shelf.

"Here—riesling for you, Mairi. A mojito that may or may not have alcohol for little Ella. And brandy on the rocks for Rune." He doles them out one by one as they come in.

"Now where are your parents?" Auntie looks around. "They were our next stop."

"Over by the hot chocolate bar. Come with me."

"Are all these people here for your parents' party?" I ask as we weave between the scattered groups of socialites.

"Crazy, huh? Can you tell my parents are extroverts?"

I'm expecting to meet two people who look something like Finn: tall, dark, and extremely good-looking. So it's mildly surprising when Finn's parents turn out to be somewhat ordinary humans. Average height, with graying brown hair. His dad is thin, with a sort of weathered look about his face, like a man who spends a lot of time outdoors in the elements.

"Mom, Dad, look who just arrived," Finn announces. "You remember Mairi's daughter, Ella? And this is Rune, Mairi's niece from out of state."

"Mairi, it's been too long—how have you been? Are you still making that lovely yarn?" His mother is a short, curvy woman dressed in a bold, red sequined dress. She has the social grace of someone who is used to playing the hostess, laying a hand on my aunt's arm as if they're long-lost friends. Maybe they are. I guess I wouldn't know.

Aunt Mairi certainly seems genuinely glad to see the woman. They chat about yarn and knitting and something about Sherri's book club in Arizona, where they're currently spending the winter.

"And your niece, Rune—what a lovely name. Rune, where are you from?" Sherri smiles at me.

"I've been living in Chicago," I reply.

"Oh, is that where you met Finn?" Sherri looks to her son for confirmation.

"No, I—well, it wasn't—" I stumble over my words, wondering how to explain the fact that I broke into her son's house and met him in a towel.

Finn looks delighted, waiting to see what I'm going to say.

"Rune's just up for a visit," Aunt Mairi says smoothly, possibly mistaking the reason for my hesitance. "Finn was kind enough to extend the invitation, since she's staying with us."

I look at her gratefully. God bless Aunt Mairi.

Our conversation is cut off soon thereafter by the arrival of more guests. When Aunt Mairi excuses herself to speak to another set of friends, Ella whips out her phone.

"I have someone I want you to meet," she grins at me, a bright sparkle in her eyes. "See that table over there in the corner? Go grab it, I'll be right back."

I barely nod my assent before she disappears through the crowd, aiming in the direction of the entrance, leaving me alone in a room full of strangers. Finn remains at his mother's side, talking to an older couple who just arrived. That leaves me, I guess. I head straight for the empty table, but another group grabs it before I make it there. Ugh. I could stand here awkwardly, or—I toss back my drink and nearly sprint to nab another table that seems freshly vacated. There are empty glasses strewn all over it, so I busy myself tidying it up, waiting for Ella to show up again.

Good thing I'm buzzed. It makes my solitude slightly less awkward. Besides, from this vantage point I can people watch. More specifically, I can stare unabashedly at the tall, stunning man working the room. He's moved away from his parents and easily engages with various groups of guests, joining into whatever conversation he happens upon. As if sensing my stare, his gaze catches mine. I can't seem to pull my eyes away as his brows lift slightly and he makes his way towards me.

I'm a grown woman who's been through a boyfriend or two, but butterflies erupt at his approach like I'm back in junior high and he's my first crush.

"Have you been abandoned?" he asks.

"Possibly. Ella said she wanted me to meet someone. She may have gotten distracted."

He looks around with a frown, as if trying to find Ella to express his disapproval. She's well and truly gone.

Finn slides into the empty seat next to me instead, and suddenly I'm all nerves again.

"This is a nice party," I say, wishing I was as full of words as Ella. "I had no idea you were such a social butterfly. I wouldn't have the energy to be such a charming host right after a work trip."

"You think I'm charming?" His eyes crinkle. "To be fair, I've been back for a couple days. I've had some time to reset my social batteries."

"Oh." That's surprising. And also—a bit disappointing, if I'm being honest. I'd had this silly little thought in my mind that he would text me when he returned, even if it was just to comment that my car was no longer taking up space in his driveway. I was wrong. I've been overthinking that damn back massage for a solid week. I take a drink of brandy to hide my embarrassing thoughts.

I'm not hiding them well enough, because his expression turns sober. "I thought about texting you the moment I got back to see how you were making out with your big northern adventure. But then I didn't."

I blink. This sounds like the beginning of a not so great conversation. "Okay."

He runs a hand through his hair. If I didn't know better, I'd say he was flustered. "It's just—there's been a lot going on with work the past few months. I've been in my head too much. So anyway, I'm glad I ran into you. Forced me to say something."

"I appreciate the invite," I force myself to say. "But you didn't have to. I would have understood if you only wanted Mairi and Ella to come."

"That's not what I meant." Finn grimaces and traces the ring of condensation left on the table by his glass. "I was hoping to meet up with you again."

Now I'm all kinds of confused. I lift the brandy to my lips to stall for time. You can't talk when you're drinking. Unfortunately, he's still silent when I finish and I feel obliged to say something.

"So, if you had texted me," I say slowly, "what would it have said?"

He lets out a breath and runs a hand through his hair again. It's mussed up and I sort of want to bury my own hands in it.

"I thought about coming up with a joke. Probably a photo of the driveway or the house and make some humorous reference about you. Very lighthearted. Then I was going to ask if you were still up north, and if so, whether you were free at all this weekend."

"And if I said yes?" Why is it suddenly so hard to breathe?

His eyes clash into mine. "Then I was going to ask if you'd like to do something with me."

Well...shit.

Before I can string together enough words to make a coherent sentence, Ella emerges through the crowd, a colorful blue drink in hand and a man with cropped sandy blonde hair in tow behind her. "Oh, hello. Sorry, Rune, I got a little distracted. Meet Sam." She twirls her hand towards him with a ta-da effect.

"Hi, Rune," says the man.

"Hello, nice to meet you," I reply. "And who, exactly, am I meeting?"

"My very latest love interest." Ella winks at me. She ushers Sam to take a seat at the table, then perches on his lap, one arm draped over his shoulders.

"Latest as in best she's ever had," Sam says, tousling her hair.

"I worked for an hour on this." She glares at him, trying to smooth the wild strands back with her free hand.

"I like it when it looks lived in," he says. "You know that. Anyway, Rune, you're the long-lost cousin from the big city?"

"Yeah. Big city girl visiting my small town cousin."

"Nice. I took an internship in Chicago my sophomore year of college."

"Really? How did you like it?"

"Hated it," he says cheerfully. "I grew up in Forest Lake, just outside the Cities, but Chicago was just too—I don't even know. Not my style."

I know people actually do really like Chicago. And to be fair, it did enchant me for the first couple years. There are so many places to see, so many activities to participate in. But with each passing day, I feel less excited about the prospect of going back there.

"How did you meet?" I ask, watching the way he leans towards Ella so that they're tucked in close together. Like even an inch is too far apart. There's a softness to her smile when she looks at him that I don't think I've ever seen on her face before.

"I work in Duluth," Sam says. "Ella came into the office building one day, armed to the teeth with pamphlets and stickers and shit." He reaches as if to tousle her hair again, then apparently thinks better of it and takes a drink of his beer instead.

"I was recruiting volunteers for cleaning up the parks and trails," she clarifies. "He was my first recruit."

"The moment she opened that smart little mouth of hers, I found myself agreeing to whatever it was she was asking for help with." He makes a grimace. "Didn't realize until too late that I volunteered to pick up what ended up being a solid fifteen gallons of dog crap."

Ella cackles. "Sam was so invested that he started campaigning for stricter enforcement and higher fines for littering. It didn't fly, but the city did put out more signs and free doggy doo bags."

"So I'm basically a city hero."

"Does Auntie know about him?" I ask.

"She knows about him, but has never actually met him. Tonight's the big night." If I didn't know better, I'd say Ella looks nervous.

"You been skiing at all lately?" Sam says to Finn, changing the subject.

"A bit. Work's been busy, but I'm hoping to get out there sometime in the next few days."

Ella perks up even more, if that's possible. "Wait, do you two actually know each other?"

"Finn and I were a part of the same cross-country ski club last year."

"It was the two of us and about eight older women." Finn chuckles into his drink.

"It was great. We were inseparable."

"I don't think you understand the definition of inseparable," Finn deadpans back.

The chatter continues and I glance at Finn, who's now bantering with Sam about some skiing thing or another. I'm dying inside, kicking myself for not blurting out an answer to Finn's maybe-question. What if he thinks I'm not interested? What if some other girl sidles up to him and he goes off with her because I haven't given him an answer? Deep down, I know it's my perpetual anxiety whispering these thoughts, but I can't shake them. So I reach for my phone, keeping it slightly hidden under the table, and tap out a quick text.

. . .

> Me: I know the conversation has moved on. But hypothetically…if I'd received that text, I would have said yes.

Send.

Immediate panic follows. Did that sound too needy? Too… eager? I watch nervously as Finn slides his phone out of his pocket and, I presume, reads my message.

I almost die of relief when I see the corners of his mouth turn up ever so slightly. Beneath the table, his knee presses against mine. I'm not sure I remember how to breathe.

Across the table, Ella sits a little straighter and tips her head to the side. Her eyes flick from Finn's face to mine.

I swear I'm trying not to be obvious about it, but it's really, really hard. I force myself to look away from him, as if I'm suddenly very interested in the decor of the place. The lights hanging from the ceiling are pretty nice. So is the exit sign above the door.

"So anyway," Sam's saying, "Ella keeps hiding her family from me. I don't know if I should be celebrating or nervous that she's finally letting me meet you guys tonight."

Ella rubs her hands together, looking around nervously. "Maybe you should just leave now. Out the back door so Mom doesn't see you." The fact that she's nervous must say something about how serious she is about this guy. He seems fine to me. And the fact that he's friends with Finn—well, I just get a good feeling about it, is all.

"You want me to come for backup?" I ask.

"I don't think we need backup, but you can come to enjoy the fireworks." Sam tucks Ella's arm into his.

I glance questioningly at Finn.

"Rune needs a refill. You guys go do what you have to," he says.

Ella takes a deep breath before striding off resolutely across the room, dragging Sam away.

"She's got him wrapped around her finger," Finn observes.

I agree. I wonder what it's like. I was always the one who was wrapped around Sebastian's finger.

The bar has become more crowded now. It takes a while before we reach the counter and flag down the bartender.

"May I order this next one for you?" Finn looks down at me.

I motion for him to go ahead, taking the opportunity to admire his profile as he orders another very classy sounding brandy for me and a whiskey for himself. I've never heard of a nose fetish before, but maybe I have one because that nose of his is absolute, pure perfection. It's straight and chiseled right down to the very tip.

He catches me staring and his eyes crinkle. "See something you like?"

"Just waiting on my drink," I lie. I couldn't care less about the drink. At this point, it's only an excuse to stand this close to Finn, our arms barely touching, pretending as if I'm not fully turned on by his proximity.

"You're undressing me with those bedroom eyes."

"I am not." I am and I need to stop.

"I'm not complaining." His hand brushes against mine as he hands me my brandy. "It's getting loud in here. Want to go find a quieter place to finish our conversation?"

Ella and Sam are forgotten entirely as Finn holds out his hand in a silent offer. I don't think twice before putting mine in his and allowing him to guide us both out of the crowded bar.

Chapter 16

Finn

The moment Rune walks into the Lounge, it's like the entire earth tilts on its axis. I'm drawn to her like a clichéd moth to a flame. With two whiskey sours behind me, it doesn't even occur to do anything besides excuse myself from a conversation with two of my dad's friends and go directly to meet Rune and her relatives.

I've already gotten the impression that Rune is far more introverted than her vivacious cousin. Her eyes are wide, scanning the room with what appears to be a mix of excitement and nervousness. Ella must notice it as well, because she steers Mairi and Rune off their original course, towards the bar, instead. Bless her thoughtful heart.

I hang back for just a moment, watching the trio as they toss back their shots. Then I'm striding towards them again, my eyes glued to Rune and that fucking dress she's wearing. It shows off every curve on her body, from the luscious slope of her breasts to the sway of her hips.

I can't help reaching out and brushing my fingertips against the sleek curve of Rune's waist as I reach her side. She stiffens for a moment, startled. But instead of stepping away, she turns towards me. Her mouth widens into the cutest damn smile and my heart is suddenly lighter than it's been all week. The girl is stunning. I could stare at her all night. Could—and do.

I try to keep up with the various conversations, playing the gracious host as is expected of me tonight. But my eyes keep finding their way back to Rune. She stands a world apart from everyone, like a goddess among mortals. Her brows are furrowed delicately; the only real sign she isn't wholly comfortable here. It takes far too long to find an excuse to go to her side.

My hands shake a little from the nerves of talking to her, of wanting to make her laugh, of putting her at ease. She doesn't seem to realize the amount of appreciative looks she's getting from the other men. She deserves to be noticed, but it's irritating me beyond belief. *Eyes on your own wife, Mr. Johnson.*

By the time Sam and Ella leave our table, I've made up my mind: I am tired of this party and all I want is Rune to myself for the rest of the night. I offer my hand to her as a sort of question. She takes it without hesitation, her eyes fixed on where our fingers intertwine as I draw her through the crowds, in search of a quiet corner where I can talk to Rune without a room full of prying eyes on us. Without my mind going a little crazy from the sheer number of other guys checking her out.

We go around the corner to the small glass conservatory that's typically used for smaller parties. A few tall tables line the brick wall, surrounding a couch and two armchairs set in a semi-circle in front of the gas fireplace in the middle of the room. It's a blessed, quiet relief after the commotion in the bar.

I twirl my hand in a flourish.

"Yes, please." She gives an adorable sigh and throws herself down onto the couch. I don't know how she moves so gracefully in that tight dress. I join her, stretching out just enough so that my knee grazes hers. Her eyes flick to my leg. A little smile graces her face as she tips another sip out of her drink.

"Your mother seems nice," she says right away, a slight inflection at the end, as if uncertain about her own opinion.

"She's really in her element here," I reply, a bit dryly. "She enjoys seeing her friends all in one place. Sometimes I'm not quite sure whether her and Dad come up to visit me or for—this." I gesture behind us. It isn't an absolutely true statement. My parents wouldn't bother coming up in the winter if it wasn't for the fact that I love it here. Even the prospect of some ice fishing for my dad isn't enough to compensate for what the bitter cold does to his arthritic joints.

"It's a nice party. I'm glad Ella made me dress up." Rune smooths out a nonexistent wrinkle on the side of her dress.

"You look incredible," I say. This time I don't try to hide my appreciative stare as I take her all in. Her hair's swept off to the side into some sort of twist that ends in a cascade of silk strands that brush the curve of her cleavage. I swallow and drag my eyes back up to find her staring at me.

"Thank you." The words are soft, obligatory, like she doesn't realize she's a faerie vision.

"I'm glad you came tonight."

"You invited me," she says. "I wanted to see you."

"Oh? And what do you think, now that you have?"

"You look nice, too." This time it's her turn to eye fuck me, and damn if it doesn't make me have to shift my position a little. Especially when she daringly flicks her eyes to my crotch.

"I'll tell you a secret: it's more impressive without the clothes."

The blush that suffuses her face makes the dumb dick humor totally worthwhile.

"So, your parents like parties?" Rune asks, abruptly changing the subject.

"It's always a whirlwind," I allow. "Their visits tend to make me question my own sanity. But I'm an only child, so even if it's not always convenient—I'm the only one they have to visit."

"Where do they live? I sort of assumed you grew up here."

"I did, for the most part. When they became empty nesters they decided they wanted to travel: Arizona in the winter, Europe in the spring and fall, and usually somewhere like Maine in the summer."

"Wow." She looks suitably impressed.

"Yeah, wow," I mimic. I guess it's cool, if you're into that kind of thing. I prefer my house with all of its familiar comforts.

"That's right, you're not a traveler." Rune seems to catch the drift of my thoughts.

"Sometimes it can be fun," I amend. "Depends on who you're traveling with—and why. What about you, Rune?"

She shakes her head, but her eyes are thoughtful. "I've never been farther than Cincinnati. I think I might like to travel someday. See some ancient castles in Europe, or maybe go camping in Scotland or Scandinavia. My sister Jules is always telling me about the places she's visited, but I would want to travel differently than she does. I'd want to find a cozy house to rent somewhere off the beaten path. Hide there, like a personal retreat from the world, and work on my drawings. Anyway. Some day." She flicks her fingers dismissively and takes another drink.

But I've already caught what she didn't say. "Drawings?"

Her mouth twists. "It's a hobby."

I stretch out my legs and lean towards her, settling in for the conversation. "Okay Rune, what's your dream career path?"

I expect her to brush off the question, maybe change the topic. She surprises me with a prompt, "I would want to be an illustrator for fantasy novels."

Well, this is unexpected. "Really."

"Fantasy romance, to be exact." She leans forward, a sparkle in those dark eyes of hers. She's actually excited about this. "I'm obsessed with it. The world-building. The layers of plots and subplots. The romance."

My kind of girl.

"Have you illustrated anything yet?"

"I've done some illustrations for my sister, who's been dabbling in fae smut." She wrinkles her nose. "Her writing is good, but she refuses to get it published. Otherwise, I have been doing fan art for my favorite series."

"Which is...?"

"*Crimson and Roses* by R.E. Andersson."

"Really." My eyes narrow.

"Have you heard of it?" Her eager expression falters at my response.

"Ye-es." I draw out the word. It's a safe answer: the books have risen to a status most authors only dream of. Every book in the 5-book series has hit the bestseller list multiple times, alongside the ongoing momentum of turning the whole thing into a TV series. "Why is that your favorite?"

"Because it's brilliant," she says, a bit defensively. "Are you judging me?"

"No, I just—why is that series your favorite?" I don't know if she's playing me or what, but I'm prepared to give her the benefit of the doubt.

"Have you read the books?" Rune demands.

"I'm familiar with the story, yes." A non-answer, but the best I can manage at the moment until I see where she's going with this.

"Well, I like the story. The plot is incredibly well-thought-out and the characters have so much depth. They're like real-life beings living in little book pages. R.E. Andersson is brilliant, and I'm obsessed with every twisted plot line she comes up with."

I choke on a startled laugh and attempt to disguise it as a cough. "She? Is it a woman? I've always pictured them as a male of sorts."

"They say it's a man, but I don't believe it," she says, leaning in as if telling me a secret. "There's too much internal character development, for one thing. If R.E. Andersson was actually a man, there would be much less of that. And probably a lot more breasts."

I almost spit out my drink. "God, Rune, stereotype much?"

She only shrugs, confident in her analysis. "I picture her being my book bestie. Someday I'll meet her and we'll hang out over coffee. I'll show her my fan art, she'll sign my favorite bookmark, and then I'll get the inside scoop on everything she's written so far: what her favorite characters are, and whether she has come up with back stories for the side characters. All fan girl stuff, you know?"

I am rarely speechless. But right now, I couldn't formulate a single word if I wanted.

"I've re-read the series at least four times," Rune continues, "and each time it just gets better, even though the last book hasn't been written yet. I'm planning a re-read for when it does come out. I even bought a cosplay outfit so I can dress up as the main character at ren fests." As soon as the words are out, she winces, as if wishing she could take them back.

Too bad she can't and now I know.

"Next time I'll make sure to insist that my parents host a costume party. Because this is an outfit I have to see." I toss a wink at her and she looks almost relieved. I realize that I should probably say something more, maybe burst that little bubble of hers, but... I'm a bit floored that she seems to honestly have no idea. Should I tell her? Or is that a dick move in this particular moment?

"Are you done judging me for my taste in literature?" Rune raises her brows at my silence.

"I'm not judging," I hasten to assure her.

"Hm. You look like you are."

"Never," I vow. "I have, in fact, read that particular series by R.E. Andersson and share your enthusiasm for the overarching story. I'd be very interested to see your illustrations."

"Maybe. I don't show many people. Are you a reader?"

"I've been known to crack open a book or two." I've amassed hundreds of books over the years. Probably more than a thousand. I'll have to count them. "And don't ask me to pick a favorite because I can't. Maybe if we could subdivide by genre, but—no, still probably not then."

"Favorite genre, then."

"Fantasy romance."

"You're teasing me."

"I swear on the grave of my childhood turtle, Shelly." I hold up my hand as if swearing in court.

"So R.E. Andersson has to be up there on your list. You can't possibly have anyone else even close."

"What about Starlight Hiddleston?" I name another popular fantasy romance author.

"I personally thought her characters fell flat. Not to mention the glaring plot holes in both *Dragon* and *Edge*."

"The spice scenes are well done." I lift a brow in challenge, seeing if she'll take the bait, but she just brushes it off.

"Maybe, but they're still cliché."

"Name one fantasy sex scene that isn't."

"Macie and Robert in book three of *Crimson and Roses*," she replies promptly. "It's one of the most surprising and emotionally raw scenes I've ever come across."

"Really." If I wasn't already smitten with this girl, I would certainly be by this point.

"I sobbed like a baby the whole way through."

"Is that how you typically react to spice? Cry?" I'm thoroughly amused now. Rune reaches over to flick my arm.

"Cry with pleasure, maybe," she says nonsensically.

I shake my head, grinning, and we both take a drink. She's so much more relaxed than when she first walked into the bar. Her eyes are bright; her cheeks flushed with the softest pink. I'm having a hard time keeping my eyes up, especially as she leans forward to take off her high heels. I wish we were really alone. I'd tug that neckline down farther—pull the whole damn dress off—and indulge myself with exploring every inch of her.

The force of that thought startles me.

I'm not a teenager who can't keep it in his pants. Even when I was a teenager, I was never that kid. To be fair, I've also never encountered anyone who tempted me as much as Rune. Those big brown eyes. That perfect little mouth. The way she's grown so animated throughout our conversation. I won't deny the powerful, physical side of my attraction, but there's something more; something that plays on the harp strings of my soul with every word, every expression that crosses her face.

Thanks to the growing volume of the music wafting around the corner and our own bantering conversation, Rune and I have drifted closer to each other on the couch. Her legs are curled up underneath her; the picture of poise and interest. Our proximity, mixed with the number of drinks I've consumed, is an absolute recipe for disaster. Possibly a great disaster that sends us both reeling. But first, there's a tiny confession that I should probably make. Soothe my conscience before I ask her to sacrifice some of her already limited time with her aunt and cousins—and spend it with me, instead.

I clear my throat. "So, anyway, funny story..."

Chapter 17

Rune

It's official: I'm obsessed with Finn.

I can't remember any other time that I've been so comfortable, so unfiltered in the presence of a masculine person I barely know. The words keep falling out of my mouth and yet he keeps looking at me like everything I say is interesting.

I rest my head against the high back of the velvet couch and wait for him to tell his funny story. He could say something about the weather and it would still be one of the most interesting things I've ever heard.

When the silence begins to stretch too long, something tugs at my tipsy brain. Something about the almost guilty expression on his face that's completely at odds with the teasing, totally relaxed Finn of just a moment ago. The one who has definitely been checking me out all evening.

"Oh my gosh, are you dating someone?" The words blurt out of my mouth before I can stop them.

He whips his head back to me. "What—no. *God*, no, Rune."

His horror makes me realize how ridiculous that thought was. It came out of nowhere. I'll just sit here, sip my drink, and patiently wait for his funny story. Which is apparently not a code for *I'm not available, so please stop thinking about us naked together.*

"Okay. Anyway, as I was going to say," Finn begins, then stops with a grimace, his gaze focused on something behind me. I turn my head just in time to see Ella come flying around the corner, still towing Sam behind her.

"There you are!" Ella smiles widely, like a kid who just found a jar of candy. "I thought you were right behind us. Or in the bathroom."

"Sorry, I got distracted." I glance at Finn, who's got a resigned look on his face.

"Well, you missed Mom meeting Sam. He passed with flying colors." She beams up at her boyfriend, bumping him with her shoulder.

"Congratulations," I say, wishing they would go away.

"Anyway, I came to find you to let you know we're heading out soon. Since you weren't answering your phone." Ella waggles her brows suggestively.

"I—sorry, it was in my purse." I blink at Ella, willing for her to get the message. I want to finish my conversation with Finn alone. Give him an opportunity to ask me out, since I'm far too shy to do that sort of thing myself. But Ella just stands there, waiting for me.

So like an idiot, I turn to Finn and go for a handshake. Formal, like we're wrapping up a business meeting. Finn all-out grins. He takes my hand and helps me to my feet, holding on until my momentary vertigo goes away, then pulling me to his side and enveloping me in the spicy musk of his scent. I guess that's fine.

"You're here a few more days?" he asks, his voice low in my ear.

"Until Sunday," I remind him.

"I'll text you," he promises. It sends a warm feeling straight through me.

"I hope your parents didn't mind too much that I showed up."

"Why would they?" He looks genuinely confused.

"Because I'm a stranger. And I monopolized your company for far too long."

"Pretty sure you stopped being a stranger the moment you walked in on me in a towel," he teases.

"I feel like I shouldn't be held accountable for anything that happened that night."

"Agreed. For the most part."

Our eyes meet and I realize just how close we are. Mere inches separate our faces. My senses are overwhelmed by his nearness and the rich scent of him. Without thinking, I run my hand along his arm, feeling the hard definition of his muscles. I'm overwhelmed with the desire to feel every damn part of this very masculine body. His eyes dart to my lips and it's all I can do not to reach up and grasp his shirt, close those last few inches between us. But I'm hyper aware of where we are, and how Ella keeps glancing over her shoulder as Sam drags her back into the lobby. Maybe I should be a little more bold, a little less timid, but—not now. Not tonight. Not with an audience.

"Goodnight, Finn." I extricate myself from his side.

"Goodnight, little stranger," he says, holding the collar of my coat as I put it on, like we're in one of those old-fashioned movies. I don't hate it. I do hate watching him return to the party after saying his goodbyes to us.

"Are you coming back with us, Sam? You're more than welcome to," Aunt Mairi offers.

Sam declines. "I might swing by closer to Christmas, if that's all right with you? I'll be staying at my family's cabin on the lake for the holidays."

I swear everyone has a cabin on that lake.

"Ok. Bye then," Ella says, dismissing him.

"Ella!" Aunt Mairi scolds.

Sam only smiles. "Goodnight, Ella. Nice to meet you, Mairi—and Rune."

❄

"So you and Finny, huh?" Ella giggles, poking me in the ribs. "I was a little worried when I couldn't find you. Imagine my surprise at finding you two all cozied up together."

We're laying in Ella's bed, dressed in comfy flannel pajama pants and warm sweatshirts, snacking on as much junk food as we could scrounge out of the kitchen.

"We were just having a conversation." It's an honest, albeit defensive, reply.

"A kissing conversation?"

I toss a puffed popcorn kernel at her face. "We were talking about books." And also maybe something more interesting eventually, had Ella not interrupted us.

"You would. Did you tell him about your fancy signed special edition book that you won't stop snuggling with?"

"I didn't, but we did talk about the series."

"Bet he loved that," she snorts. "Rune: winning hearts, one book at a time."

I roll onto my back on the soft comforter, tucking my hands behind my head. I'm still feeling the effects of the alcohol, loosening my tongue and making me feel more hopeful than my usual cynical self. "Is it silly to have a crush on him? It's not like I live here."

"This isn't the nineteenth century. You don't have to live within an hour's ride on horseback to date someone. Or bang them if that's all you're looking for. There's this thing called a cell phone, you see," Ella squeals as I fling a few more popcorn kernels at her.

"Ha ha, you're so clever. I'm serious, though. What if I'm making Finn a rebound thing? Or what if he's not even interested and I'm making an absolute fool of myself. I felt up his fucking arm tonight."

"I know, I saw," Ella chortles. "How did it feel?"

"Super strong. And like I really wanted to feel the rest of him."

"Yum," she sighs. "I'm happy with Sam, but I have seen Finn without a shirt before. It was unforgettable. I wish that experience for you."

"What about you and Sam? How long have you been together? Why have I not heard of him before?"

"That's like a million questions. Slow down." Ella raises her hand to shush me. "We've been going out for eight months. Hardly anyone knows about him because he's my person and I don't want to share."

"Since when?"

"Since I actually want to keep this one."

"Does he know that?"

"I think he might."

I reach out and retrieve some popcorn from her hair. "Well, isn't that cute. Think you'll get a ring for Christmas?"

"Think you'll get a ring for Christmas?" she retorts, rolling her eyes. "I'd give both of us an equal probability."

"Equal? You've been dating the guy for eight months."

"Yeah and Finn's not one to mess around. If you want him, let him know. He seems happy to oblige." She gives a horrible snicker.

"Why am I even friends with you?"

"Because you love me and I'm more fun than Courtney, who only has time for law school crap these days." There's a strong note of bitterness in Ella's voice. "Besides, we're family, so I have your back, no matter what. You want to bang Finn, you go for it. Who am I to stand in the way of a little seasonal lust."

I join in her laughter, even if I don't fully agree. I'm no prude and have done my fair share of sleeping around in college, but it doesn't sit right when I think about Finn. Maybe my perception of him is skewed. But so far, everything I've seen of him makes me suspect that I might not be satisfied with a one-night stand. It would probably only make me want more of him...and probably ruin me for any other man. I don't know if I should pursue anything that sends me off the deep end like that. I hardly have a handle of my life as it is.

"I can already tell you're overthinking this whole thing."

I rub my heart, half-mocking, half-serious. "I know. I just—I'm directionless right now. I don't want to latch onto the first person who catches my eye." As if Finn wouldn't have caught my eye even when I was dating Sebastian. Pretty house aside, I have a strong suspicion that Finn's about as kind and genuine as they come. "Besides, I've only been single for like a week."

"Please. From what you've told me, it sounds like you've been single a lot longer. Besides, it's not like you're thinking about marrying the guy." She gives a big yawn and glances over at the sparkling mermaid alarm clock on her nightstand. Five past one. "I'm getting old. I don't know how many all-nighters I pulled in college, but midnight is definitely my limit these days."

"I couldn't even pull an all-nighter in college," I admit. My phone died sometime on the drive home and I grope around for a charger. By the time it lights up, Ella's flipped off the lights and snuggled under the covers next to me.

I should just go to sleep, but—there's a single notification that I have to tap into.

> Finn the Hero: I already said this, but I'm glad you came tonight.

> Me: Likewise.

Almost immediately, the typing bubble pops up.

> Finn the Hero: Why are you still awake?

> Me: We're having a sleepover. Will probably regret it in the morning.

> Finn the Hero: Know what would cheer you up?

> Me: …a few glasses of water and some sleep?

> Finn the Hero: Water & sleep, yes. But also: skiing

> Me: Are you suggesting that conceptually or are you inviting me to something? I can't tell.

> Finn the Hero: I'm inviting you to come skiing with me tomorrow :) Tell Ella that Sam will be out, too, if she wants to join us.

I don't bother to clarify what type of skiing he's talking about. I am one hundred percent down to do absolutely anything with this man. Up to and including taking off my clothes and climbing into bed with him.

"Stop flirting with Finn and turn that off," Ella grumbles.

"Who says it's Finn?"

"That stupid smile plastered all over your face."

"He just asked if we wanted to go skiing tomorrow. Sam's going to be there. What should I tell him?"

"How is this even a question? Say yes. I want to see my boyfriend. And you can go out with Finn. Drool over him a bit more."

"I don't know if it's going out," I muse. "Or just like...hanging out."

She snorts loudly. "Based on the way he stared at you all night, I'd put good money down on it being a date. Either way, make him sweat it out a little before you answer."

It might be good advice, but—

> Me: Ok.

Chapter 18

Rune

Aunt Mairi is already awake and working on a crossword puzzle when I stumble my way into the kitchen a little after eight. I only had three drinks at the party—and one when we got home—but I feel like death. I guess my binge drinking days from college are well and truly gone. I was so wrapped up in my head that I didn't even think to drink water. Or eat any of the food. Or sample the hot chocolate. I'm an idiot.

"Do we have plans today?" I ask Aunt Mairi, pouring myself a glass of water.

"I don't think so. You girls can do whatever you want. Courtney and I will be heading out a little later this morning, but should be back tomorrow early afternoon."

"You're going with her?"

"It's a bit of a drive. I figured I would keep her company and get some shopping done while she's at her event. There's plenty of food for you and Ella, and I've got extra wood stacked on the porch so you don't have to go outside at night to keep the fire going."

That's Aunt Mairi for you: thoughtful and generous to a fault.

"Ok." I clear my throat. "I was thinking maybe I would go out skiing this morning. I'm not sure if I'll be back before you leave." I try to sound nonchalant, but it comes out like a question. For her or for me, I'm not quite sure.

She sets down her pen and looks at me more closely. "By yourself?"

"No, with Ella and Sam...and Finn." I mentally curse the heat that rises up my face. She doesn't appear at all surprised.

"Do you need money? If you're going downhill skiing, the lift ticket and rentals can get a little pricey." She makes as if to reach for her purse.

"No, of course not. I'll be fine."

"Maybe he'll pay for you?" It's as close to prying as she'll get: a subtle question as to whether or not this is actually a date...and if I'm even interested in that sort of thing.

"We'll see, I guess." I shrug like it's not that big of a deal. Like I haven't been wondering the exact same thing.

"You'll have fun either way."

"Thanks, Auntie." I lean down to give her a quick peck on the cheek.

A short text conversation with Finn later determines that he'll pick Ella and I up around ten. Which means my work is cut out for me. I go upstairs to Ella's room and throw open the shades, revealing the utter mess of her room, full of empty dishes and clothes strewn over nearly every surface. I peel the blankets off her.

"Go away," she moans.

"Get up. Your prince charming is waiting. Or will be."

"My prince charming can go fuck himself." She sits up and swipes at the tangled strands of hair before tucking them aggressively behind an ear. "Although I wouldn't mind watching him attempt that. It sounds kinky."

"That's sick and twisted."

"Oh, please. Someday when you're an adult like me, you too can have a sexual thirst trap who makes you feel alive in a way that your private school upbringing never could."

"My mother would drown you in holy water for that comment alone," I say sternly. "If you're not ready by the time Finn comes to pick us up, I'm leaving without you."

"Is that really the thanks I get after letting you spend the night in my bed?"

I dodge the crumpled dress she throws at me.

Once I'm showered and dressed, I scroll obsessively through the few texts I've exchanged with Finn over the past week. It's silly to analyze, but—I'm about ninety percent sure that he's interested in me. That's what this means, right? The question is how much and what does he intend to do about it? Perhaps more importantly: what do I intend to do about it?

I don't know how to answer that question.

My head says to take it slow and just see what happens. My heart—or maybe it's my neglected sex life—says to go all in and enjoy it while it lasts.

Too bad I don't have a great track record when it comes to relationships. The whole Sebastian situation has been disheartening and humiliating. But Finn? I have a sneaking suspicion that if I were to ever date Finn and then lose him, I would be absolutely shattered over it. Maybe even ruined. I can't imagine ever meeting anyone more perfect than him.

By the time Finn's truck pulls into the driveway, Ella is just stumbling out of her room, hair still wet from her shower.

"You're going to freeze like that." Aunt Mairi looks askance at her daughter.

"I'll sit in the chalet until it dries," Ella promises, pulling on her coat.

"Have fun, girls." Aunt Mairi gives a little wave. "I'll see you tomorrow."

"Thanks, Auntie." I hurry out the door, black ski boots tied together and draped over my shoulder. The skis I've been using all week are leaning up against the garage, next to Ella's. I hand both pairs to Finn, who puts them in the back of the truck.

"I want the back to myself so I can stretch out my legs," Ella insists.

I don't know if she's telling the truth or just trying to get me to sit next to Finn in the front. Either way, I won't complain.

"Cold?" Finn asks.

"Never," I lie. Even the short walk from house to truck has me shivering. Thank goodness for the toasty warmth of the cab. I'm not sure how I'm going to survive a whole morning outside.

"Do you ski much?" He puts his arm across the seat back, twisting around to see better when backing out of the driveway.

I crinkle my nose. "Define *much*."

That pulls a laugh out of him. "Let me rephrase: do you know what skiing is?"

"Asshole." I rub my mittened hands together. "We've been cross country skiing almost every day this week." It's the truth, even if last week was the first time I ever remember putting skis on. Ella mumbles something from the back seat.

"So you don't want to spend some time practicing on the bunny slope? Or making laps across the yard?"

I scoff. "I wouldn't ruin your ski day like that."

"Ruin it? Rune, it would be delightful to see you master the bunny slope. You and the other toddlers." He chuckles at my expression, then nods at the black matte travel mug in the cup holder nearest me. "That one's yours, by the way, if you want it."

"You're incredible."

"Why, thank you."

"Where's mine?" Ella asks.

Finn glances in the rear view mirror. "In the cup holder on the other side."

"No it isn't—oh. Yes, I see it. Thanks, Finny."

He shakes his head good-humoredly. We drive in companionable silence for a while, the latest hits playing softly on the radio.

"Did you get some good sleep after the party last night?" I ask.

"I was awake a little after seven. Once the sun starts to rise, it's hard for me to stay asleep."

I nod. I'm the same way. I've tried everything from sound machines to blackout shades, but I always seem to be awake at the ass crack of dawn. The thick forest of snow-clad trees flash past the window as we drive down the highway, fresh and pristine against the pale blue of the winter sky.

"Are your parents early risers, too?"

"They are. Fortunately, they rented a place across the street from the Lounge and stayed there last night."

"They didn't want to come skiing today?"

"I didn't ask. They know I usually need at least a day to recover from their parties, so they made other plans. I thought it might be a good opportunity to spend some time with a certain girl today."

Bold. I glance over my shoulder, but Ella has her ear buds in, oblivious to our conversation.

"Am I coming along to be your wingman?"

"That is definitely not—" He turns his head with a frown. I can't hold back my grin as he realizes I'm joking. "Good one, Rune. Proud of yourself?"

"Yeah, actually." I don't often get the upper hand in bantering sessions. I'll take what I can get.

"Hope your aunt doesn't mind that I've stolen you away."

"She's heading out of town with Courtney for the night. And honestly, I don't think she minds having a little bit of quiet in the house. With all of us around this past week, there's been a lot of activity."

"Do you come up to visit often?"

I'm totally unprepared for the stab of guilt that accompanies that question. "No. I should, but this is the first real visit I've had in years."

"They must be glad to have you."

I shrug. "Either that or they're counting down the days until I leave. In all fairness, I'd originally planned to go home yesterday. But Ella talked me into helping with the holiday fundraiser. So I figured I'd at least stay until then."

"Are you telling me I have Ella to thank for your company this morning?" His voice is so dry that I giggle.

"I guess so."

I'm shamelessly taking him in as he drives: the strong, high cheekbones, thick black lashes, and a five o'clock shadow that has me wanting to rub my fingers across his jaw. Pure eye candy is what I would call him from a distance, but there's a softness, a thoughtfulness to his expressions that has me thinking all sorts of thoughts. Like white dresses and expensive bouquets. Normal shit.

And I'm not the only one. Finn turns the head of every female, from the parking lot to the front desk of the ski resort, where he and Ella both flash their season passes. Finn has his credit card out to purchase my day pass before I can even remember which pocket I put mine in.

"I can pay," I insist, because it's the polite thing to do. Even though my credit card balance has started giving me anxiety. He waves me off.

"Really, you're doing me a favor. You're saving me from spending a long day with two very hungover parents."

"They seemed nice," I offer, shifting my weight from one foot to the other. No matter how badly I want this to be an actual date, it's a little uncomfortable watching him spend money on me.

"They are in public," he smiles, tucking his wallet back into his coat pocket. "It's the one-on-one time that can get...long."

"Sam says he's running late, I'm going to wait for him," Ella announces, looking up from her phone. "You two go ahead."

"We could all wait," I suggest. It seems rude to leave her alone and run off with Finn.

"We'll catch up," she assures us. "My hair needs to finish drying, anyway."

I look at Finn, who shrugs. "Sam's always late. I don't mind heading out right away. We could do a warmup loop and meet back up here to go on a longer trail together."

Ella doesn't look like she's interested in much beyond increasing her caffeine intake by ordering a latte from the chalet coffee shop, so I go with Finn.

"We can start with the low trail. It's easy but scenic," he suggests once our skis are on.

"Lead the way."

Finn takes off with a lithe grace that has me feeling all kinds of feelings. It's like I can almost see those muscles rippling, even under his winter jacket. He shoots effortlessly through the forest, like some woodland god.

A god, that's what Finn is.

I'm more like a troll. A bumbling, awkward troll. I can't imagine how bad his parental visits must be if he thinks it's better to spend a morning watching me struggle on the trails. The first time I fall, it's terrifying: I'm picking up speed down a slope one moment and the next I'm hurtling face-first into the snow. Every time after—well, at least Finn finds it entertaining.

"You lean into it," he tries to instruct me. "Keep your center of gravity low."

"I am leaning," I argue, "but my skis are so much faster than my body."

"Impossible." He taps his ski pole against his foot. "Your skis are attached to your body."

"I don't understand how you stay upright with a hill and a turn," I huff, trying to brush the snow out of my jacket, where it's currently freezing my neck.

"So when you said that you've been skiing everyday—?" He lifts his brows, waiting for my answer.

"We go on the flat lake like civilized people," I grumble, finally getting my right foot free so that I can untangle myself and get to my feet.

He laughs. "But snow looks so good on you."

I look up, preparing a haughty retort. The words fall away as I see the expression on his face. One of those half-smiling, I-know-what-I-want kind of looks. The kind that directly precedes a guy leaning in and doing something about the budding attraction between us...except that he merely glances down at our skis with an amused huff. My heart twinges with disappointment when he slides backwards instead to give me space to put my ski back on. I take off my mittens to tighten the laces on my boot.

"How much farther do you want—" Finn's words fall away abruptly.

I look up curiously from my crouched position and see his face has turned unnaturally white.

"Finn, what is—?"

"*Rune, don't move.* No, don't turn your head. Stay still." His voice is low, quiet, and laced with what I think might be fear. Which makes me start to freak out.

I tense, all senses on full alert as I do my best to imitate a statue. My knit winter hat muffles my hearing somewhat, but I catch the soft crunch of something walking in the snow behind me. It sounds slow...and big.

It can't be a bear, right? Those hibernate in the winter.

What is it, I want to scream, but Finn's finger is on his lips. His jaw is tight, his whole body tense as his eyes move from me to —whatever is behind me. Dear God, please don't let him be contemplating whether he should just glide away and leave me here. I am fully helpless with just one ski on.

No, I'm sure he's not thinking that, but—I already know I'm doomed. It will take a solid ten seconds before I can even get my boot connected to my ski again. Maybe it would be faster to just take the other one off? But then what? I can't fucking run through the deep snow.

I've begun shaking from the cold that's seeped into my bones just as the sound of the footsteps pauses. Since I'm going to either die of cold or from that *Thing* that I can't see, I decide to risk turning my head. If I'm about to be eaten, I want to know what is going to eat me.

Standing no more than forty feet away, taking up the entire width of the trail, is a huge bull moose.

I might not live in northern Minnesota, but I've seen pictures of these things before. None of the pictures prepared me for the sheer size of a moose in real life. It's far bigger than a horse; its shoulders must be taller than my head by two feet. And it's staring at me. It knows damn well that I'm here.

I can barely breathe. If a moose attacks, I'm pretty sure you're supposed to go hide behind a tree. But I won't be able to move with these skis. I'll just...die. Trampled to death by a moose. All because I wanted to go skiing with Finn. Fuck my life.

I guess the bright side is that Finn will likely survive. He can probably out-ski the animal, especially if I'm between them, acting as a distraction. The thought is strangely calming.

The moose turns its head, as if debating its next course of action. Then, after what could be a minute or an hour, it gives a low snort and trots away. It's out of sight in seconds, lost behind a thick grove of spruce.

I'm still staring at the place where it disappeared when I hear the slide of Finn's skis closing the short distance between us. Seconds later, his skis are off and he's down on his knees, pulling me into his arms and pinning me tight to his chest.

"Fucking hell, Rune," he mutters, before putting me at arm's length. His wide eyes scan my body, as if looking for some injury even though I literally just crouched on the ground like a terrified mouse.

"I'm fine," I assure him, my voice a little breathless. Maybe because of the freakiness of the giant moose or maybe because my face is inches from Finn's.

"Thank God," he breathes and then his lips are on mine.

Chapter 19

Rune

I've imagined kissing Finn many times over the past week. I thought that he would be excellent at it.

My imagination did not prepare me for the pure luxury of what it actually feels like to have my face pressed up against his. There's hunger and a slight edge of desperation. His hand nudges my chin into a better angle as his tongue sweeps into my mouth. He's skillful, somehow both passionate and tentative, like he's posing a question and wants to know what I think about it.

I fist my cold, bare hands on his jacket, anchoring myself as I give my reply. A very enthusiastic, *fuck yes.*

I've never thought of myself as particularly talented at kissing, but the way Finn gives a shuddering intake of breath makes me think that maybe I'm not too bad at it. Maybe I just needed to do it with the right person. I'm vaguely aware of the way his arm draws me snugly up against his body. All of my focus is on his mouth, his taste, and the feel of his breath on mine.

We're both breathing hard by the time he draws back, our eyes locked with the same hazy expression.

"You're shaking," Finn says.

"My hands are a little cold," I admit. Maybe the rest of me is, too, but I can't make my brain focus right now.

"We should keep going." It's a reasonable thing to say. Before the moose showed up, I was sweating profusely from the exercise.

"Or you could warm me with your body heat," I suggest.

"It would take longer," he says, although he looks like he's actually thinking about it.

"It would also be more fun."

"I wholeheartedly agree." He picks up my mittens, brushing the snow off them before handing them to me. "Do you want to turn around or finish this loop? I think the moose is gone. Probably."

I accept his assistance putting my ski back on and helping me to my feet. I'm stiff from crouching so long in the freezing snow. "Let's finish the loop. Maybe we'll get to see more wildlife."

Finn barks out a laugh. "I'm not sure my heart could take another encounter."

That makes two of us.

As it turns out, the rest of the trail is much more level. I don't fall any more, but am dripping with sweat once again by the time we get back to the chalet. Ella's skis are still sitting exactly where she set them when we arrived this morning.

Finn's hand drops to the small of my back as we go inside, sending warm shivers up my body. We find Ella and Sam just chilling in the cafe, drinking Bloody Marys together.

"I thought we came here to go skiing?" Finn demands.

"The view's fine from where I sit." Sam smirks.

Ella gives him a high five. "Nice." Then, to us, "I needed a little food in my belly. We're ready to head out now."

"Food's not a bad idea. You want anything, Rune?" Finn looks at me.

"I could eat something," I admit. Now that I think about it,

I'm starving. In my haste to over-analyze my romantic prospects this morning, I forgot about breakfast.

"They have really good blueberry muffins," Ella says.

Finn offers a quick smile and heads across the little cafe. I just stand there awkwardly, unsure whether I should accompany him or remain with my cousin. I hate situations like this. I never know what to do.

"There's space for you here." Ella pats the black vinyl upholstered seat next to her.

So I sit.

"How was your morning?" I ask, for the sake of saying something.

"Fine. Good," Ella says with a little laugh like it was a joke question. "How was yours?"

"Very athletic." I feel like I should tell the story about the moose. That would be a really great thing to talk about. But my thoughts are far too fragmented to do the story any justice. The only real thing on my mind is the man standing across the room and the way he kissed me.

"Do you like to ski?" Sam asks politely.

I open my mouth to respond, but Ella beats me to it. "Rune likes the idea of skiing."

Sam smiles. "It can be challenging."

A vanilla thing to say, but I'm spared the necessity of answering by Finn returning to the table with a tray of assorted bakery items. He sets it on the table and slides next to me on the booth seat.

"I didn't know what you like," he says.

"So you bought the whole bakery?" Sam scoffs.

"If you ask nicely, maybe we'll let you have our leftovers," Finn tells him.

I just nod, my mouth already full with a blueberry muffin that has cream cheese in the middle. Finn's knee brushes against mine under the table. I glance over at him and see the slightest twitch at the corner of his mouth. I push back with my own knee and the twitch turns into a smile that triggers butterflies in my stomach. The tiniest hint of a dimple graces one of his cheeks. I wonder how he's managed to stay single this long, or if he's just in between girlfriends at the moment.

"*Rune*." Ella's voice breaks into my thoughts. She sounds mildly annoyed.

I finish chewing before I reply. "What?"

"For the *second* time, I asked if you wanted to go out to lunch at that burger place we went the other day?"

"I'm literally eating a muffin right now," I point out.

Sam grins as Ella throws up her hands.

"I was talking about after we're done skiing. God, Rune, did you not listen to a word I say?"

"I tried not to," I reply with a shrug, like I hadn't been accidentally distracted by Finn's good looks and the heat of his knee against mine. "I'm game for whatever."

Two muffins and a slice of quiche later, I'm finally full.

"Thanks for that," I say.

"It was the least I could do," he returns with a meaningful look. I think he's referring to the moose incident.

Ella and I make a stop at the women's restroom before hitting the trails. The moment the bathroom door closes, she rounds on me.

"Ok, spill it," Ella demands. "What happened out there? You two are being weird."

"How are we being weird?" I ask, feigning ignorance.

"Other than the fact that Finn bought out the bakery because he 'didn't know what you wanted'?"

"He didn't actually buy out the bakery," I point out needlessly.

There were only like six muffins plus the quiche. "I think he felt guilty because we ran into a moose on the trail. It was a little freaky." I think back to the size of the creature and the way it stood there looking at us. As still as a statue, except for its breath blowing like smoke in the cold air. Simultaneously majestic and terrifying as fuck. Put that down as one of the top three things I never want to repeat. Just after seeing a girl in bed with a guy I thought was my boyfriend.

Ella's mouth falls slack. "Holy fuck, are you serious? Did it see you?"

"Yeah, it definitely did."

"Did you get a picture?"

"No. I was more focused on hoping it wouldn't attack."

"Oh." She thinks about this for a second. "Why didn't you say anything at the table?"

Other than the fact that I mostly forgot about it after Finn kissed me? I shrug and turn to my reflection in the large bathroom mirror. I look windblown and my hair is weirdly flat from my winter hat, but overall, the look isn't *terrible*. "I guess I forgot."

"You forgot?" The skepticism is back in her voice. Maybe it's because I know she'll eventually find out, or maybe I am secretly dying to talk about it, but—

"I forgot because I kissed Finn," I blurt out.

Ella's eyes widen. "You're shitting me."

"I shit you not."

"You two actually—oh my God, I cannot believe this." She chews on her lower lip, a dangerous spark of excitement growing in her eyes. "Sam thought it would take dinner and a few drinks before either of you made a move. I thought maybe a sauna might be in order. The kind where you go in naked."

Now it's my turn to stare. "Do you mean to say that while

Finn and I were moments away from possible death by a moose on the trail, you and Sam were in here playing matchmaker?"

"Yes?" She gives a small, apologetic smile.

For a long moment, we just look at each other. Then her smile widens and she leans on a hip, fully invested in this moment.

"How was it?"

"Incredible," I admit. "I'm still seeing stars."

"I'm swooning already. Do you want more? You look like you want more."

I give a *how is that even a question* look. She nods, brows puckered slightly. "Then we'll have to make sure you get some. Come on, I have so many ideas for how to make it happen."

"No, don't. If this is meant to happen, then it will. I don't want to mess anything up by trying too hard."

"It's obviously meant to happen, so let's focus on making sure nothing gets in the way of fate." Her mouth is set, determined. I'm a little afraid of what is about to be unleashed.

"Please don't be obvious about this. Don't let him know I told you," I beg.

"Give me a little credit," she sniffs. "I wasn't born yesterday."

Her assurance will have to do.

The guys have their skis on by the time we get outside, and are in the midst of a debate as to which route we should take next.

"We have two trail options," Sam tells us. "There's the Pine Hill trail and then that one that winds around the river to the south. I don't know what everyone's up for?"

"Which one is better?" I wonder aloud.

"The Pine Hill one," Ella says promptly. "Except it's a little more challenging."

"In what way?"

"There's a hill."

"A big one," Finn adds seriously.

Everyone looks at me.

My eyes narrow. "I survived a moose. I can probably handle a hill or two."

"Too soon," Finn mutters.

Ella beams. "That's my cousin."

It's a solid two minutes before I regret my decision. I honestly thought I'd do a lot better this time around. If we're counting the number of falls, I am definitely doing better. But everything is uphill. My thighs are burning and I'm generating so much heat that I have to unzip my jacket. Finn kindly skis next to me, even though I'm slow as a snail. I glance over at him several times, wondering if he's regretting that kiss yet. I'm clearly not in his league. Poor as dirt and a shit skier.

And that's before I round the curve and see where the trail veers up. Way the heck up.

"There is absolutely no way I'll be able to get up there. You have fun. I'll stay here and—uh, make camp."

"The view at the top makes it all worth it," Ella assures me.

"Maybe, but not if I die in the attempt." I turn to Finn, expecting him to sympathize or suggest that I should turn around to get a head start for the way back. But he just winks.

"Like you said, what's a little hill after a moose attack?"

It's a challenge and I feel obliged to take it as such, knowing full well that I'm only doing this in a pathetic attempt to impress Finn. Ella and Sam race ahead, insisting that they'll wait for us at the top. I sigh and try to emulate the way he uses a side-step to work his way up the hill. It's tedious and by the time the ground levels out again, I'm barely able to lift my legs. I don't know how I'm going to get back down.

"This way." Finn turns off the trail into the untouched snow. Ella and Sam are no longer anywhere in sight.

"Is this even legal?" I ask nervously, like there's going to be some kind of woodland warden who orders us back onto the groomed trails. Finn either doesn't hear the question or chooses to ignore it, and I'm left to scramble after him through some leafless trees—birch, I think, with curling paper-like bark—and a thick spread of pine. Then, suddenly, I realize why this whole venture was worth it.

The world falls away beneath us, opening up a dramatic landscape of miles upon miles of pure, untouched wilderness. It's the kind of view that makes your heart surge.

"This is incredible," I breathe.

"This is one of my favorite places in the world." Finn's voice sounds low, almost reverential.

I take off my skis and let myself fall backwards into the snow. It's so deep that it makes a kind of chair where I fall. The chickadees are singing merrily from all sides; somewhere in the woods beneath us, a blue jay is calling. I close my eyes, indulging in the forest sounds and the feeling of the midwinter sun shining warm on my face. Finn removes his own skis and joins me in the snow.

"I used to come here with my grandpa in the summers," Finn says after a while. "There's a patch of wild blueberries a little ways down this cliff, down by where those red pines are growing. We always had to pick enough so that my grandma could make a pie. Sometimes it was a quick task. Other times—well, let's just say that there were some long, miserable afternoons and I learned the true reason why they say the mosquito is Minnesota's state bird."

"That sounds fun."

"It was hell," he says, but there's a smile in his voice. "Even on a good day the bugs were bad. But Grandpa passed away when I was ten. I try to come up here a few times a year to honor his memory."

That's unexpectedly sweet. I squint open my eyes. "Thanks for bringing me here. And for everything."

"Everything?"

"You know...letting me stay the night during the snowstorm. Helping with the car. And—everything."

He's quiet for a moment. Then, "I'm sorry you lost your job and went into the ditch. That's just shit luck. But I'm glad, too. I wouldn't have met you otherwise."

I meet his gaze. *Why are you glad you met me*, I want to ask. But that sounds too much like I'm fishing for compliments, so I settle with, "I feel the same."

"I'm also sorry about the moose."

"Why?" I ask, startled. It's not like he summoned it.

His mouth tightens as he looks back towards the view. "I felt so helpless. All I could think was that the moose was going to charge you and there was nothing I could do. Besides stand really still, that is."

"What would have happened if it had charged?"

He huffs out an embarrassed laugh. "I probably would have waved my poles like a maniac and skied off the trail to try to distract it."

I'm floored. "That's some serious hero shit."

"We didn't have many options. Not when you only had one ski on."

"Even if I had both, I wouldn't have gotten far."

"Yes, I'm aware." He tries not to smile, but the corners of his mouth twitch.

"It turned out well, though," I say, thinking of the kiss. "Your post-moose comforting tactics were thoroughly distracting."

"It wasn't a tactic. I just couldn't think straight to stop myself."

"Did you feel like you had to? Stop yourself?"

He drags his eyes to mine. "I should have asked first. I'm sorry."

"Don't be," I whisper. "You read the signs correctly."

We stare at each other, then he reaches out to softly cradle my face in his hand, running his thumb across my bottom lip. I didn't notice him take his mittens off.

"May I kiss you again, Rune?" His voice drops an octave.

I reply by tugging his face towards me, my lips parting with a sigh as his tongue slips into my mouth. He rolls, pressing his body over mine, brushing the powdery snow away when it threatens to fall in my face. Even through a thick winter jacket and snow pants, I can feel the hard lines of his body. And damn if it doesn't make me want to escalate things.

"What are you thinking?" I ask when he slows his kisses and just...looks at me. It's a stupid question, but I want to know anyway.

He winces, as if caught red-handed. I think he might not answer, but he says, "I'm thinking that I wish we were doing this somewhere warm, so I could feel your body against mine."

Oh.

I summon all my boldness. Not too difficult, considering how turned on I am right now. "What's stopping us?"

He gives me a humorous look. "Your cousin?"

"Why did you want her to come along, again?"

"I thought maybe you'd be more likely to say yes if I invited her."

"I would have come if it was just the two of us," I tell him honestly. "I would have said yes in a heartbeat."

When he moves in for another kiss, it's with an expression that has my breath catching.

"You're incredible," he breathes, blue eyes piercing as he looks down at my face. "Beautiful. Fearless. So full of life."

I laugh because I am neither of those things. I'm just a scared little mouse who's trying not to fuck up her life too badly.

I'm seriously thinking of taking off my jacket, maybe letting him get a little handsy, when the sound of voices echoes through the trees. Ella and Sam are calling for us. Finn laughs at the disappointment on my face. He rises easily and reaches down to help me up.

"To be continued," he murmurs. A girl can only hope.

We ski back to the trail, where Ella and Sam have magically appeared. The fact that they don't comment on our side venture tells me that maybe they were similarly occupied.

"Ella and I were just talking. What do you think about maybe finding a hot tub somewhere?" Sam looks at us.

"And where were you thinking of looking for a hot tub?" Finn eyes him suspiciously.

Sam gives an innocent shrug.

"Fine. Come on over to my place." Finn's tone is begrudging, but there's a good-humored slant to his expression.

"Provided Rune can get back to the chalet," Ella points out.

"I take offense to that," I lie. I, too, wonder if I'll be able to make it before nightfall.

Chapter 20

Finn

Rune is a trooper. A beautiful, determined little trooper. I've lost count of the number of times she's fallen today. That she hasn't given up is impressive, especially considering the terrifying moose encounter this morning. She seems to have recovered and has made several questionable jokes about it. I'm still seriously shaken and it's triggered a wave of extreme protectiveness. I'm afraid to let her out of my sight. If I'm being honest, I don't *want* to let her out of my sight. I thought that I'd be able to shake my fixation on Rune by talking to her at the party last night. Or by spending time with her this morning.

I was wrong.

It turns out she's like a drug. An addictive one.

Here I am, inviting people into my home—my sanctuary—because I'm not quite ready to say goodbye to her.

"I'll ride with Sam," Ella announces once our gear is loaded back into my truck. "We'll stop by Mom's and grab some swimsuits. Rune, you want to come with us?"

"Rune rides with me," I say firmly. There's no way I'm letting her in the car with Sam. He isn't the best of drivers on a good day, let alone when the roads are icy. Rune climbs into my truck without complaint, albeit a bit stiffly. She's going to be sore as hell.

It's easy to work up a sweat when skiing, but the chill hits hard the moment you stop. My truck takes about nine minutes to heat up when the temperatures are this cold, so it's only just starting to blow warm air by the time we turn into my driveway. Rune, bless her heart, doesn't complain once.

"You want hot chocolate or coffee?" I ask once we've peeled off our snow gear and left it to dry in the entryway.

"Hot chocolate for sure," Rune says. "Please."

"Better drink this while I make your hot chocolate." I hand her a tall glass of water. I noticed she didn't drink anything since the coffee I brought for her this morning. "You need to rehydrate."

"Okay, *daddy*," Rune rolls her eyes but accepts the glass anyway. She freezes, hand outstretched, then winces as her own words register. "That came out very wrong."

"You have a dirty mind." I smirk when she snatches the water out of my hand. She very intentionally makes eye contact as she drinks it down. I never thought I'd live to see the day that drinking water would be considered sexy, but here we are.

"Happy?" Rune demands.

"Immensely. Now go change into something dry. Your shirt is soaked."

"I didn't bring anything else. It's fine, I'll survive."

It is not fine. I locate the same sweatpants and t-shirt that she wore last week and offer them to Rune. "You know the drill. We'll put your clothes in the dryer. It shouldn't take more than half an hour for them to be wearable again."

It shouldn't make me feel this pleased when she complies—or when I see her emerge from the bathroom dressed in my clothes once again. Rune deposits herself on one of the kitchen bar stools, leaning her elbows on the island counter and watching me move around the kitchen.

"Enjoying the show?" I tease.

"It's giving me hibachi vibes. Only...hot chocolate."

I slide the steaming mug towards her, complete with marshmallows and some crushed peppermint candy pieces. It looks pretty damn professional. She hums her appreciation.

The sound goes straight to my groin.

"Do you need any help with anything?" she asks, absolutely unaware of the growing discomfort in my pants.

"You could put these out on the table." I take the two large pastry boxes out of the refrigerator, filled with last night's hors d'oeuvres. Anything to get her out of the kitchen while I calm the fuck down.

Her eyes light up at the sight of them. "I was so nervous at the party last night that I didn't eat any of it. Which is very unlike me, I might add."

"You didn't eat at all?" I mentally kick myself. I was so eager to get her away from the party, I didn't realize that she was hungry. "Dig in."

She barely needs the encouragement and dives into the array of delicacies with unabashed enjoyment.

"This is absurdly good," she says around a mouthful of bite-sized caramel cheesecake.

"Believe me, I know. Why do you think I snuck the leftovers home with me?"

"Smart and good-looking. You're such a winner, Finn." Rune munches happily on her food.

"Good looking, huh?"

She gives me the side eye. "Are you playing coy with me?"

I snort. "Coy? Who even uses that word?"

"That's what they say in the books. It means, like, you're pretending to be shy and unaware."

"I know what coy means."

Her brows rise at my indignation and she rests her chin on her hand. "You can't honestly claim to be oblivious to the way girls—women, I mean—look at you. I've only been around you for like two days and I can see it. Like the front desk lady at the ski resort this morning, for example."

"I thought I caught a glimmer of approval."

Now it's her turn to scoff. "Please. She was basically drooling."

"What about you?"

She is suddenly very interested in the mini pies. "What about me?"

"What do you think about me?" I press.

"I already told you: smart and good looking," she says curtly. "Did you want me to go on?"

"If you don't mind. I'd love to hear what else you think of me." I smile, leaning towards her. I thought that shy and proper Rune was adorable. This half-flustered side of her is even better. I'm taken with the urge to push all of her buttons, to see what other facets she'll reveal.

"You order a very nice brandy on the rocks and really know how to make a killer cup of dairy-free hot chocolate." She pauses for a breath, then adds in a softer voice, "You're also thoughtful, kind, and far too generous."

My mouth feels a bit dry. I was not expecting the sincerity, the slight edge of vulnerability in her tone. "Basically an all around nice guy, huh?"

Her mouth tilts up. "Basically."

We share a quiet smile for all of three seconds before the back door opens with a slam as Sam and Ella let themselves in.

"I'll take a mocha latte," says Ella right away, eyeing Rune's cup of hot chocolate. When I level a deadpan look at her, she shrugs. "Don't pretend like you can't do it. I see the espresso maker on the counter."

Of course she does.

The girl is a force of nature, but you have to admire the way she has Sam twisted around her little finger. Sam and I hit it off immediately when we met last year. I like his laid back approach to life. He's the kind of guy who's up for anything, even if we've gone weeks or months without hanging out. An invaluable friend, especially with my schedule and its long, self-imposed bouts of solitude. I have him to thank for keeping Ella occupied today so I can monopolize Rune's attention. And fuck, if I don't want to maintain that monopoly a little longer.

"I can't believe you started eating without us." Ella looks miffed.

"We needed a head start." Rune grins at her cousin's scowl.

I'm impressed at the amount of hors d'oeuvres we're able to consume in the span of twenty minutes, followed by a frozen pizza baked in the oven. Afterwards, Rune throws herself down onto the couch with a groan.

"I don't know if I'm *happy* full or *too* full. I'm such a pig when I'm hungry," she says.

I nudge her leg aside to make enough space for me on the couch next to her. Sam and Ella have gone upstairs to change into their swimwear. I hope that's all they do up there.

"I think I said this already, but this is an amazing couch." Rune curls up into a little ball with a sigh of contentment. "I'm going to have a hard time not falling asleep. My muscles are like jelly."

"Take a nap if you want. I don't mind."

"That's being bad company."

I smile at that. I don't think she could be bad company if she tried. "It's a napping kind of day."

"Hurry up and change, you two," Ella calls to us as she and Sam make a beeline for the hot tub outside on the heated stone patio. I ignore the demand and put my feet up on the ottoman. I still have half a cup of coffee to drink and zero intention of letting Ella boss me around. The couch is facing away from the hot tub, but I can see everything if I turn my head. I shoot Sam a text, telling him to keep his hands to himself.

His phone must ping from where he's set it near the edge of the hot tub, because he picks it up almost immediately. He lifts one hand and shoots me a rude gesture.

"I want to go in the hot tub, but I also don't want to go in there with them," Rune's wry voice sounds beside me.

"Same." I lift my arm and she accepts the invitation immediately, snuggling into my side. I breathe in her scent, the faint coconut smell of her hair and the wood smoke and pine of my sweatshirt. I like knowing that she'll walk away from here smelling like me. "We can wait until they get out. The hot water might be nice on "

"How much longer do you want us to stick around?"

"You have somewhere else you need to be?"

"I just don't want to overstay my welcome."

"You won't."

"You say that now, but if our visit goes downhill later, you have only yourself to blame. I was willing to quit while we're ahead."

As if. "Rune, you could move in and still not overstay your welcome."

She stills a little, taking in my words. Then she turns so that her eyes meet mine. The sleepy softness is gone, replaced with wariness. "Finn, I'm not very good at reading between the lines. I wasn't aware that my last boyfriend wasn't actually dating me anymore until I found out he was sleeping with someone else."

I know she's hinting at something else, but this truly pisses me off. "That's called cheating, Rune."

She blushes and looks away. "It's on me. I should have been more aware. Asked him what he thought about us. If I'd put more effort into communicating, I wouldn't have been so blindsided. But it doesn't matter anymore. It's over."

"No, Rune, it actually does matter. That's on him and he's the biggest fuckwit for trying to pull one over on you."

Rune winces. "He didn't exactly try to pull one over. He answered the phone when he was in bed with her. It doesn't even bother me that much that he wanted out. I would have understood. But..." Her words trail off. It's the way she says it, with the shock and hurt still evident in her voice, that makes me feel the need to comfort her. I pull her across my lap, wrapping both arms securely around her. I'm a generally nonviolent person, but I could beat the shit out of that dickhead.

"You don't deserve that, Rune."

She gives a small smile. "Thanks."

"I'm fucking serious." I want to say more, but I have a feeling that words are just words to Rune. So instead, I kiss her. A gentle, nipping kiss on her lower lip. The lower lip that I can't stop staring at. Her soft intake of breath has me hard in an instant. I grasp her hip and pull her tighter against me. She feels incredible; all soft curves and warmth.

"You taste amazing," I murmur. I'm only talking about her mouth, but—fuck, I bet she tastes incredible elsewhere, too.

I can feel her smile against my lips and she slides her hand from my chest to my stomach and lower. She will be the death of me. Even with her clothes on, she feels better than any woman I've ever had naked. The curve of her breasts, the arch of her back—absolute perfection.

Desperate to feel skin, I slide my hand under her sweatshirt, feeling the swerve of her hip. I stop there and make her look at me. "Rune, tell me what you want." The words are harsh, desperate. I could consume this woman whole and never look back. But I need to know what she wants. What she expects.

"I want you to keep going," she says breathlessly.

That's not good enough. I pull back. "Is that you talking or the oxytocin?"

"What kind of a question is that?"

A stupid one, probably. "Just answer it. Please."

Her eyes narrow as she drags her gaze from my face, downwards and back up. It's a challenge. A dare. "I want you to kiss me. And grope the shit out of me."

"Thank fuck." I reach to pull her face back to mine, flipping us so that she's lying beneath me on the couch. My hand slides up her side, pushing the sweatshirt up so that I see everything. Including the fact that she's not wearing a bra. "You came prepared."

"My bra was drenched with sweat." She sounds apologetic.

"I really don't mind." I gently cup one breast then the other, with a feeling that can only be described as reverence. Then I lean in and pay homage to them with my mouth. She writhes in response, grinding up against me. It's too much and not enough, all at once. I'm all too aware of the fact that we aren't alone. That it's impossible to pull her clothes off the way I want. So instead, I reach down and trail my finger up her thigh, up the seam of her leggings.

She lets out a soft, breathy moan.

"Like that, huh?"

I do it again, slipping my hand beneath her waistband. "Tell me if you want me to stop."

"Do not fucking stop."

I tease her, running my fingers back and forth, never quite touching where we both want them to be. But then I do.

And then the sliding door opens.

Ella and Sam troop in, laughing loudly. Just like that, our moment is over. Rune scrambles to extricate herself from me, nearly falling off the couch as she untangles her legs from mine. I pull the throw over my lap with a silent, vehement curse.

"Nap time's over. Wake up, Rune," Ella says in a singsong voice.

"I'm awake, you idiot," Rune snaps, struggling with her ponytail.

Ella's smile turns catlike. "I hope we're not interrupting anything."

"You aren't," Rune says, but she glances at my lap and her already flushed face gets a little more pink. I wish I'd thought to take it upstairs. Or lock Ella and Sam outside until we were finished.

"Good. I just got a text that there's a party in the ice fishing village in the Perch Bay ice village this afternoon. Some of my old friends from high school are going to be there. Sounds like there's brats, beer, and chips for everyone. Think you'd want to go? With Mom and Courtney are gone, we're on our own for food." Ella's voice is hopeful. She has the boundless energy of a golden retriever, which is both amusing and incredibly exhausting for an introvert like myself.

Rune shakes her head. "Go without me. I'm so tired from skiing."

"I'm not going to abandon you," Ella objects. "You only have two days left with us."

"I won't be bored. I can read or work on my art. Besides, we still have all day tomorrow, which is more than we were planning on in the first place, before you extended my trip."

"Well, maybe Sam and I will just swing by there for a bit. Just to say hi to everyone. We can drop you off at home on our way."

"That's the opposite direction for you. I'll bring Rune back," I offer quickly. There's no way in hell that I'm willing to watch her just walk out of my life at this point. Not before finishing what we started on the couch. And even then...well, we'll have to see where the rest of the day goes. To find out whether the thoughts behind those brown eyes match the ones currently wreaking havoc deep within me.

Chapter 21

Rune

When Ella and Sam disrupted the moment I was having with Finn on the couch, I was teetering on the line between horrifically embarrassed and straight up pissed. Now it seems I have a second chance. That doesn't mean I don't feel some guilt about turning down Ella's invite.

When Finn goes out to help Sam load some firewood into the back of his vehicle (a donation for the bonfire at the ice village party), I follow Ella into the bathroom.

"You don't mind that I'm not coming with you guys, do you?"

"Why do you think I suggested that in the first place? I figured you'd turn down the invite and Finn's hero complex would jump into play one way or another." Ella quickly changes out of her swimsuit into a warmer set of clothes.

I spin around. "What the fuck, Ella."

"I know, I'm a genius. Besides, you have a sex addled look. It's making me hot and bothered, even though I know for a fact that I'm going to get some today."

Oh, great. "And just where are you going to *get some*?"

She winks.

"I feel like you should not be encouraging this," I mumble, glancing out the window. Finn's carrying an armload of wood across the driveway. It's freaking attractive.

"Please. You're both consenting adults. From where I stand, you both want this. Do you have an actual reservation or are you just overthinking?"

"I don't know. What if I'm just using him to scratch an itch? And using him the wrong way? I had plenty of the bedroom activities with my ex. It was fine, but I want more than that."

"*It was fine*, she says," Ella mocks with an exaggerated eye roll. "Tell me your ex sucked at sex without telling me that he sucked at sex."

"You're missing the point."

"What I'm missing is some special adult time with my boyfriend. Which, for the record, is what we're actually heading straight off to do now that I've successfully pawned you off on Finn. You don't have to do anything with Finn if you don't want to. If you'd rather sleep alone tonight, just ask him to bring you back to Mom's house. Although I may or may not be there tonight, doing really raunchy things with Sam."

"Doesn't he have a cabin nearby that you guys can use?"

"I prefer my bed. Stop panicking and enjoy your little love adventure." She opens the bathroom door and strides into the kitchen, decked out in sweats, her swimsuit tucked into a plastic bag.

The front door opens just wide enough for Sam to poke his head in. "You ready to go, Ella?"

"Just getting my coat on," she assures him. Lowering her voice, she adds, "I left you a little present in the backpack, but it's your call if you want to use it or not. I'm one hundred percent sure that Finn's not going to pressure you into doing anything. If you want what he's offering, take it. If not, don't. He'll respect your decision either way."

"Is it that simple?" I wonder aloud.

"It better be." She plants a disgusting kiss on the side of my face, cackling at my expression as she walks out the door.

Leaving me alone in Finn's house.

I sit awkwardly at the table, waiting for him to come back in. When he does, he takes a long look at me, a tiny crease forming between his brows. I tense, wondering how well he can read me… hopefully not very well. My thoughts are just embarrassing. Maybe he knows that, because he relaxes somewhat and pours himself a cup of coffee from the glass carafe before joining me at the table.

"You want to go back to your aunt's right away, or do you want to stick around for a while longer? I wouldn't mind hanging out in the hot tub for a bit, but I can do that later if you're dead set on leaving me."

And there it is. Another notch on the stick of Finn's many attractive traits: making either choice sound just fine, removing the pressure that I'd built up for myself in my head.

"I don't mind staying a little while longer, if that's ok."

He smiles. If I didn't know better, I'd say he looked pleased. "You want to join me in the hot tub, or are you just going to watch?"

"That all depends on whether Ella thought to leave a suit for me."

A little digging in said bag tells me she did, in fact, leave a swimsuit. A very skimpy string bikini that only just covers my bits. It's far less coverage than I'd have with my underwear and bra. Is this her grand plan? I stand in front of the bathroom mirror, debating whether I'm confident enough to pull this off. I'm typically more of a crop top and swim shorts type girl.

Through the door, I hear Finn call out. "I'm heading outside. There's beer in the fridge if you want one."

I wait until I hear the sliding door open and close before finally emerging from the bathroom, a towel wrapped over my swimsuit. Through the window, I can see Finn walk across the patio to the hot tub, his magnificent body on display in the fading afternoon light. He's all lean muscle, which I remember vividly from the first moment I saw him. I catch the slightest glimpse of those incredibly well-defined abs before he slides into the steaming water. My knees feel a little weak.

While I stand still, debating what to do, Ella's words replay in my head. *If you want what he's offering, take it. If not, don't.*

Okay but seriously, is it that simple?

Because there is no doubt in my mind: I most certainly want what he offered earlier on the couch.

So maybe I'll just head out there and see what happens. Let my raging hormones make some decisions for once. Taking a deep breath, I grab a beer and walk outside.

Finn's head turns the moment the door slides open, his gaze pinned on me as I make my way across the patio. The stones are heated and warm against my bare feet. Pushing away the shyness, I unwrap the towel and set it on one of the patio chairs that's been cleared of snow. Cautiously, I put my toe in. It's scalding, but I'm not about to stand here, my body on full display. I force myself to step in quickly, hissing a little when the water reaches my waist. My boobs, barely covered in this skimpy suit, are still more than visible, but I can't seem to force myself any lower. Not until I acclimate to the temperature.

"It's really hot," I say.

"I think that's where it gets its name," Finn teases, his expression a mixture of amusement and—well, you know. Since my boobs are pretty much in full view.

It takes a couple minutes, but finally my body grows accustomed to the temperature and I sit down, the water coming up to my shoulders. I let out a sigh, relaxing in front of one of the jets.

"It feels like an exotic destination vacation out here, surrounded by all these snowy trees," I comment.

"I wasn't sure you were going to come out," Finn says, taking a sip of his beer.

"I wasn't either," I admit.

"But you did."

"Yeah." Obviously.

"What made you change your mind?"

Besides seeing how he looked without a shirt? "I just figured it would be nicer to hang out than stand around inside and overthink."

That pulls a smile out of him. A real one that crinkles the corners of his eyes. He lifts his bottle and taps it gently against mine. "Cheers to that." With a quick glance at my chest, where the top of my bikini is just visible, he adds, "And cheers to that suit. You look stunning in it."

I burst out laughing. I saw what I looked like in the bathroom mirror. Stunning was not one of the words that came to mind. "Courtesy of Ella. It's a little small."

"Is there such a thing?" Finn looks serious, apart from the little smirk that tells me he's up to play. "I would imagine you'd look just fine with nothing at all. The suit is just a nice extra."

Another line thrown out. A test to see what I want.

"I thought the rules were: No skinny dipping in my hot tub," I say lightly, trying to mimic the tone he took when Ella suggested such a thing.

"Those rules are for your cousin and in mixed company. They don't apply to you."

"Really." The way he's looking at me now sends a jolt of pure heat swirling low in my stomach. Heat that has absolutely nothing to do with the freakishly scalding temps of this hot tub. I take another swig of beer, then set it down on the side and tuck my hands under the water to hide how they're shaking. From nerves or anticipation, I'm not quite sure.

His eyes are dark, hooded. "You call the shots, Rune."

"Generous of you."

"Trust me: generous really isn't the right word for it."

"Oh?"

"Try desperate. Or enamored. Or better: wholly captivated." His eyes are all-consuming, so intense that I couldn't look away if I wanted.

"Those are good words." I don't know what I'm saying. *Shut up, Rune. Just stop talking.*

"I'm wondering how I managed to convince you to spend time with me, wondering what I have to do to get you to stay a little longer."

Because I know what I want—and maybe to test his sincerity a little—I reach back to tug on the strings of my bikini. I tied them tight, intending to make sure there weren't any embarrassing nip slips. After a moment of struggling they loosen and I pull the whole thing off. I drape it over the side, next to my beer; a flash of hot pink against the muted browns and grays of winter.

Finn lets out a low, breathy laugh. His eyes don't leave mine. "Bold, Rune. What's your plan now?"

What is my plan? I don't have one. I'm operating on pure instinct and desire. I lean back against the wall of the hot tub, my body still mostly covered by the bubbling water. "Now it's your move." My voice comes out deeper than usual, less timid. I don't know this part of me. I've never explored it before. But Finn— Finn makes me feel safe. Confident. Desirable.

When he reaches out his hand, I take it. I let him pull me

across the hot tub and settle me on his lap. It's impossible not to feel how hard he is. I'm basically wearing nothing. My breasts are now fully exposed above the water, nipples tight from desire and the cold air. I feel mildly unhinged. I want to rub myself up against him, run my hands over every part of his beautifully sculpted body. I want to rip off the rest of my swimsuit and do all kinds of things with him.

"Feel that?" he says in my ear, moving against me. "I've been hard for you all day."

That sounds uncomfortable. "I'm sorry," I say.

"I'm not."

We look at each other and lean in at the same time. It's a slow, intentional kiss. One that makes my toes curl, my body long for more. My attention wavers between the masterful way he strokes into my mouth with his tongue and the way his hands slide up my legs, pulling me tighter against his hard length. If I was on fire before, this is an inferno. I shift against him, my eyes fluttering closed at the pressure, the maddening hint of friction.

"You sure you're okay with this?" he asks, breathing hard.

I choke out a laugh and gesture to my bare chest. "Yeah, I'm pretty sure I am."

He bites back a smile. "Right."

And with that, he lowers his head to my breast, pulling it into his mouth as I arch backwards. I can't help the strangled moan, the way my hands grip his arms. I'm on fucking fire and all I want is more.

I reach down and stroke him. He shudders against me.

"Rune, what do you want?"

"That stupid question again," I mutter. If I were thinking critically, I might be impressed with his integrity. But right now, all I want is to not think.

He takes me by the wrists, pinning my hands behind my back. I writhe in his lap, so turned on with how his eyes heat even more.

"Use your words and tell me exactly what you want," he grits out.

I pin his gaze with mine. "I want to get naked and *do* you."

I am unprepared for the sudden flash of desire mixed with vulnerability. He leans until our foreheads are touching. "It would be my pleasure."

"Finn?" I whisper. "You can keep holding my hands like this, if you want."

He gives a short laugh, but complies. "Getting a little kinky, aren't we?"

I could burn with how he's looking at me, watching my reactions to the way he changes his hold so that one of his hands spans my wrists. His other hand grasps my shoulder, trails down my breasts, rolls a nipple. An embarrassing moan is wrung out of me. Through the haze, I realize that Ella was probably right: maybe Sebastian actually was terrible at sex. I don't remember ever being this turned on with him. We're not even fully naked yet.

Finn apparently notices the same thing, because he hoists us both out of the pool and carries me into the house, my legs wrapped around his middle.

I'm about to object when he sets me on the couch and turns away—but it's only to add some logs to the dying fire. He stares at me, approval evident as he drags his gaze up and down my body.

I've never felt so appreciated, so beautiful. But I'm not a painting. I want to do things. I rip off my bikini bottoms at the same time that he drops his trunks. I am purely, utterly without words. He could be a fucking statue—that famous Michelangelo one—his muscles are so perfectly put together, down to the deep V that leads to the exact part of his anatomy that I want the most right now.

"So," I say.

His eyes brighten and crinkle around the edges. "So," he repeats. "I don't even know where to begin. I have so many ideas when it comes to you. So many places that I want to explore."

"Better get started then, huh?"

He laughs, low and rough, as he reaches me, pressing me down with his hand until I'm laying on my back, my legs falling open for him. He runs a gentle finger up my center, smiling as I draw in a quick breath. He does it again, his other hand worshipping my breast at the same time, sending threads of pleasure coursing through my whole body.

"I could play with you all night," he murmurs, watching me closely. It's terrifyingly intimate.

"Please don't," I say. "Just fuck me already."

"Bossy much?" he asks, but doesn't sound at all displeased. I shriek as he drags me up against him. "Couch or bed?"

"Bed, in this case." I don't want to risk the welfare of that beautiful couch. Finn drags me to him, our naked bodies fully flush. I wonder if we'll even make it to a bed. It feels so very far away.

But somehow, despite barely breaking our kiss, we stumble up the stairs and down the hall to a bedroom. My eyes widen when he flips on a low light, taking it all in while Finn goes into the attached bathroom to dig out a condom. There's a king-sized bed in the center and an entire wall full of windows facing the lake, complete with a bench and cushions that look perfect for reading. It's nicer than any hotel I've ever stayed in and three times as cozy.

I turn to say as much when I catch the sight of him watching me. All other thoughts empty out of my head and I hold my hand out for the condom, indulging in the feel of him in my hands as I slide it onto him. Then his mouth is on me and he's dragging me to the bed, pulling me with him.

Together, we're a raging fire: hot and passionate and determined. Every touch is pure luxury as he works his way up and down my body with his mouth. Then, with a clever twist he's underneath me, settling me into position. His hands stabilize me as I seat myself deeply onto him. My breath catches at the sheer decadence of him inside me. *Fuck* and fuck again.

Sweat beads on Finn's forehead as we move in tandem, every roll of my hips met with a thrust of his own. He seems to sense the moment my energy flails and he flips us around, driving himself into me from behind. I try to brace myself against the pillows, but his hands hold me exactly where I need to be. Where we both need to be.

I'm so close—creeping closer to the edge with every breathtaking thrust of his body. When his hand reaches around and finds my clit, I see stars.

His grip on me tightens as his body shudders with his own release. For a long moment, I can only pant, trying to catch a full breath. He plants a trail of kisses along my neck before slowly pulling himself out, leaving me to collapse in a boneless heap on the cloud that is his bed, chest heaving from exertion.

"I've never—that was—" Words truly fail me.

"I know," he says, staring back at me with the same look. Wide-eyed and amazed. "Rune, I know."

His hand trails up and down my arm, soothing my heart rate. I want to stay here forever. Right here, like this. So I'm immensely relieved when I return from cleaning myself up in his bathroom and find that he's turned the sheets down. He must have gone downstairs; my phone and a glass of water are sitting on one of the nightstands next to the bed.

He lifts the sheets to help me slide under them, both of us still naked. A massive yawn threatens to split my jaw.

"I'm sorry, I don't know if I can keep my eyes open. I've had more exercise today than I've ever had in my life."

"So stay with me. Sleep here tonight," he says, like it's the obvious choice. Maybe it is.

I roll over and shoot a quick text off to Ella, in case she actually is expecting me back. Then I let Finn tuck me into his arms, kissing me gently on the curve of my ear as he pulls the blanket over us. Exhausted and fully sated, I nestle into him. The last thing I'm aware of is his arms around me; the soft pattern of his breath lulling me to sleep.

Chapter 22

Finn

I awake to the warmth of Rune's body, still cocooned in my arms. The soft gray light of the sky tells me that it's early morning. I don't want to get out of bed. Her hair cascades around us like spun silk. I can't help but run my fingers through the ends of it. She rolls over, blinking at me through sleep heavy eyes. One hand reaches for me and I let her draw me in for a kiss.

"Good morning," I murmur.

"Hi," she replies. Her smile is a little shy. "Thanks for last night."

I'm over-aware of the fact that she's lying naked in my bed. I close my eyes and breathe her in—the scent of her body, her hair. I could wake up to this every day. "For the record, that wasn't at all how I pictured last night going."

"No?" She props herself up on an elbow. "How did you picture it? Did you imagine that I would have bigger boobs?"

"What the fuck, Rune." I caress her breast, palming it gently. It's so soft, so mesmerizing. "They're perfect. No, I meant...I had every intention of seducing you with some measure of romance. A nice dinner, some fancy wine. But when you took off your swimsuit, I sort of...forgot." I'm an idiot. She might as well know it.

"I'm sorry I ruined your plan." She doesn't seem sorry. If anything, Rune looks pleased with herself.

"You didn't. My plan ended up with us getting naked, too." I pull back the blanket, an appreciative sound humming low in my throat as I run my hand down her side. Her skin is incredibly smooth. It's pure instinct to press my cock against her. She pushes back, well aware of what she's doing to me. I force myself to add, "Can I make it up to you? I'll cook breakfast."

"Breakfast is good," she replies. I mentally prepare to drag myself away when she tugs at my arm, letting her knees fall open. A request. Breakfast is momentarily put on hold as we continue where we left off last night. I pride myself on being both perceptive and imaginative as a lover, but I feel like a starved man who's presented with real food for the first time.

This bed is perfect for sleeping in. It's even more perfect, I realize, for discovering the best way to draw those small gasps of pleasure from Rune. She's on her knees, face cradled in her arms on a pillow, and we're both so obviously close that I'm tempted to finish us quickly, but in the end...I flip us to indulge in the sight of Rune riding me, driving us both to a gasping, sweaty completion.

We stay that way for a while, her straddling me, tracing the contours of my chest, my abs, the muscled curve of my thighs. I keep my hands patiently on her hips, letting her explore. Her eyes are on me the whole time. Because I'm watching her, too, I see the moment her mind starts to wander. The wrinkle of her nose, like she's just been told a particularly bad joke.

"What's that look for?" I smile, reaching up to cradle the side of her face with my hand.

"You're like an aromatic god and I am in desperate need of a shower."

My laughter doubles as she rolls off me. "You smell like sex and me. Please don't wash it off. Ever."

"Gross." Her nose wrinkles even more. She runs a finger across my cheekbones, my nose. I close my eyes and revel in the soft, tentative touch. "You wouldn't mind me sketching you, would you?" she asks suddenly. "Specifically, your nose. For my illustrations."

"Only if I can see them," I bargain. I've been wanting to see her portrayals of the *Crimson and Roses* series since she mentioned it at my parents' party.

"You can, but they're not finished yet."

"Show me," I plead. She looks at me, wavering in her decision. I put on my most innocent face. "I just want a peek."

"Fine. Here." She swipes a few times then hands her phone to me.

I'm floored. The illustrations are good. *Really* good. The colors, the shading, the expressions—all far beyond what my most vibrant imagination could ever conjure. I zoom in to catch the details. "Rune, these are incredible."

She ducks her head, embarrassed but pleased. "There's a lot of things to fix before I would consider them done. Before I would ever let the author see."

I freeze as a wave of guilt washes over me. I've tricked her and I didn't mean to. But maybe—a sudden, wild idea starts to form. It may be possible to fix this—all of it.

"Were you serious when you said you wanted to be an illustrator?" I ask.

"I guess I don't really know since I've never tried. But I think so. I thought maybe I could try to sell some prints in an online shop or something and then just see where it goes."

"You could." It's a sensible starting point. A safe one. Too safe, considering how skilled she is. "I might have a contact who would like to see these. Someone who works in the publishing industry," I hedge, not wanting to promise anything until I have a chance to talk to Amber and flesh out this budding plan a little more.

Although Rune's eyes light up, she worries at her lip. "I don't know if I'm good enough for that kind of project yet."

I swipe back through the photos, landing on one illustration in particular. The two main characters from *Crimson and Roses* are at odds—a classic enemies to lovers story—and the male is held at knifepoint by his love interest. I turn the phone back to face her. "Rune, this is more than good enough. This is the kind of thing authors dream of for their books."

"If you think so." She sounds doubtful.

"I'll reach out to them, and will let you know what they say." I return Rune's phone, another idea in my mind. "In the meantime...the shower is probably large enough for two people."

"Probably?" She laughs at the word choice.

"I've never tried before," I admit. I don't typically invite women to my house and certainly don't invite them to shower with me in my private bathroom.

"Well then, we'd better test it out." She flutters her lashes.

It turns into more of a striptease and I honestly have no idea what's gotten into me. I can't get enough of her splayed out naked in front of me. It goes far beyond simple lust. I want her here in my house, touching my things, leaving her clothes strewn around to disrupt the sterile, pristine life that I've built for myself. She might be leaving tomorrow, but I have no intention of letting what we have end. And if my idea comes to fruition...well, I'll just keep my fingers crossed.

"Coffee? Breakfast?" I prompt, pulling on a pair of black gym shorts. I'm not sure where her clothes are—downstairs, somewhere —but I hand her one of my shirts so she doesn't have to walk around naked. Not that I would mind if she did.

"Yes and yes." She accepts the t-shirt, pulling it straight on, completely nude underneath. I swallow. She notices my stare and gives a pointed look at my bare chest.

"You could put a shirt on. I'm not sure I can think straight if you're walking around like that."

I toss her a wink. "That's the plan."

She rolls her eyes, a smile playing at the corner of her mouth.

As we walk into the hall, Rune's gaze catches on the open door to my office. It's the kind of room that would probably be a haven for her, too: floor to ceiling bookshelves lining two walls, with a large desk set into a corner and an armchair with a matching ottoman up against a window. But I don't want her in there. Not yet.

"My office," I tell her, breathing a sigh of relief when she moves past it without another word.

Downstairs is a veritable mess compared with my usual orderly cleanliness. There are empty mugs and beer bottles on the table, along with boxes full of crumbs from our afternoon snack. Pillows are strewn about in the living room. My swimming trunks are probably still on the floor where I left them. An absolute disaster. And one that makes me smile when I think about it. I set about cleaning things up while the coffee brews, putting the boxes in the garbage and rinsing out the beer bottles before tossing them into the recycle bin. Wordlessly, Rune comes over to help, washing the mugs by hand.

When the counters are clean, I pour fresh brewed coffee into two mugs.

"For a successful sleepover," I say, clinking our cups together.

"Best I've ever had," she replies.

"Fuck yes." We smile at each other and I'm about to suggest we snuggle on the couch while drinking our coffee when I hear a car pull up in the driveway. Rune and I share a look. It's only nine in the morning. Too early for unannounced visitors, unless Ella and Sam have decided to show up to gloat. When I look out the kitchen window, my heart drops.

"Who is it?" Rune asks warily, noticing my reaction.

I swallow, my throat suddenly very dry. "My parents."

"You're joking."

"I fucking wish."

She looks around, panicked. "Should I hide? I could go upstairs until they leave."

That startles a laugh out of me. "Absolutely not." We're both consenting adults. She's not a medieval mistress that needs to remain a secret.

"I need to put my bra on. I don't know where it is." She claps her hands over her chest, a growing look of horror. "Finn, I'm not even wearing *pants*."

I allow myself one long look of appreciation at her bare legs before striding into the bathroom, where I fish out a clean sweatshirt and shorts from the dryer. They're mine and at least two sizes too big for her, but they're better than nothing. I wait while she pulls them on. Only then do I answer the knock at my door, pulling it open to reveal my parents. They're standing on the porch, smiling like this is the best thing in the world.

"Surprise!" Mom's arms are full of shopping bags and boxes. "We brought breakfast."

Behind her, Dad just grins, clearly thrilled at the fact that they pulled one over on me. "Just getting up, huh Finn?"

"Mom, Dad, this is...a surprise. Come on in."

"We both texted and I called twice this morning," Mom scolds, kicking her shoes haphazardly against the wall, like a child. "I figured you were busy working or maybe lost your phone, so I thought: why not swing by and bring you something to eat."

"How much do you think I eat?" Judging by the number of bags, she's brought enough food for a month.

"Oh, you know, I thought I'd bring a little extra. Some of these are your Christmas presents and—oh!" Mom's chatter falls silent when she realizes that I'm not the only one in the house. Poor Rune is standing uncertainly in the kitchen, her face noticeably paler than it was a minute ago. She looks terrified. I don't blame her. I'm a little nervous myself.

"Mom, you remember Rune," I say.

"It's nice to see you again, Mrs. Sigurdson." Rune offers a tentative smile.

Mom's look tells me that she absolutely does not remember her.

"You met her at the party," I remind them. "Mairi's niece."

"Oh. *Oh.*" I don't like that look on Mom's face. The one that reads far too much into a situation. She's going to scare the girl off before I can convince Rune to stay in the first place. "Of course."

"You want coffee, Mom? Dad?"

"Of course, sprinkle a little cinnamon in mine, would you, honey?" My heartbeat kicks up a few notches as Mom takes her coffee over to the table. "So, Rune, I'm afraid we didn't get much of a chance to chat at the party. You're on vacation from Chicago, if I recall?"

"Yes, that's right," Rune says. I send her mental well-wishes.

And what are you doing in my son's house? Mom doesn't voice the question, but it's written all over her face as she turns from Rune to me, waiting expectantly for an explanation.

Too bad I have no intention of giving her one.

"So what are you two doing out and about so early?" I ask instead. "Isn't it like six in Arizona time?"

"It's past eight there, Finn, and we are on vacation. Late to bed, early to rise." Dad gives me a sage nod, as if imparting some wisdom.

Mom only rolls her eyes. "Your father doesn't understand what a vacation is. We're having brunch with Mr. and Mrs. Lakso—you remember them, Finn? Mrs. Lakso was your eighth grade English teacher. We thought we'd drop off some food for you on the way. Rune, we brought French toast and bacon. Is that something you like?"

"Yes, it's one of my favorites."

I relax a little. I can tell from Mom's shift in demeanor that she's noticed Rune's discomfort and has decided to put her at ease. For now.

"Now you'll have to remind me. What is it that you do?" Mom asks, believing this is safe ground. I close my eyes.

"I've worked in marketing for the last couple years," Rune replies quickly.

"How interesting. Marketers are so valuable." Mom takes a polite sip of her coffee. She has a personal bias against marketing, for whatever reason. She's told me more than once that all marketers are scammers at heart. "Have you enjoyed your vacation?"

Rune nods. "The cold takes some getting used to, but we've been out skiing a lot."

"It's always cold here. I was so glad when Finn decided to install that hot tub. It's so nice when it's—when it's—well, anyway, the cold is a pleasant break from Arizona's heat."

Confused by the abrupt change of direction, I follow Mom's gaze out the window and wince. Rune's pink bikini top is dangling over the edge of the hot tub in plain sight. Right next to her half-finished beer. It doesn't take a genius to figure out what all went on. Rune's painfully traumatized gaze meets mine, pleading for help. I should have let her escape when she had the chance. My mistake.

Mom darts a very obvious *what the fuck* look at me, as if it's my fault that she and Dad showed up before I had a chance to put the place in order again. To hide the obvious signs of last night's sequence of events.

Fully oblivious to the underlying tension between Mom, Rune, and I at the table, Dad wanders into the living room.

"Didn't like the pillows on the couch, eh Finn?" I close my eyes, begging for strength at his dry humor. I was born tidy, or so my mother likes to say. The sight of my couch pillows in disarray is probably as jarring for my parents as it is for me.

"Feel free to put them back in order, if you want." I don't dare look at Rune. I know for a fact that those pillows fell off when I had her naked on the couch. Right after she took off her—oh shit. Rune's thinking the same thing, sending me a panicked look that has me scrambling to my feet. I have to distract Dad before he can find the matching bottoms to the hot pink bikini top that's dangling over the edge of the hot tub.

I'm about three seconds too slow. I see the moment he spots them, his brows furrowed as he tries to make sense of what he's holding. Slowly he looks from the bottoms to the swim trunks that are also lying in the middle of the floor. He clears his throat awkwardly before putting them back down, this time on the edge of the hearth.

"You know, you have to hang up your wet clothes if you want the fire to dry them, Finn," he says offhandedly. "I thought we raised you better."

For once, Mom is completely without words. She makes an attempt at finishing her coffee as if nothing has happened, even making some small talk with Rune about how she heard there was a new exhibit at the art museum in Chicago that might be worth checking out. After a few minutes, even that proves to be too much.

"Well, Pat, we'd better be off or we'll be late for brunch. Come along, we'll leave these two to their, er, visit." Mom casts one of her social queen smiles at all of us. The one she uses when she's stuck in a social situation and wants to escape to get shit-faced drunk.

Dad follows meekly, unable to look any of us in the eye. He mumbles a subdued, "See you, bud," before shutting the door behind him. Leaving Rune and I alone once more.

"So that was—" Rune starts, her face flaming.

"Fucking awkward," I say wearily, dropping back into my chair.

She opens her mouth as if to disagree, but then deflates. "Yeah," she agrees. "It really was."

Chapter 23

Rune

"I'm so sorry, Rune," Finn apologizes for what must be the hundredth time as he drives me back to Aunt Mairi's house.

"It's fine," I reply tiredly. Ella sent a text with a pointed suggestion to hurry if I wanted to make it before Auntie and Courtney return. I'm not scared of them finding out, per se, but I'd rather tell them on my own terms.

"I didn't know they were coming," he continues, looking as frazzled as I feel. If it wasn't so scarring, I would probably laugh. The whole thing unrolled like a bad comedy. "I shouldn't have forced you to stay downstairs to meet them. I was just—I just didn't want you to feel like you had to hide. I fucked up."

"You weren't the one who left a freaking bikini lying around someone else's house," I retort. I couldn't have been more obvious if I'd left a sign with red letters: *I got naked and had sex with your son*. I think of Finn's dad and the face he made when he put two and two together. I let out a strangled moan. "Now both of your parents have pictured me naked. I can only imagine what went through their heads."

"There's no way they thought about you naked," he lies, trying to soothe me.

"They know we did it."

"Yeah." There's no denying that part.

I let out a half-laugh, half-sob.

"I'll make this up to you," he vows. There's a pleading look in his eyes, like he's begging me to give him another chance.

I could tell him not to worry about it, that it's all fine. But honestly, if he can think of something that will make me feel less awful, I don't mind. I'm not ashamed to have people know we were together. There's just something about the manner in which it happened which might have scarred me for life. I'll never be able to look either of his parents in the face again. Not unless I'm really drunk.

Finn turns into Aunt Mairi's driveway. There's no sign of her car yet.

"So…will I see you at the fundraiser tonight?" I'm leaving in the morning, but neither of us has addressed that. Nor do I feel up to that conversation at this particular moment.

"Yes. I'll find you there."

"Awesome. Cool." I unbuckle my seatbelt.

He reaches over to grasp my hand. "You ok?"

"Yeah, I'm just going to go inside and die of residual embarrassment." I bury my face in my hands. The whole thing keeps playing on repeat in my mind. "Fucking bikini bottoms."

Finn pries my hands away from my face with a sort of panicked gentleness. He kisses each palm before drawing me in. Some of the tightness in my chest lightens when our lips meet. He feels and smells like home, which is even more unsettling than anything else.

When he drives away, he takes all of my good feelings with him. I'm left with an overwhelming sense of nervousness, like I'm back on the very edge of a downward spiral and don't know how to make it stop.

❄

Ella only barely contains herself as I walk inside and toss my bag into the guest room where I've been staying. My clothes are scattered around; I should spend the afternoon packing. I won't have time in the morning, not if I want to get on the road at a reasonable hour. And with a nine hour drive ahead of me...I definitely want to start my journey fairly early. I find my pajamas and tuck them into my suitcase. Four sweaters quickly follow.

Fuck, I should have just talked about my upcoming departure with Finn. I don't like this feeling of not knowing where he stands. But I doubt either of us was capable of thinking straight this morning. First from the sex, and then—the surprise visit.

"Well?" Ella asks finally from the doorway, breaking into my depressing thoughts.

"Well, what?"

"Was it not good? You look like you're having serious regrets."

"I'm not. It was great. I had a good time."

"Just a good time? Not *mind blowing*?" Her fingers flutter dramatically.

"It was fine. Very enjoyable." I locate my last sweater and set it aside to wear tomorrow on the drive.

Her brow puckers. "Why are you being weird? I thought you'd be a little more excited. You've been pining over him since you got here. Either it was really awful or you're stuck up in your mind again."

Or both. I'm saved from a reply by Aunt Mairi and Courtney coming into the house.

"Oh look, my favorite sister is still here," Courtney says, giving me a big smile.

"Ha ha," Ella snorts.

"We passed Finn on the way in," Aunt Mairi says. Is it my imagination or did she give me a look? So much for secrecy on any front. We might as well put a public notice in the local newspaper.

Ella looks at me expectantly, her face scrunching up when I shake my head.

We sit in the living room, eating popcorn while Aunt Mairi and Courtney recap the highlights of their trip, from shopping finds to the dumb drama at the Christmas party.

"And how was skiing with Finn?" Courtney asks. "I hear he asked you out."

"It was nice. I saw a moose." I manage to speak normally, but my palms are sweating.

"Those things are so awesome. I've only ever seen one once, and it was just a blur. How close was it, do you think?" Aunt Mairi looks between me and Ella.

"Oh I wasn't there," Ella holds up her hands. "It was just Rune and Finn. Like the little lovebirds they are."

"Lovebirds, huh?" Courtney looks amused, which is just a little bit annoying.

"Ella wasn't with us because she decided she wanted to hang out in the chalet and wait for Sam," I say, giving Ella a warning look.

She stares straight back at me.

"Did anything happen that I should know about, or is this something that needs to stay between you two?" Auntie asks warily. A question that she's probably asked a million times since we were kids.

Ella's eyes narrow, as if daring me to say something. And maybe I'm just sick of secrets, maybe I need to process it more, but the words start tumbling out. Once they do, I can't stop them. "It was fine. Skiing was fun. We went to hot tub at Finn's and I ended up staying the night, but his parents showed up unannounced this morning. They know we weren't fully clothed at some point and it was the worst experience of my life."

Three stunned faces stare back at me.

"I was not expecting that," Ella admits.

"Just to clarify, was it the worst experience because his parents showed up, or because he's really...you know, bad at it?" Courtney asks.

I choke out a horrified laugh. "The part about his parents."

"You don't have to talk about this if you don't want to," Aunt Mairi says quickly. She looks like she's torn between intrigue and the knowledge that she is the only real adult in this room and isn't sure whether she should be a part of this conversation. "Why don't I make some tea and snacks."

While Auntie prepares food in the kitchen, Ella drags me into the living room with Courtney.

"Okay, before Mom comes back in, I have to know the details," she whispers. "He's got to be an amazing kisser, is he?"

"Yeah," I hear myself saying. "He's not bad."

"Did he get handsy? Was there tongue? Was he—you know, *big*?"

"Ella, we do *not* need to know this." Courtney looks revolted.

"So what else did you do besides each other and flaunt your shenanigans in front of his parents? Let me guess: you had him write a special little message in your fancy book. With little hearts over each *i*?"

It takes a moment for me to figure out what she means, and when I do, it still doesn't make sense. "I don't get it."

"You know, like, *Rune, love of my life, this story was written for you*."

Courtney's monitoring my confused expression and she suddenly sits a little straighter, amused expression wiped away. "Ella, just stop."

"I'm just joking. It's not like I'm saying he had to write the L word, but a personalized message is a little more special than—"

"Shut the *actual* fuck up."

Ella's mouth falls slack. Then she glances at me and a disconcerting understanding dawns across her face. "Do you seriously not know?"

"Know what?"

"It's not really a secret, but," Ella's eyes dart towards Courtney.

"Fucking Finn," Courtney says under her breath. "Did you know that Finn's a writer, Rune? That's how he makes his money."

"I didn't," I say, unsure why they continue to look at me like that. Maybe that's what he was referring to when he got all serious about my art this morning. Maybe he has author connections. "That's pretty cool."

Courtney continues, "He's the author of that one series you're obsessed with."

I look from Courtney to Ella, now thoroughly disoriented as the words sink in. Of all the ways I expected this conversation to go...well, this wasn't it. "Are you sure? I thought R.E. Andersson was a woman."

Ella bursts out laughing. "What the fuck, Rune? There's pictures of him on his website. Don't tell me you haven't seen them."

"I haven't," I admit, feeling suddenly nervous.

"That's on you, then. Ignorance is not bliss." Her fingers fly, tapping on her phone. A minute later, she turns it towards me. "It doesn't look exactly like him, but you can tell it is."

I stare at the black-and-white photo of R.E. Andersson that

Ella just pulled up. It is most definitely Finn. And I would have known, had I not been a complete idiot.

"So embarrassing," Ella cackles, clearly enjoying this. "Also, why did you think the author was a girl? How do you even come up with something like that?"

I briefly explain my theory. The one I shared with Finn at his parents' party. I thought it made so much sense, but seeing the way my cousins are staring at me...well, I'm starting to have some doubts.

"That is so sexist," Courtney says. "Your theory sucks."

"I pictured the author being some sort of girl book bestie, okay?" I defend myself, despite knowing that what she says is true. "Instead of a super hot guy that I want to bang."

"That you *did* bang," Ella points out.

"Well, at least he doesn't know," Courtney says soothingly.

I give her a tortured look. "Oh he knows. I told him on Thursday." I remember the look on Finn's face when I told him my theory about the author's gender. The way he looked at me with that quizzical expression.

Courtney gives a sharp, incredulous laugh. "That's...God, Rune, I can't help you here."

"Why didn't he say anything?" I lament. "Is it a secret?"

"Because he's a dumb idiot, like all men." Courtney shrugs. "And yes, I'm well aware of how sexist *that* is."

"Maybe he didn't want to embarrass you by pointing out how stupid you are." Ella gives me a shitty grin.

"This sounds like a conversation that might be best finished between Rune and Finn," Auntie says, gliding into the room with a plate full of snacks: cold cuts, cheese, pickles, and pita chips.

It looks amazing, but I'm not hungry. I feel stupid on so many levels. Surprisingly, the fact that I didn't recognize him is the least of my concerns. That he didn't say anything, though, is perplexing

—was it because he felt bad for correcting me? Was he concerned about how I'd react? Afraid that I'd go out and advertise the fact that I slept with fucking R.E. Andersson?

I wouldn't have.

"I wouldn't worry about it if I were you," Aunt Mairi breaks into my thoughts.

"I won't—I'm not. I'm just disoriented."

"Are you planning on confronting him? I hope you do," Courtney says, sounding a little vicious.

Am I? I'm not even sure I'm brave enough to show my face after this.

"Honestly, it's fine," I say. "I'll just ask for his autograph next time I see him." The humor falls flat, but my aunt and cousins pretend as if they believe my lie, kindly steering the conversation towards much safer topics, like the menu for Christmas dinner and whether they should bother with hanging twinkle lights on the woodshed this year.

All the while, I'm wallowing in a mix of misery, confusion, and embarrassment. I made a fucking assumption of the author's gender based on nothing but my own very limited analysis, and it was dead wrong. Was that offensive? I hadn't meant for it to be. Surely Finn wouldn't have withheld information about his writing because of that...would he?

And if so, why did he sleep with me? I'm such a freaking idiot. It wouldn't be the first time that I had sex based on superficial attraction, but I thought it was different between us. I was hoping we'd have connected on a deeper level. Instead, I probably just insulted him and—oh, shit.

The first fucking thing I did this morning after being intimate with him was to shove my illustrations in his face. Why did I even show them to him? I don't show them to anyone. What is *wrong* with me?

The thing with his parents this morning was awful. But this—this just might be worse.

I'm going to have to say something when I see him tonight. I owe it to both of us. Even though—even though it feels off. Wrong, somehow. I trust Finn, I swear I do. But maybe all of the circumstances surrounding our little winter romance skewed our perception of reality.

It's felt like a dream these past few days, but maybe I'm the one who's been out of touch with reality. It's probably time that I wake up and move on with my life.

Chapter 24

Rune

It seems like the entire community shows up for the fundraiser, from young parents with babies to retired folks who look like they're all geared up and ready for the social event of the year. Ella was right: the room looks far better in the evening light than it did when we were in here decorating. The strings of fairy lights and long evergreen garlands cascading over almost every wall feels very cozy and Christmas-y. The savory smell of roast beef and loaded mashed potatoes pervades the room. I'm hungry, but there's been a tight knot in my stomach all afternoon and it's currently ruining my appetite. As I follow my cousins through the crowd, I keep my eyes peeled for a man with dark hair and mesmerizing blue eyes.

I don't know whether I'm pleased or disappointed when I realize he's not here yet. He said he would come tonight. I hope he doesn't come with his parents. I don't know if I could handle facing them again so soon.

I did go for one last ski sprint this afternoon with Courtney, which helped stabilize my raging emotions and settle the sick feeling in my stomach somewhat. There's something about wide open spaces and solitude that helps to calm the soul. I'm determined to tell him what I know, if for no other reason than the fact that I'm out of time. I'm leaving tomorrow morning. I don't want to walk away with misplaced hope that whatever happened between us could turn into something more. And let's be honest: why would he think any different?

I was only ever going to be here for a few days, and it's not like either of us talked about making a long-distance relationship work. Not when he hates traveling and I don't have the money for it.

Aunt Mairi bids on a few items at the silent auction table. I put a five dollar bid down for a basket of three wine bottles and a pair of stemmed glasses. I'm willing to go as far as ten. Ella has gone wild, putting twelve dollar bids down for everything, insisting that she'll have to luck out on something.

Then, with plates full of buttery rolls, green bean casserole, and a dozen other dishes, we find four seats together at the end of a long table. I'm worried that I won't be able to enjoy it, but after the first bite, my appetite returns with a vengeance. I eat everything on my plate and go back for seconds that I definitely do not need and probably don't have room for in my stomach. But I eat those, too.

Finn still isn't here. Maybe that means he isn't coming after all. Maybe his parents wanted to do something else, or maybe he just wants to stay home and write another best seller.

I check my phone again, just in case, but there are no messages from him.

Ella abandons us without a word, hurrying towards the other side of the room. I catch a glimpse of her flinging her arms around a man with red hair.

"Why does Sam show up everywhere like he's some weird latent shadow? Why can't they just go places together like a normal couple?" Courtney rolls her eyes.

I don't have an answer for her.

The gray haired lady sitting two seats down from me leans towards us, asking if we know when the silent auction will begin. Aunt Mairi tries to explain that it's already begun, but the woman can't hear over the clamor of conversations. I cringe a little as Auntie raises her voice and repeats the explanation. Pure chaos.

Courtney elbows me in the side. "He's here," she says, nodding towards the silent auction table. I turn and there he is, indeed. Right next to his parents.

Maybe he senses my stare because he turns and looks in our direction. I whip my gaze back to Courtney.

"I can't talk to him with them there," I say, panicked.

"So don't. Text him. Ask him to meet you in a dark secluded corner. Or better yet, let me talk to him first." The glint in her eyes suggests that

"Absolutely not." I will not take the coward's way out. I'm not that desperate. Yet.

I watch them out of the corner of my eye and am relieved when they find a seat on the other side of the room. Relieved...and disappointed. I'm pretty sure he saw me.

Maybe I'm going at this all wrong—I can't possible separate him from his parents, just so that I can tell him I know his little secret.

"You're chickening out, aren't you," Courtney says flatly. "I can see it on your face."

"I guess I'm okay if this is all that ever happens between us," I insist. "It was nice, it was great, and now it's going to fade into memory."

"Just stop. You're making this way weirder than it has to be. The only thing that happens if you leave without talking to him is a whole lot of unnecessary angst."

She's right. I know she is. But I am going to need some liquid courage before I can approach him. Courtney, bless her, pours me two consecutive glasses of red wine.

"Go get him, girl."

"This is a bad idea," I say, rubbing my hands together nervously.

"It's the only idea worth acting on. You can do it and you will. Wave if you want backup."

I give her a wan smile and force my legs to take me across the room. He's still with his parents, which means I have to break into the conversation before I lose my nerve. I'm just reaching for Finn's arm, to make him aware of my presence, when his dad's voice registers.

"You're going there again? I thought you just saw her. "

"I swear, Amber takes up more of your life than any normal girlfriend would," his mom says.

I freeze. *Amber*?

"You can always come with me. Then she can take you out on the town instead of guilting me into it," Finn replies in a dry voice.

"We'll all go out to dinner together. It's been far too long since we've done that."

Well, this is strange. I don't know what I've walked in on, but maybe I should just walk myself back out. I don't know who this Amber is, and it is absolutely no business of mine, but—isn't that the real problem? I know so little about Finn and my heart is disproportionately attached to what I do know about him. He said he wasn't dating anyone, but what if this is an ex that he still talks to? That he still *visits*? My mind is buzzing with possible scenarios, but I don't feel comfortable asking for clarification in front of his parents. In fact, I would be relieved if they forgot I existed in the first place.

With that thought in mind, I shuffle back a few steps, fully intending to disappear into the crowd, when Finn's mom catches sight of me. She clears her throat, gives a pointed look, and Finn turns in his seat. A flash of something crosses his face. I'm so nervous I can't tell if he's happy to see me or not.

"Well, hi, stranger," he says.

"Hello, I just thought I'd come say…hello."

His parents' faces are curiously blank, as if they know the evening entertainment is about to begin, but they're not quite sure what it's going to be.

Finn's brows furrow slightly. Do I look as frenzied as I feel? Fuck, I hope not. A man bustles past, clapping Finn on the shoulder as he goes by. Finn gives a quick smile at the man and exchanges a few words. I can't hear what they're saying, but it's the smile that jolts me back to reality. That and the full plate of food in front of him.

I can *not* do this.

We're at a fundraiser-slash-party. He came here with his parents to eat and socialize. And here I am, ready to be the asshole who turns the evening into a confrontation. And for what? To demand that he tell me all of his secrets? *For fuck's sake, Rune.*

"Anyway, just wanted to say hi and nice to see you. Hope you enjoy the food, it's really good." I nod at the table and force myself to meet the still somewhat blank stares of his parents with a smile. Finn opens his mouth to say something, but a harried mother darts between us, grappling with an enraged toddler. By the time she captures him, screaming and flailing, I'm waving and out of earshot. There. Totally normal social exchange.

"You chickened out, didn't you?" Courtney pushes my wine glass towards me when I slink back into my seat, red-faced and defeated. I take it and gulp it down. It will have to be my last for the night, unless I want to drive to Chicago hungover tomorrow. Which I don't.

"His parents were staring at me. I—I don't think it's the right time."

"Ella would say that now is the only time you have, since you're leaving tomorrow."

"What would you say, though?" *Please let it be something sensible.*

She smirks and takes a drink of her own wine before answering. "*Courtney* would say that, as fun as all this drama is, you guys literally have each other's phone numbers. You could just text or call him or whatever. Totally not that big of a deal. And if it is a big deal...well, he might be hot and super rich and kind of funny, but is that really the kind of relationship you want? Secrets and stress at every turn?"

"That's far too sensible." I've lost sight of Finn across the room. Damn, I hope he's not coming to find me. I'm in no state to converse like an adult. There are too many thoughts in my head. Thank you, anxiety, for showing up at the worst possible moment and derailing any hope of having a normal, relaxing evening.

"You look like shit. Do you need to go home?" Courtney asks, peering at my face.

"No. Maybe I'll just go hide in the bathroom for a while."

"The bathroom? Really?"

I nod, feeling a little dizzy. "Come get me when we're ready to leave. And, uh, please don't tell Auntie."

"Whatever, weirdo. I'll check on you in five minutes. Text if you need me before that," Courtney says, pulling out her phone. She's used to Ella's unhinged behavior. I don't think my sudden freak out phases her at all.

It takes me a moment to make sure I have everything with me: my purse, my coat. And the—nope, that's not my scarf. I set it back down and give an apologetic smile to the old lady next to me. I'm not sure she even noticed.

I should definitely not have had that third glass of wine. It takes far more focus than it should to exit the room, following the bathroom signs that lead across a wide hallway, the floor wet from melted snow. I catch myself on the first slip, but on the second, my left foot twists and slides out from under me. I flail, trying to regain my balance, knowing that I'm going to land on my ass.

A strong hand catches me by the arm and I find myself with my face pressed up against a white button-up shirt. One that only barely masks the hard, muscled chest beneath. I lift my head and stare at the horrifically beautiful eyes of Finn.

"Careful," he murmurs.

"Thanks." I cast around for something to say. Something light-hearted to pretend like I'm feeling the same feelings that I was this morning, before all my anxious doubts began to accumulate. But when I open my mouth, I blurt out, "Who's Amber?"

He freezes, the slight smile fading as he takes in my expression. "What do you mean?"

"I heard you talking to your parents. I just wondered. And I know your pen name." This fucking wine. I can't seem to stop the words from falling out of my mouth.

"Okay." He clears his throat and darts an uncomfortable glance around. We're the only two people in the hall right now, although the double doors to the main area remain open. The longer the silence stretches, the more uncertain I become. He doesn't appear to know what to say.

Which is maybe the answer that I have been trying to avoid facing: Finn doesn't want to tell me about that part of his life. I blink away the blur in my eyes that accompanies the stinging sense of rejection.

"Anyway. Congratulations on your success," I mumble and try to dart around him, but Finn moves with me, blocking my path.

"Rune, what's wrong?"

"Nothing."

"Something is bothering you. Tell me what it is, please." There's a hint of something like desperation in his voice.

I draw in a breath, steadying myself as I stare past his shoulder. It's easier than looking into his eyes. I can't think straight when I look in his eyes. "I happened to find out this afternoon that you are R.E. Andersson."

"Is that bad?" he asks warily.

"I don't know, is it?" I throw my arms up in frustration. What a strange question. "Why didn't you tell me? There were several opportunities. The topic certainly came up more than once."

"I didn't—" he takes a breath, then, "—we haven't had time to talk about a lot of things."

"No, we just went straight to fucking."

He flinches.

"I'm sorry," I blurt out immediately. That was a really shitty way to voice my frustration.

"It's fine," he says tightly.

"Clearly it isn't."

He looks away, a muscle ticking in his jaw. I wait, desperate and a little angry at the same time.

"Why didn't you tell me?" I whisper. I want him to say something to fix this emptiness deep in me, but he just shakes his head and I deflate. I don't need him to tell me everything. I just want to know why he won't. The words I need to tell him this refuse to move past my lips. I don't think I can do this. I don't know if I *want* to do this anymore.

"Was it funny, Finn?" I ask quietly, my voice cracking. "Did it make you laugh when you realized I had no idea who you were? When I went on and on about your books, absolutely oblivious?"

"God, Rune, it isn't like that." His eyes flash. "I was intrigued.

I wanted to spend time with you and I—I just wanted to tell you at the right time."

"Which was going to be when?"

"I don't know—tonight? Tomorrow? I didn't want it to affect us."

"Except that it has."

His hand tightens around me. "You have to understand that when I meet people these days, it isn't really me that they're seeing. People don't give a shit about anything besides how I play into their little fantasies about novels that I fucking wrote. So yeah, when you showed up and treated me like a human being and didn't ask me to autograph your books, it was a nice change. Because then I knew it would be Finn you thought of when you were kissing instead of some fantasized version of me."

"Well that would have been impossible, because I'm straight and my fantasized version of you was a girl," I retort.

He stares at me.

I glare back.

Despite the heat of the moment, the corner of his mouth twitches. "Because I don't write enough about—" he glances down at my chest. I remember that he kissed me there this morning.

"Amongst other things."

He lets out a long sigh and I allow him to draw me into a gentle hug. A peace offering, maybe.

"I didn't mean for it to be like this," he says. "I'd hoped to have the opportunity to tell you myself, before you found out from someone else. I'm sorry."

I force a smile. "It's fine."

For a long while we just stand there, my cheek resting against his chest; his thumb rubbing gentle circles on my back.

It feels wonderful and painful all at once.

"I'm leaving tomorrow," I say finally.

"I'll see you again." He says it like it's a certainty. But there's no follow up. No promises to stay in touch. No requests to visit. No passionate kisses to convince me that our time together was as real as it was brief. And that, more than anything, is what makes me realize that this getaway fling is well and truly over.

I'm afraid to step away, out of his arms. Because then the spell will be broken and real life will return. But eventually, I do.

Chapter 25

Rune

"You'd better hurry. The forecast said it's going to snow. Don't want to run into that."

"I know, I know." I heft my worn duffel bag into the back seat of my tiny little junk car, next to my suitcase.

"You sure you'll be ok?" Aunt Mairi shivers in her wool coat, hands tucked deep into her pockets. I've already said my goodbyes to a very sleepy Courtney and Ella. It's only six-thirty and still dark as night outside.

I hold up my travel mug of coffee. "I've got this to stay awake and the radio to keep me company."

"Still, if you get stuck—" her worry hangs in the air, deep lines creasing her forehead as her brows knit together. I think she's a little scarred about the ditch incident that occurred on my way here. I'm surprised I'm not.

"I'll be fine. The old bucket will get me back to civilization." I pat the chipped, rusty blue paint of my car.

"This is plenty civilized for me." She waves a hand at the buildings behind us. Her log home—warm yellow light shining through the windows—and an old woodshed filled to the brim with freshly cut birch wood to last through the long winter. I'm really going to miss this place.

Aunt Mairi brushes a chunk of graying hair out of her face as the wind picks up.

I give her a big hug and breathe her in one last time. She smells like woodsmoke and cedar. The smell of winter in northern Minnesota. "Miss you already."

"Don't be a stranger. You're welcome here anytime. I love you, sweetie."

My eyes tear up a little. "I love you, too, Auntie."

And with that, I begin my drive back south. The roads are clear and nothing slows my journey down to the North Shore, through Duluth, and across the whole fucking state of Wisconsin. I stop once for a bathroom break, once to eat lefse at a Norwegian restaurant, but otherwise—I just drive. I was afraid that I would cry, but I don't; a numbness descends, blanketing my exhausted emotions. I feel far more burned out by the emotional rollercoaster of the past week and a half than I think I ever experienced during the entirety of my relationship with Sebastian. And that's including the final, fatal video call.

And this is why we don't act impulsively, my irritated brain lectures me. *It can only end badly.*

A few texts roll in throughout the day. Most are from Ella and one is from Danielle, confirming my ETA. Only one comes in from the person I really want to talk to. And when I read it, I'm disappointed by everything it doesn't say:

Finn the Hero: Safe travels.

Me: Thanks.

. . .

Ugh.

I'm tired and cranky by the time I turn onto my street and find a parking spot within walking distance of my apartment. Even though it's a solid thirty degrees warmer here than in Minnesota, it somehow feels much colder. I hurry through the slush of the unshoveled sidewalks, dragging my suitcase behind me. It's a wet, slippery mess. My feet and legs are soaked by the time I make it to the door of my little, dilapidated apartment. The one I can't afford to pay rent on anymore.

As soon as I step inside, I'm assailed by the smell of pizza and the soft murmur of voices. The lights are on in the kitchen and there's a half-finished wine bottle on the counter. Danielle must have a friend over.

"You're back!" Danielle shrieks from the living room. A second later, her arms wrap around me in a lung-squeezing hug. "I missed you."

"Missed you, too." I look over to see who she's visiting with—and do a double take at the woman standing by the couch, dressed in jeans and a lumberjack style red button up. Her dark chestnut hair is much longer than it was the last time I saw her. On her face is a brilliant, affectionate smile.

"*Jules?*"

"Surpriiiiise. You going to give me a hug or what?" Jules' teasing smile is like sunshine to my sad, frozen little soul. I fling myself towards my sister, tackling her onto the couch. Or I try to, anyway. She's got muscles I never had and lifts me up, twirling me around like I'm a little kid.

"Why are you here? Aren't you supposed to be in like, Sweden or something?"

"I was in Finland, dumbass."

"But—why? How?"

"An airplane, and because I wanted to spend Christmas with my baby sister."

"And how was your trip, Rune?" Danielle butts in. "Do we get the full story? Can I get you some wine? Food? Cozy slippers?"

"Wine and cozy slippers," I decide. There's a lot to tell. I only sent a few texts throughout the past week and a half, mostly photos of snow and comments about the frigid temperatures. Nothing about anything that really mattered. At first, because it seemed premature, and then—well, it's just easier to spill the tea in person.

Five minutes later, we're curled up on the lumpy L-shaped couch, cuddled under an array of blankets, since the heat doesn't seem to be working as intended.

Then, with one glass of wine down and several to go, I begin to tell the story of my Minnesota vacation. I don't spare a single sordid detail: I might adore my cousins and aunt, but Danielle and Jules are my people. I hold nothing back. When I reach the part where I confronted him, where we had our last conversation, the ongoing commentary from Danielle and Jules falls silent. They just sort of...look at me.

"So that's it?" Danielle says, brows furrowed.

"He texted me '*Safe travels*' today, and I said '*Thanks*' and it's been radio silence since then."

Jules is staring at me like I'm an alien. "Can you repeat the part again where he swept you off your feet, invited you into his mansion, showed you what a real fuck is like, and then you get all pissy because he's also your favorite author of all time?"

I groan. "Don't say it like that. It was the timing: first his parents, and then the secret identity, and then I got all up in my head. I wasn't pissy." I don't *think* I was, anyway. I was just...

confused. Worried. Helpless. So many pathetic words piled up to describe my emotions at the moment.

"That's never a good place to be." Danielle gives a sympathetic smile. She's an over-thinker, just like me.

Jules purses her lips. "You've self-sabotaged. Hardcore. And now let me guess: you've decided it's best to just let things die."

I hate that she knows me so well. "It's one thing to be in the middle of a winter romance, feeling all the feels. It's another to be back home, looking around at the dingy apartment walls that scream *this is my reality*. I just need to get used to it."

"Oh, please," snorts Jules. "It's like you're being intentionally illogical."

"Can't you be on my side? Say nice things and make me feel better?"

"Would it work?"

No, it would not. "I have less than five hundred dollars in my bank account. What am I supposed to do, beg him to take me back and start a relationship when I could very well end up in Florida with Mom and Dad by February?"

"You're so dramatic, and I'm almost positive you're not counting the money I sent over." Jules rolls her eyes. "Just move in with me if you can't afford rent."

"She can stay with me! I'm not kicking you out because you don't have a job," Danielle argues.

"Anyway," Jules continues, "the relationship is obviously already there. What you're doing is sabotaging it. I hope you realize that the reason you ran away to Minnesota in the first place was to avoid confronting the fact that you lost both your job and your boyfriend. Sounds like when things got confusing up there, you ran away again. You can't keep running from your own life. At some point, you'll have to actually *live* it."

I hate what she's saying. I hate that it feels true. "I was living it! But I don't want to start a relationship where there's secrets."

Jules leans on her elbows. "Finn isn't Sebastian, Rune. Judge him all you want for his own mistakes, but you can't base your treatment of him off the trauma in your past. Not every secret is a harmful one. It sounds like he intended to tell you."

Well, now I feel like shit.

"Anyway, whatever," she continues. "You screwed up and he probably should have apologized in a more epic way. All water under a bridge, as they say."

"Thinking positive. I like that," I say wryly.

"Since we can't go back in time, what say we take a few days to forget about stupid romance, which is clearly overrated, and focus our attention instead on making this a cozy little Christmas?"

"I'm all for that," Danielle toasts emphatically. Hypocritically, too, since she has a boyfriend.

"Cool, so let's finish this bottle of wine and start on the next." Jules wraps her arm around me. "Little Rune can drown her boy problems in a nice cheap bottle of blackberry wine."

"Yeah, give her something more to regret," Danielle giggles.

I smile despite myself.

Having my sister here is comforting in a way I didn't realize I needed. Growing up, it was always Jules and I *contra mundum*. We held each other's secrets and relied on each other exclusively through every phase of growing up with emotionally distant parents. Even our personalities balanced perfectly: despite the fact that I'm two years younger, I was the motherly one and she the adventurer. Where I'm shy and indecisive, Jules is confident and quick to take action. I hope she rubs off on me while she's here.

In fact—there are a lot of things I will shamelessly lean on her for during the two weeks she plans on staying with us. Starting with my living situation.

"Do you still want to move in with Brian?" I ask Danielle the next morning, when the three of us are eating a breakfast of fried eggs and English muffins together. She decided to take the whole week off work to use up a sick amount of PTO.

"Yeah," she admits. "But it's not like, super urgent or anything. We have time to figure things out."

"And by *things* you mean me?" I clarify. Before she can protest, I continue, "Does his offer of a room in the basement still stand? If so…I think we should definitely move before this apartment lease renews."

I kind of expect her to jump at the idea. Instead, Danielle looks torn. "Is this because it's what you want to do? Or is it like one of those sad *I can't be with my love so you might as well be with yours* things?"

Jules snorts into her coffee.

"I don't think that's a thing," I say. "Anyway, it's not like this apartment is a winner. It's been good, but maybe holding onto it is also holding us back from something else."

"Maybe," Danielle says carefully, "but is Brian's house really the *something else* that you want?"

"If I hate it, I'll just find another place to live," I point out. "Do you think Brian will give me a little friends and family discount?"

"He definitely will." From the look on Danielle's face, I wouldn't be surprised if she sets that as one of her own stipulations for moving in with him. She's a good friend like that. And Brian's a good enough guy who will hopefully just go along with it.

"Ok, well—" I glance at Jules, who nods. "Want to start moving this week?"

"Wait, are you for real?"

"The renewal is on the fifteenth, which means we have three

weeks to vacate our place. Since there are three of us here, I figure we can just tackle the worst of it right away.

"Okay, but is that really how Jules wants to spend her vacation?"

"Please, it's far better than sitting here and listening to Rune's sad stories. Stop glaring at me, you know it's true," Jules adds to me.

I give her a rude gesture with my hand.

"I'll give Brian a call," Danielle says, brightening considerably. "See if he's up for that."

As it turns out, Brian is, indeed, up for our idea. He even pledges to take a couple afternoons off work to help us transport some of our stuff.

Which is definitely good news, since Danielle and I both have collected far more than we realized in the years we've lived here. Every now and again, I hear her swearing in her bedroom as she tries to cram her life into a sensible number of cardboard boxes.

Normally I'd offer to help her, but—after a few days, things really aren't going any better with my own belongings. There's an entire box with just knick-knacks in them.

"I should donate these," I muse. A lot of them are souvenirs that Sebastian picked up for me on his journeys. I don't need them in my life, even if they are really pretty.

"So do it," says Jules. "Things weigh you down. It's time to start a new life."

Sometimes I really do hate how much sense she makes.

In the end, I donate three large boxes, the contents ranging from the stupid knick-knacks to old clothes that I was saving for...I don't even know. Nostalgia, I guess.

Jules volunteers to do the driving to and from the donation center. I suspect she's just tired of being cooped up in our musty little apartment, because she takes a suspicious amount of time—and comes back with coffee.

"Are you going to give away your smut books?" Jules laughs, reaching into my pile of books for a paperback with a shirtless man and neon letters on the front.

"Absolutely not. It's probably the most action I'll get for the rest of my life."

She rolls her eyes. "Speaking of...are you going to invite your boyfriend down for the big housewarming party next week?"

I wince. Brian is dead set on throwing a big party for us, probably to show off his girlfriend to all his entrepreneur friends. Which is fine and all, but I don't think that a party with strangers is the right place to meet up with Finn again...if he wants to meet up, that is.

"I'm not sure."

"Why not?" she demands. "Have you officially ended your thing?"

I narrow my eyes. Jules looks far too innocent for a question that she already knows the answer to. Have I texted him? Yes. And he texts back. But the spark just isn't the same over text. Sexy winks and comments have been few and far between. I've been having a hard time figuring out whether he's sending me messages to be polite or because he actually *wants* to.

Regardless, I'm far too self-conscious about my living situation to invite him down for a housewarming party with a bunch of strangers.

"We never officially started it," I say finally. "Anyway, it's Christmas tomorrow. Can we just not talk about him?"

"Yes, let's get into the Christmas spirit," Danielle agrees from the doorway. "We can sing carols to each other in front of the fake Christmas tree."

I snort a laugh at the mental image that evokes. She brought one of those two-foot-tall fake trees home from a nearby thrift store. We intend to re-thrift it the moment we move out of the apartment.

"To kick things off, I have an early Christmas present for you." Jules produces a small thin box wrapped in newspaper, with an extravagant ribbon taped to the top.

"My Christmas present to you is free housing for as long as you're here," I joke, unwrapping the package to reveal a thick black satin paper sealed with a gold stamped wax seal and a spray of tiny etched leaves. It looks fancy. It looks expensive. When I open the envelope and realize what it is, I'm not sure whether to laugh or cry.

Two VIP tickets to the Faelight Fantasy Ball on New Year's Eve, a week from now.

"How did you get these? The ball has been sold out for months—and VIPs are by invite only." I turn them over, awed.

"I have my ways." Jules looks smug.

"Okay, but how—"

"Please, you've been resharing the posts for months on social media. It doesn't take a genius to know that you want to go. So I made it happen."

"That's definitely not how it works," I argue. "How did you get the invites? Who are your connections?"

"Just say thank you, Rune," Danielle says, sounding mildly exasperated.

"Fine. Thanks." I turn them over again, taking in every luxurious detail of the tickets. "I assume this means you're coming with me?"

"Unless you want to invite your man."

"I don't have a man." And also, it's New Year's Eve. I'm sure he already has plans with his family. I'm very scared of rejection if I ask and he turns me down. Better to live with a teensy bit of delusion than hopelessness. That's my new motto.

"In that case, yes. And just wait until you see the dress that I got. It's all kinds of classy and boobylicious."

Chapter 26

Rune

"So you seriously aren't going to invite Finn down for the big housewarming party?"

I wince at the accusation in my sister's voice. I wish she'd stop talking about Finn. It's hard enough pretending that I'm okay with how things are turning out without having to constantly speak the lie out loud.

I force a smile. "I'm going to assume that you forgot about the fact that this is New Year's Eve and that I'm currently getting dressed up for the fantasy book ball of my dreams tonight. Bringing Finn up is just tasteless."

"You are literally dressing up as the main character in his novel," Jules points out.

I stare at my reflection in the full length mirror that we've propped up in the living room. Most cosplays of Macie, the main character from *Crimson and Roses*, tend to focus on the extravagant, revealing dresses that she's described as wearing when she appears at royal court. I decided to take an alternate approach. I created my own interpretation of an outfit that she wears during a midnight rendezvous with her love interest. One of those classic enemies-to-lovers moments.

Granted, in the books, it simply says: *She was dressed all in black, with a cloak of shadows.*

So I took some artistic liberties.

I'm wearing a tight, low-cut sleeveless wrap that falls into a series of tattered ruffles down to my knees. Underneath is a sheer black chiffon skirt that shows off both my legs and my cool leather medieval-style slippers. They aren't terribly sexy, per se, but they're wildly comfortable. For a cloak, I found some shimmery transparent fabric that sometimes looks black and sometimes silver, depending on the lighting.

And, because she's a good big sister, Jules spent a solid forty minutes working on my makeup to give me smokey eyes and sensual red lips.

I look fabulous. I wish I could dress like this every day.

True to her word, Jules is wearing something that borders on classy and downright trashy: a silver dress with sparkles and sequins that reveals all of her back, framing the crescent moon and stars tattoo along her spine that she got to celebrate her high school graduation. Mom and Dad were pissed when they saw that tattoo.

"I don't understand how you get your boobs that high without a bra," Danielle says, impressed.

"It's amazing what can be done with silicone these days." Jules pats her perfectly rounded cleavage with a pleased smile.

Together, we're a matched set. I'm the night sky and she's pure starlight.

"You're going to Brian's tonight?" I confirm with Danielle. I do feel a little bad that she's not coming. She seemed to like the Renaissance Festival that I dragged her to last year.

"Yeah. This place is creepy without our stuff."

She's not wrong. After a solid week of packing and moving our personal items over to Brian's house, the only things left in the apartment are some clothes and the beds. Even the living room furniture and kitchen set sold yesterday.

It's a little sad, but far less sad than I thought it would be. It definitely helps that Brian's place is actually pretty cool. The basement is a walkout, so I even have my own door. It's clean, private, and relatively upscale. A great way to start the next phase of my single, jobless life. Which I've decided I'm very excited for, by the way. I hardly even think about Finn anymore. I definitely don't check my phone every hour or two, agonizing over a text that never comes.

"Does it feel weird? Dressing up like one of his characters?" Danielle asks.

"I've just gone back to pretending that *he* is a *she*," I joke. It's only half a lie. I do try to forget that I'm wildly, sexually attracted to the author. After so many years of thinking of R.E. Andersson as my girl bestie, you'd think it would be easy. The reality is that I can't stand to look at my autographed book anymore. The one he touched. The one I spent over a hundred dollars on. I packed it away in a box along with the other paperbacks from his series. I'm sure I'll eventually put them out on my bookshelves. Or maybe not. I'll figure it out. After I figure out if *we* are going anywhere, that is. These past couple weeks back in Chicago have felt like some of the longest of my life.

But how do you have *that* conversation when you're too embarrassed to ask them to visit? When you have too much pride to beg them to invite you back? When neither of you have brought up the kind of important fact that he's an internationally bestselling author?

What you do for work doesn't define who you are, but...it's still unnerving that I was so obviously oblivious to it and he let me make a complete fool of myself, showing him my drawings and telling him my dumbass theories. I try not to think about it too much, I could die from embarrassment.

"Come *on*, Rune, our ride is outside," Jules urges, half-dragging me down the stairs as I scramble to double check that I have my wallet and phone.

"Have fun. Don't do anything I wouldn't." Danielle laughs at our departing backs, offering her middle finger as a farewell. We return it with gusto.

"I really like that girl," Jules says.

"I know, right? I think we—what the fuck, Jules." I stare in complete shock at the vehicle parked in front of our building. I expected a taxi of some sort. Instead, there's a shiny black limo, with a woman in a suit who opens the door for us to get in.

"Surpriiiiiiiiise." Jules gives me jazz hands. "We're riding in style. VIP *all* the way."

"I've never ridden in a limo before." My mouth might be stuck open permanently. I try to take in every detail of this moment as I whip out my phone and start snapping pictures of the sleek lines of its exterior. Inside, there are two black silk bags in a basket, with the Faelight Fantasy Ball logo stamped on them in gold ink and filled with woven leather wristbands, a granola bar, some chocolates, and two drink tickets.

Not to mention the champagne and charcuterie which comes courtesy of the limo, apparently.

"How much did this cost?" I demand in a whisper, not caring if it's tacky to ask.

"Not as much as you would think." Jules looks as excited as I feel. "Just freaking enjoy it."

It isn't hard to do what she asks. I feel like royalty.

"I bet you regret not asking your boyfriend now," Jules says, pouring herself some champagne.

"Hell no," I say, which is a very obvious lie. I very much regret the fact that I wasn't ballsy enough to ask Finn to be my date. I'd like a chance to impress him with something classy like a limo and champagne. But I bury that thought deep within me. Tonight I will have no regrets.

None.

❄

I've never been in an actual ballroom before. This particular one is all Grecian pillars, marble stairs, and dark blue tapestries. It's breathtaking. The room has tall molded ceilings and extravagant chandeliers that reflect in the shiny white marble floor. The floor is already flooded with partygoers dressed in every kind of outfit I could possibly imagine. Even the members of the stringed quartet, perched on a smallish platform, are dressed in black sequined outfits with golden masks.

There's an energy, an excitement to the room: grown adults indulging in dressing up as fae, vampyr, elves, and yes, I do spy a few hobbits.

"This is incredible," Jules says, her eyes wide. "Rune, we need to make this a tradition."

I nod my agreement, my senses fully overwhelmed by the colors, the rich extravagance of it all.

Still buzzed from the champagne, I wade arm-in-arm with Jules through the groups of people, making small conversation and collecting some bookish souvenirs from the tables tucked in a series of alcoves.

It isn't long before the event formally begins with a cascade of twinkly fairy lights coming to life just as a voice over the loudspeaker introduces the male MC to the ball. He appears, masked, wandering around the ballroom as he acts out the dramatized storyline of a handsome prince who stumbles into faerie and comes upon an elven queen. The queen glides down the grand staircase to meet with him, stars glittering in her silver hair.

Together, they step to the center of the room and lead the way into the first of the night's dances. It's amazing and cliché...and I really fucking love it.

It doesn't take long before more couples join in the dancing, and soon the entire floor is alive with twirling, glittering dresses and laughter.

"That's our cue." Jules drags me onto the floor. My feet get tangled in my skirt and I stumble into a tall red-headed nymph.

"I'm so sorry!" I say, but she just laughs and blows me a kiss.

I last through several dances—old-fashioned reels intermixed with iconic pop covers—before my breath gives out. I need water, followed by something alcoholic, since my buzz has worn off. Jules shouts something as I walk away, but the words are lost amid music and laughter. I assume she wants me to bring her back a drink. Maybe I will.

As I wait in line, the music shifts from loud and pulsating to sweet and gentle. An old-timey waltz. All the dancers are pairing up and I look around to see if Jules is sitting this one out. I finally spy her on the dance floor, twirling away with some dude wearing large black wings. Good for her, I guess.

I turn back to examine the menu of fantasy-inspired drinks:

Vampyric Tonic — *Bloody Mary*
Valinorian Sunset — *Peach schnapps, vodka, orange juice*
Elven Tears — *Blue curaçao, vodka, lemonade*
Woodland Potion — *Gin and tonic*
Wingspan Vision — *Apple whisky sour*

I want to try them all. A woman with shimmery green skin and moss woven into her long black braid takes my order.

With two Woodland Potions in my hand, I turn to find my way back to Jules. She's still in the arms of the dude with wings, looking fairly animated.

Excellent. I guess I'll just stand here and watch her have fun, since it seems dangerous to traipse the dance floor with two drinks in hand. I down one quickly and start sipping on the other. Jules looks so carefree, wholly in the moment with her head flung back as she laughs at something the bat dude says. I wonder how she manages to live so freely, without bending to the anxiety that haunts my every step.

I wonder if I could learn to be more like her, instead of the mess of a human that I am.

A hand brushes against my arm and I instinctively move to the side, making space for whomever it is in the crowded sidelines. They stop next to me, and I glance over to see a black sleeve with rich gold embroidery trailing from elbow to cuff. Fancy.

"When you said you had a cosplay of Macie, I did not envision this," a male voice says in my ear.

I stiffen. Despite the music, the hum of voices, I would recognize that voice anywhere. I lift my eyes past the gold embroidery and look straight into the face of Finn, who's staring back with an enigmatic expression on his face.

He's dressed up—like *actually* dressed up in one of the classiest outfits I've seen yet this evening.

Gold dust lines his cheekbones; his dark hair is somewhat unruly. He looks like a mix between my favorite Holly Black character and a medieval knight. My knees go a bit weak.

"Cheers to the Faelight Fantasy Ball," he says, holding out his own drink and tapping it against mine.

"What are you doing here?" I stammer when words finally find me. "Are you—?" I don't know how to finish that. *Mad at me? Here with another woman? Ready to tell me all of your secrets?*

"I'm participating." He gestures to his outfit with a funny expression on his face, like he doesn't quite know how he manages to pull off looking absolutely dashing in literally anything.

"Oh," I say. Jules is still out dancing, perfectly oblivious to the panic that's starting to take over. It never once occurred to me that Finn, of all people, would be in attendance at this ball. Even if he's written at least a third of the characters that attendees are cosplaying tonight.

"Did you have a nice drive?" I ask lamely, when I can think of nothing else to say.

"I flew."

I nod. Of course he did. Why drive when you have the money to fly? He probably flew first class and everything. I glance up at his face, and am confused by what I see. He looks grave and far too serious. He obviously didn't expect to see me. Maybe he regrets that I'm here. I'll just excuse myself, and—

"Rune, can we talk?" he asks, with a gesture towards the large doors at the entrance to the ballroom.

"Of course." I try to ignore the shiver that tingles up my spine when his hand settles on the small of my back. He guides me through the throng of revelers, out into the comparative quiet of the hall beyond. We stop near a giant potted fern that may or may not be artificial. I don't know if I'm happy or nervous or terrified, but my hand shakes as I tip my glass again, swallowing the last half of Woodland Potion in one go. Finn notices and his jaw tightens just a bit.

"So, this is a pleasant surprise. I didn't realize you'd be here," I say brightly.

"I hadn't initially planned on it, but there was someone I wanted to see." He stares intently at his drink, giving the glass a little swirl. If I didn't know better, I'd say he looked nervous. My mind sifts frantically through every conversation, but I come up blank.

"Oh yes? Who?" I ask automatically.

A flash of surprise mingled with disbelief flickers across his face. "You, Rune."

I take another drink. This doesn't add up. "I didn't even know I would be here until last week."

"Let's call it a lucky guess."

Obviously it was more than that, but fine. Another secret.

"Why?" The word comes out barely audible.

He reaches for me, then seems to think better of it and lets his hand fall. "I made a mistake. I shouldn't have let you leave the way you did. Not without doing a better job of explaining myself. But I thought maybe you wanted space. Maybe you needed it. I was a little blindsided. I wasn't exactly thinking straight." He offers a small, apologetic smile.

"So you're here to—?" I'm not quite sure how to finish that.

"I'm here to grovel at your feet. To beg your forgiveness. And yes, to explain, if you'd still like to hear what I have to say."

I might not know where we stand, but I do know that his uncertainty is like a knife to my heart. So despite the fact that I am desperate to hear his explanation, I can admit that he doesn't owe it to me—certainly not in such a public place when we're at risk of being overheard by revelers.

"I shouldn't have made such a big deal about it," I say hurriedly. "You don't have to tell me. I really don't need to know."

Conflict battles across his features at my words. He clears his throat. "I'm sorry, I thought—well, it doesn't matter. You look like a vision, Rune. It's nice to see you again. I'll let you get back to your night with your sister."

I watch as he takes my hand and presses it to his lips in a gentle kiss. But it's the sadness, the hurt, in every line of his face when he begins to turn away that cuts me to the core.

Chapter 27

Rune

The moment he breaks eye contact, I know that I've said everything wrong.

"Finn, wait," I beg, my fingers tightening around his.

He stares at our hands, then back at me.

"Yes?" he says.

"I didn't mean it that way. I'm not trying to push you away, I was just trying to be polite. I do want to know what you have to say. I want to hear everything—anything—that you want to tell me." I'm vaguely aware that I'm babbling, that Finn's hand is trapped in mine, but I can't seem to tear my eyes away from his. Especially when he has that look on his face.

"You do, huh?"

"I do. I know things got a little weird, and I swear I'm trying to be okay with the fact that what we had was great and fun, but—"

"Is that what we had? Fun?" Those blue eyes blaze at me.

I hesitate, unsure if I'm willing to admit the truth aloud. To put myself out there in a way that makes me fully, wholly at his mercy. From where I stand, my time with Finn was eons beyond mere fun; it was magical, soul-healing, unforgettable. I left a piece of my heart with Finn. It's the only explanation for why, despite my confusion and angst, I feel whole right now.

"I don't know what you want," he continues. "Or need. But I'm going to put my cards on the table and admit that I've fallen for you so hard and fast that it truly defies all logic. I haven't stopped thinking about you once since the night you came into my life. I've been out of my fucking mind since you left, trying to give you the space you need. Trying to convince myself that it would be stupid of me to chase you down, to beg you to give me a chance—give us a chance."

I don't know what I'm hearing. I might be hallucinating. "You want me to give us a chance?" I confirm, incredulous.

He swallows and nods.

"Are you saying this because you feel bad?" That seems like a Finn thing to do: over-the-top kindness. "Please tell me the truth, even if it's going to hurt me."

He gives a soft huff of laughter. "I'm saying this because I'm fucking obsessed with you. I want to know everything about you. I want to go back in time and tell you all the stupid little things about me. Everything we haven't had time for yet. Including the—er, *thing*—that led to our misunderstanding."

He glances around at the people milling around. I nod, encouraging, as he continues, "You don't have to give me an answer tonight or even ever. Just know that I came here to beg you for a second chance."

My breath shudders as the words hit me. I thought I was well on my way to losing him. I thought he was never mine in the first place.

"I've spent most of my adult life wanting to be left alone to pursue the fleeting inspiration of my own imaginings," he continues, oblivious to the tears forming in my eyes, "but everything shifted from the moment I first set eyes on you. I'm asking if you would be able to forgive me for skipping over the more important parts of a relationship and allow me to try again—the right way, this time. Secrets and all."

A tear escapes and I quickly dash it away. Finn catches my hand and presses another gentle kiss on the back of it. I really like what he's saying. I also can't believe that he's saying it to *me*.

"Are you asking me out?" I clarify.

The hand holding mine trembles slightly. "Yes, Rune. I am."

Well...shit. "Okay, then."

A slow smile spreads across his face. "Okay? As in, you accept?"

Now I'm smiling. Even though I have no doubt as to what my answer is, I take my time to look at Finn—really look at him. Despite the tension in his strong hands, his face is clear, hopeful. For some inexplicable reason, Finn didn't just come here to apologize. He wants me, maybe even as much as I want him. It doesn't change the fact that I'm terrified of what might happen if we wade into this deeper together, but I am persuaded by the vulnerability shining in his eyes. If he can put his heart on the line, I suppose I can find the courage to do it, too.

"Yes, Finn. My answer is yes."

I melt a little inside from the way his features light up at my response. The way he drags me up against his body, our lips meeting in a heady, intoxicating kiss. I catch his bottom lip between my teeth as his tongue sweeps into my mouth. Searching, demanding.

I throw my arms around his neck. I cannot get close enough to him to chase away the fear, the dread, the sadness that have been clinging to me the past couple of weeks.

Too bad we're standing in a very public place, surrounded by complete strangers. When we both pull back, there's a telltale sheen in those blue eyes.

"Did you really come here just for this? For me?" I say in awe.

"I really did," he confirms, pressing a kiss to my forehead. "I have a lot to tell you. Stuff we didn't get a chance to talk about yet." He takes a deep breath, as if ready to tell it all now. I shake my head quickly.

"Not here," I say. Not where there are so many people who could overhear. "Later."

He nods, his gaze raking my body. "Have I told you yet that you look incredible?"

I give an embarrassed laugh and grip his hand tighter. "My interpretation."

"Better than I could have imagined."

"How did you know I'd be here?" I ask.

"There may have been some mild subterfuge involved," Finn says offhandedly, like it's no big deal, but...it kind of is. Because Finn is here at the Faelight Fantasy Ball, far-outshining any other man in attendance. I'm not the only one who thinks that, if the interested glances from the other women are anything to go by.

"Like...?" I wait expectantly.

Biting back a smile he leans in to whisper in my ear. "Where do you think your sister got the tickets?"

My eyes widen as everything suddenly clicks into place. The Faelight Fantasy Ball has been sold out since early October. VIP tickets were by invite-only this year. I turn and find Jules standing at the entrance to the ballroom, a wide smile on her face with a glass of something lifted in a toast. The wing dude is ghosting around behind her. She's clearly got him charmed. I'm going to have to ask her about him. Later.

"You two know each other?" I ask.

"We've met. Somewhat recently."

"Did you—how—?" Words fail me.

"I know the organizers behind this event. They gifted me a pair of VIPs earlier this fall. I brought them to the fundraiser that night, planning to ask you if you wanted to go with me, but our conversation went a little differently than I hoped."

That's putting it mildly. Now I really do feel like a big jerk.

"Your sister could probably tell you far more nuanced details of what all went down. Long story short, I asked my contacts if they had one more. They did, fortunately. I met up with your sister on Wednesday to deliver them. And now we're here."

"Now we're here," I repeat, amazed. I reach out and touch the brocade accent at his collar. "So now what?"

The muscles of his neck contract as he swallows. His hands run lightly down my sides, coming to rest on my hips. "I thought maybe we could dance."

"Okay," I say.

I've never danced with Finn before. It shouldn't surprise me that he's really good at it. Or that it only takes half a song before every bit of reserve I'd amassed over the past two weeks has melted completely. It's difficult to stay mad with someone who looks at me like I'm the only woman in the room. Which I'm not.

Once we start dancing, I'm surprised at how many people actually recognize Finn. He's beset by admirers, swarmed by them, actually, all of them asking for autographs and selfies with him. He takes it all in stride, laughing easily and chatting with them. It doesn't take a skilled analyst to see that he has them all fully charmed. Who wouldn't be?

"Look how famous you are," I comment when we're dancing together again. "Who knew?"

He smirks down at me. "Imagine my surprise when one of my biggest fans thought I was a woman."

I can't help blushing. From now on, I'm going to research the fuck out of every author I read. No more surprises. "I'm sorry," I say.

"It's really fine," he replies.

"But seriously, it was out of line. I know I shouldn't have assumed—"

"Rune," he interrupts me gently. "I'm not at all offended. It's actually kind of an honor. I would hope that my writing transcends gender stereotypes."

I look at him gratefully. He twirls me once, before pulling me in for another kiss.

Even with over-excited and somewhat tipsy fans approaching us repeatedly, it feels like the night ends far too quickly in a blur of dancing, drinking, and sparkling lights. I ask Jules repeatedly who her winged partner is, but she only shrugs and said he calls himself Cass. A glaringly obvious fake name, considering his attire. Apparently it doesn't bother her and she leaves without exchanging numbers.

Once again, the limo is waiting for us. This time, Finn comes with.

Chapter 28

Finn

I am the luckiest fucking man alive right now. I don't know what I've done to deserve this. Pen a few novels? Let a half-frozen stranger stay the night? I'd do so, so much more for the beautiful woman who's currently nestled in my arms, looking up at me as if I'm the sun, the moon, and the stars. I don't deserve her—I certainly don't deserve the quick and wholehearted forgiveness that she's bestowed on me.

"I feel like this is too easy," she murmurs, making me laugh. We're laying on her bed at her apartment, which is as charming as it is sparsely decorated. There's only one bathroom, which Jules claimed as soon as we arrived. She's in there now, showering off the sweat and grime that comes standard with a night of dancing.

"Do I need to prove myself? I feel like I could go on a quest in this outfit." I flick my fingers at the hem of my tunic. It's actually pretty awesome.

Rune chokes on a laugh and traces the fancy pattern along my sleeve. "No, but I might need to. The cynical part of me is waiting for the other shoe to drop. Like maybe I haven't suffered enough to deserve having you here, holding me."

There's no sadness, no bitterness in her tone, but the words send a pang through my heart. It doesn't take a genius to see that Rune deserves the fucking world. The fact that she's overwhelmed by my mere presence—when there's literally nowhere I'd rather be than at her side—makes me feel uncomfortable. I've been such an asshole to her, without even meaning it.

"I don't know why I let you leave in the first place," I tell her. "I convinced myself that the best thing was to give you space. That maybe you didn't want me around after I hadn't been entirely forthright with you."

Her eyes widen. "Impossible."

I lean down and kiss her gently on those sensual red lips. I'll have to ask her to wear that color more often. It does things to me. "I owe you an explanation."

She stiffens just a little. "You don't have to," she says, which is ridiculous.

"Of course I do. I left you with the impression that I didn't want to share certain things with you. It really couldn't be farther from the truth. Maybe I should have told you the moment I met you. Or at the very least, the moment I found out that you knew about my books. But I got sidetracked. It wasn't an exaggeration when I told you I couldn't stop thinking about you. I felt like I had to make up for lost time getting to know you. It felt ridiculous to spend time discussing my writing when what I really wanted was for you to know *me* and who I am beneath that." I let out a self-deprecating laugh. When I say the words out loud, they sound so pathetic. Like the worst cliché in a Hallmark movie.

Rune's just looking at me, and I don't know what she's thinking right now. I force myself to continue, "I swear I was going to tell you. In fact, I had a gift for you in my truck that night of the fundraiser. I was going to give it to you that night, before you came back to Chicago. It would have explained everything. But I sort of lost courage. I thought—I thought I'd already screwed it up and you didn't want anything more from me."

"I feel like a bitch," Rune moans, covering her face with her hands.

"You aren't—and weren't," I assure her, drawing her hands away. That's the last word I would ever use for Rune. "You just looked so confused, so sad. It shattered my heart and I didn't know what to do to fix it."

Her fingers close around mine and I swear I do not deserve this woman. The way she looks at me adoringly while I'm confessing how big of an idiot I was.

"So the thing you were going to give me?" she prompts. "How would it have explained everything?"

I open my mouth to tell her, but am interrupted by the emergence of Jules, fresh out of the shower, dressed only in a bathrobe, holding a paper bag.

"Jules, put some clothes on. Stop trying to steal Finn," Rune snaps, earning a laugh out of me. As if.

"Not even interested," Jules says. "No offense."

"None taken," I reply.

"I just happened to overhear Finn's confession. Figured this would be the right time to deliver this." She plops the paper bag on the bed.

"What—?" Rune looks at it, completely mystified.

"Open it," I prompt. And I watch as she pulls out four leather bound books. The sequels to the *Crimson and Roses* copy she bought earlier. She doesn't say anything as she runs her fingers along the gilding on the covers. Nor does she make a sound as she opens the cover and reads the message I penned the morning that I woke up with her by my side:

To Rune,
I thought you might like a complete set.
Love,
R.E. Andersson
(Finn)

The fact that she's still not saying anything makes me a little nervous.

"It's okay if you don't want them," I tell her.

"Finn, you're so ridiculous," she says finally, a catch in her voice. When she lifts her head to look at me, there are tears shining in her eyes. "These are beautiful. This is perfect." She reaches for me, but I put my hand up.

"I, er, have one more thing to show you." Because if I start touching her, I'm fairly sure I won't be able to stop. Not until we're both sweating and fully spent. I pick up the envelope that has half fallen out of one of the books and hand it to her. Jules quietly backs out of the room, closing the door behind her.

Rune's brows furrow as she scans the letter inside. "Finn, what is this?"

"I pitched your work to my lawyer, Amber," I add, and am glad when Rune's face registers recognition at the name. "I've been looking for an illustrator for an exclusive edition of *Crimson and Roses* that I want to publish when the final book is ready. It's up to you, of course. There's the proposed commission amount on the back, along with a five percent royalty on all copies sold. I had my lawyer write up the contract, but you can certainly negotiate terms further. Amber represents quite a few big time authors and publishers and agreed that there will likely be a high demand for your work once it's published. She's already showed some of your illustrations to her friends and there are at least three other authors who are interested in working with you in the future, if you ever wanted to."

I'm barely finished speaking before Rune throws herself at me, tears streaming down her face.

"I can't believe this. I don't deserve this," she whispers, her head tucked against my shoulder. I tighten my arms around her.

"You absolutely do. You have incredible skills and vision. And Rune," I lean back, looking her straight in the eyes. "It would be a fucking honor to have you illustrate the series. But if you don't want to, I won't be offended. It's just an offer I wanted to put out on the table. Turning it down won't change anything between us. All I want is you, if you'll have me."

She shakes her head, smiling through her teary eyes. And then her lips are on mine, her hands on me, tugging at my tunic. I pull it off in one smooth movement, letting it fall to the floor next to Rune's leggings.

It feels a little like role-play, helping her undress from the outfit of one of my book characters. I really like it. We'll have to do this more often. Which is the last coherent thought I'm aware of as she stands there, fully naked. For a moment, all I can do is admire her. She's pure and utter perfection; her face coloring a little at the intensity of my gaze.

"So, are you just going to look at me all night, or—"

I don't let her finish, dragging her into bed with my mouth on hers, indulging in the magic that is her body. We explore each other long into the night until finally, breathless and somewhat satiated, we fall asleep, my arms wrapped around her.

❄

"Wake up, bitches, it's the New Year," Jules sings, bursting into the bedroom. I drag the sheet up to hide my naked body.

"Nice, I finally understand what she sees in you," she snickers at my abs.

I'd been nervous as hell to meet up with Jules a few days ago. After I'd fucked things up with Rune, I expected pure hostility to greet me when I walked into the predetermined coffee shop. That was until Jules came sailing in, a mix of their cousin Ella's boldness, Courtney's sharp observational skills, and Rune's absolute charm and beauty. We hit it off immensely. I'm glad to know that Rune has a sister like Jules to take care of her—even if I secretly intend to take over the majority of that role from here on out.

"Get the hell out of here, Jules," Rune murmurs, half-asleep.

"Only if you promise to get up. I've made breakfast and we have things to do."

"Like what?" Rune sits up, clutching the blanket to her chest.

"You'll see. No raunchy things this morning, please. The walls are paper thin and I do not want to hear it."

I laugh at the frustrated look on Rune's face and slip my hand between her legs. A good morning caress. "I'll make it up to you later. Promise."

"Stop it and come out here," Jules calls from the kitchen.

I force myself to stare at the wall as we get dressed to avoid temptation. Since all I have is my costume, I'm thankful when Rune is able to scrounge up a pair of her roommate's boyfriends' sweatpants and t-shirt. Even if they're slightly roomy for me.

"I can pick up my own clothes this morning," I tell Rune when she tries to apologize.

"From where? Where is your car?"

I lean in and kiss her. "Secrets."

She gives me a suspicious look. Thankfully, not the kind she was giving me last night when I showed up at the ball. This one is a tad bit friendlier. After our breakfast of scrambled eggs, Jules excuses herself, insisting that she has a few errands to run. The obvious wink she gives us as she departs makes Rune's eyes narrow.

"Ok tell me what's up," she demands, turning on me.

"Even better: I'll show you. But first, let's go get some coffee."

I let her show me around the neighborhood in her ancient car. There's a clunking sound in the engine that makes me fucking nervous. Rune insists that it's just the car's way of trying to communicate with us.

"Is it communicating that you should stop driving it?" I ask wryly.

She just rolls her eyes. "Tell me where to go to get your stuff. You're wearing Brian's morning-after-sex clothes and it's a little weird."

I direct her to the neighborhood of my Chicago house. While I obviously prefer the log home I built up in Minnesota, both for its aesthetic and location, I do take a bit of pride in the place I bought for myself here. It's in a quaint but classy neighborhood, with cute shops and a spectacular bookstore that I fell in love with. The moment I saw this particular house for sale, I snatched it up. It has a charming style, like a New England cottage, and painted a sort of blueish gray with white accents. It was a little bit of a financial stretch at the time, but I was tired of living in hotels. I wanted a place I could stay during my work trips and when I needed a change of scenery and pace.

Rune goes quiet as I direct her to turn into my driveway, my card opening up the gate so we can continue to the house itself.

"Why are we here?" she asks in a strange voice. The smile dies on my face.

"This is my house," I tell her. "My second home."

To my utter surprise, she bursts into tears.

Chapter 29

Rune

Finn owns my dream house.

He fucking *owns* it.

"You have a house here. In Chicago," I say flatly.

"Ye-es," he says slowly.

"You didn't mention it before."

"Was that important?" He's looking at me nervously, uncertain how to read my mood. I don't know how to read my mood. This is pure insanity.

"Not really. Except I've walked past this house a thousand times and dreamed of living here someday when I was rich and successful." I laugh at the absurdity of that statement. "This was the first place I came when I found out my ex was cheating on me. The second was *Rowanberry Nook*, the bookstore around the corner where I found your book. The owner said you'd dropped it off earlier that day."

His face has gone slack. "I walked to the bookstore that day."

"We could have passed each other on the street."

We share a look of awe. Then he smiles, big. "I'm claiming this as a fucking sign. Come on in, let me show you around your dream house."

It shouldn't come as a surprise that the inside of the house is as beautiful as the outside. But it truly is. Every so often, I tear up a bit and Finn holds my hand a little tighter. Neither of us can stop smiling. Neither of us can stop touching the other. Which means that it isn't long before he gives me a tour of his bedroom and we make very appropriate use of the beautifully soft bed.

"You hungry?" Finn asks when we've finished, his finger trailing down my arm.

"Probably," I reply, stretching contentedly. Finn's beds are amazing. I wonder where he gets them from. "I don't want to leave this bed. I wonder how long it would take you to get sick of me if I just stayed here forever."

His eyes take me in. "Honestly, I'd probably be ok with it."

"I wish I knew where Jules went off to. She's not answering my texts."

"Hm," is all Finn says. But it's the way he says it that has me suddenly suspicious.

"Do you know where she is?"

A clanging sound echoes from downstairs.

"Oh look, the doorbell. Why don't we go see who's here?" Finn doesn't bother trying to hide his grin as he gestures for me to lead the way.

I fling open the door, expecting either a food delivery or my sister. And yes, Jules is standing there—along with a small group of very familiar people.

"Happy New Year," Danielle waves wildly with one hand, the other holding tight to Brian's arm. Aunt Mairi, Ella, and Courtney are just behind, carrying an assortment of shopping bags.

"What—how?" I step aside to let everyone in, returning hugs as they're handed out.

Finn efficiently directs the bags towards the kitchen and soon has everyone settled into the living room with drinks and cozy ambient music playing in the background. Multi-colored holiday lights line the ceiling; in the windows are white Scandinavian-style candelabras.

"How did you get here?" I ask to no one in particular, while Jules animatedly recaps the highlights of last night's ball.

"He flew us down," says Ella. No need to ask who *he* is. "He must really like you."

"I guess," I say. I catch Finn's glance and offer a little smile. I hope he understands. I hope he knows how much this means. He merely winks.

"It's also a little bit over the top, if we're being totally honest," Courtney says, but she looks amused more than anything.

"It is." And I really fucking love it.

As it turns out, Finn wasn't the only mastermind behind this New Year's get-together and the full story quickly unfolds with contributions from nearly everyone.

"I'd already been planning a surprise visit with Danielle's help," Jules begins. "Thankfully, Aunt Mairi promised to make sure Rune returned to Chicago to make my surprise work."

"I was told to make sure you made it home by Christmas morning, even if I had to kick you out of the house to make it happen." Aunt Mairi smiles.

"The one real variable was Finn. Fortunately, he did his part to ensure that you did, in fact, leave when you said," Courtney says, earning a pained smile from Finn. I slip my hand into his and give it a little squeeze, which he returns.

But it was Finn who reached out to Courtney, of all people, for advice. And since she knew about Jules' intended visit, she put him in contact with my sister.

"The rest is history. I got to claim credit for a really awesome

Christmas gift and play the role of matchmaker at the same time." Jules gives Finn a high-five.

I don't think my heart could get any more full.

Not today, not ever.

"Happy?" Jules asks later, curling up next to me in the corner of the massive L-shaped couch. Courtney and Ella are arguing about vacation destinations and Aunt Mairi is deep in conversation with Danielle.

"Yeah," I say, looking around. "I can't believe this."

"And to think just yesterday you were willing to throw it all away." She gives me a knowing look. She's going to hold this over my head for years to come.

"I'm an idiot," I admit.

"You are. Good thing you have a really spectacular big sister who's willing to save your ass, huh?"

"Good thing," I grin at her, even though a twinge of anxiety accompanies her teasing. I really was about to tuck all of my feelings away, all because I was scared of opening myself up. Of being truly, wholly vulnerable. Jules was right—I can admit that now. Just as much as I can admit that I'm wholly, completely undeserving of Finn. While I was mentally preparing to let him go, he was working hard to give us a real chance.

"I'm so lucky," I breathe, stretching out my foot to prod Finn, who's chatting entrepreneurship mumbo jumbo with Brian. He reaches down to wrap a warm hand around my ankle.

"You deserve good things, Rune," says Jules, watching the small interaction. "Seems like he might, too. Cheers to a new year and new love, baby sister. May only good things be on the horizon."

I wiggle my toes again and Finn glances up at me. My breath

catches in my lungs at the look of pure affection on his face. I shift onto my knees and lean towards him.

"I can't believe you did this," I say, laying my head against his shoulder.

One arm wraps around me, holding me close as he presses a kiss against my hair.

"I can't believe you said yes."

Eight Months Later...

Finn

The sun's just rising, casting an array of reflections on the rippling lake water. It's so fucking early, but I've been thinking through a new story. One that's a little different than my usual strain of epic fantasy with kingdoms and torture. Something a little bit sweeter.

My fingers fly across the keyboard, the quiet tapping hardly audible with the songbirds trilling merrily outside.

I'm lost in my world, visions swirling in my mind as I plow my way through the first draft. It's always a race to see how quickly I can capture the clear images that are in my head. I know from past experience that if I wait too long to write them down, they disappear.

Not that I've run into that problem very often since Rune came into my life. Every moment I spend with her seems to only fuel the ideas simmering beneath the surface. So that's kind of a nice side effect.

Eventually, I hear soft rustling sounds from the bedroom across the hall. Rune's awake. I smile to myself and type just a little bit faster. It's been eight months since we "got back together" as

Rune likes to say. I didn't realize I'd been that close to actually losing her. I might be able to write some fucking awesome love stories (per one reviewer), but I definitely have to learn how to make it work in real life.

Footsteps pad across the floor and I turn to greet Rune, catching her by the hand and pulling her into my lap. Her fingers clasp behind my neck as we indulge in a slow morning kiss. A kiss that I don't ever truly want to end.

"Good morning," she murmurs.

"I missed you," I say, which makes her smile. I take her left hand and lift it to admire the ring on her fourth finger. I've been wanting to buy her jewelry and she said she wanted a ring. So I gifted her with this diamond one last week, along with a plea for her to extend her stay with me indefinitely. Even though it wasn't the kind of ring she'd meant, she said yes.

"What are you writing now?" she murmurs, pressing a gentle kiss to my neck.

"A story," I say, closing my laptop.

Her brow lifts, waiting.

"Ours."

Acknowledgments

Where to even begin...there are so many wonderful people in my life without whose support and encouragement I could never have written this book. While it isn't the first book I've written, it is the first to be published...and hopefully, not the last, as I have so many more stories brimming up, desperate to be recorded.

Miia, your excitement and encouragement on that magical walk through a magical Finnish forest made me realize I wanted to take my noveling seriously. I've appreciated every conversation and accountability session that keeps me on track and energized.

Emma, your developmental edits and feedback not only made the book more coherent, but also helped me hone in on the heart of this story.

Danielle, my work-bestie-turned-book-bestie, your editorial commentary has been invaluable...as have the tens (or hundreds) of thousands of texts that we've exchanged over the years on all things books, work, family, and more.

And then, of course, my husband, who inspired this love story in the first place between a girl with a dream and the freakishly good looking bachelor who won her heart.

Bonus Epilogue
Rune

"This might be the worst idea you've ever had." Jules spares a brief, helpless glare, swiping at the cloud of mosquitos.

"Don't I fucking know it," I groan. No amount of bug spray seems to help; the little monsters are ruthless. "Just pick faster."

Jules mutters a curse under her breath that's obviously meant for me to hear, which is probably fair. To be honest, I didn't think it was going to be this bad.

"Maybe you brought the wrong bug spray."

"Maybe." I give a little nod to placate my sister. I know for a fact that I brought the same spray Finn and I have used every time we've gone out adventuring in the forests of northern Minnesota—which has been a lot, by the way, since I moved in with him in February.

As Finn says, there's definitely a reason why they claim the mosquito is Minnesota's state bird.

Granted, it's been a while since we've had an opportunity to go off and do fun things like hike or whatever, thanks to Finn finding what he calls a "treasure trove of inspiration" for the final novel in his best-selling series. He's spent the last three weeks holed up in his office, typing away furiously at the story I can't wait to read.

When Jules heard that Finn was otherwise occupied, she jumped on the chance to come for a visit. And since it happened to coincide with some kind of falling out that she had with her boss, Jules hasn't been in any hurry to leave. With Jules here, I've taken a break to go adventuring all over the area, visited with Aunt Mairi, spent innumerable hours swimming in the lake, and roasting any kind of food we can think of over campfires in Finn's yard. All in all: it's been a pretty good two weeks of summer bliss.

Kind of idyllic, actually.

Apart from this hellish morning.

"How much do we have so far?" I call out.

Jules glances into the plastic bucket. "Maybe another half a cup and we'll be done?"

"Fucking hell." I move to find a better spot, crouching to locate the clusters of berries hidden on undersides of the low bushes.

"I really hope your boyfriend appreciates our sacrifice."

I silently agree. The thing is, this whole ordeal was inspired by a story Finn told me on our first date. Apparently he and his grandpa used to come to this very blueberry patch, fighting bugs and heat until they had enough wild blueberries to make a pie.

I thought it was a cute story.

Now I get why it was such a big deal: you actually have to be committed. I'm pretty sure we've picked thousands of tiny wild blueberries by this point, but the volume is growing at a snail's pace. Unlike the collection of mosquito bites across my body.

It's another twenty minutes before Jules declares our mission complete. We scramble through the thick underbrush just as the heavy clouds overhead release the rain that's been threatening us all morning.

"I'm going to itch for days," Jules complains, scratching furiously at a bite on her shoulder.

"You won't," I promise. "We have an herbal salve at home that works wonders."

"Sounds sketchy."

I roll my eyes. "You'll be changing your tune soon."

The steady rain turns into an all-out downpour and I turn the windshield wipers higher. Good thing I took Finn's truck, since my car's wipers barely remember what their job is. A thunderclap sounds just as we reach Finn's house and make a dead sprint for the door. Any part of me that wasn't soaked before certainly is now.

"Well, what a great outing you planned," Jules deadpans, checking her bedraggled appearance in the hall mirror.

"Super awesome," I reply. "Very successful."

"What was successful?" Finn calls from the kitchen. He's sitting at the island in the middle of the kitchen, cup of coffee in hand.

"We went on a forest outing," I inform him. I'm dripping from the rain and reek of bug spray, but that doesn't stop him from pulling me to his side when I lean in for a kiss.

"The bugs were bad," Jules adds, subtly tucking the bucket of blueberries out of sight.

He takes one look at the expressions on our faces and I can see him fighting a smirk. "Those little fuckers."

"Where's this herbal witch salve you promised?" Jules demands, scratching at her arm again.

"Bathroom cupboard. Little round tin." Her desperate dash towards the bathroom would be more funny, except that I, too, am absolutely miserable from the itching. "Bring it here when you're done, will you?"

"Want some coffee?" Finn asks, making to get up, but I wave him back.

"I'll get it. You sit."

"Awesome. I need it," he jokes, referencing the fact that he's literally been sitting on his ass all day every day, writing his book.

"How's your book going?" I ask, pouring some of the steaming black liquid into my cup.

"Well, that's the thing." He clears his throat.

"What thing?"

"I finished it."

It takes a moment for the words to register. "Like...all of it?"

He gives a small, almost shy smile. Like he doesn't quite believe it himself. "Yeah. Every last sentence. Minus copy edits, of course, and—"

I set down my coffee and throw myself into his arms. He catches me easily and tucks me to his chest, angling his head to capture my mouth with his.

"I couldn't have done it without you," he breathes, leaning his forehead against mine.

"You've been writing professionally for like a million years. Pretty sure your skills pulled through for you. I'm just wearing out your couch and distracting you." I give a little laugh. Sometimes Finn says lovely, wonderful things about me that are straight up not true. "But thank you for the sentiment."

"The sentiment?" He leans back, a bemused expression on his face. "I'd lost sight of every vision I had for this series. I'd lost faith in it, in my ability to tell the story. I was terrified that I'd be one of those authors who leaves his readers hanging until the day I die. But it was more than that. I'd lost sight of myself in the process. And then you walked in on me in a towel."

"I think we can forget about that part." I am still embarrassed by the reminder that I did, indeed, break into Finn's house that one winter night. It's definitely not nearly as funny as Finn likes to claim it is.

He smirks. "I like to think that it played a key role in our story. Love at first sight."

From the bathroom, Jules snorts loudly.

"It definitely didn't hurt." I run my hand down his chest, feeling those delicious abs through his t-shirt. Sometimes I still have a hard time thinking coherent thoughts this close to him. His hands tighten on my hips, and I'm fairly certain that both of us are only thinking about one thing now. At least, I am. And from the heat in Finn's eyes, I would bet good money that he's on the same page.

For Jules' sake, I push on. "Anyway, I'm your muse and you're the incredibly brilliant human who came up with the best fantasy romance series of our generation. Win-win."

"Win-win," he repeats, his thumb finding the skin just about my waistline. I shudder, shifting my hips towards him in response.

"How long until it works?" Jules comes out of the bathroom, rubbing a dab of salve onto her bug bites. "Also, please keep your clothes on."

I pull my hand back from where it was creeping lower on Finn's body. "A couple minutes, maybe?"

"I'm never going to stop itching," she mutters. "Do I hear celebrations are in order, my good man Finn?"

"Celebrations are always in order, my good woman Jules." Finn grins. I really, really adore how well he gets along with my sister.

Whereas I'm still somewhat in awe of his writing, Jules is not. She writes fae smut, and although she has yet to publish anything, she's passed a few chapters to Finn, insisting that he could benefit from expanding his reading material. Not only did he read what she sent him, but he's embraced several memorable quotes of hers and uses them ad nauseam. I haven't decided if it's funny or annoying.

"In that case, why don't you make yourself scarce. Rune and I have a surprise for you," Jules says, making a shoo-ing motion towards the back door.

"Can Rune make herself scarce with me?" he asks, waggling his brows suggestively.

"Absolutely not."

"Fine. I'll head into town and go pick up some groceries. It's been a hot minute since I made a good meal."

Jules and I are okay at cooking, but Finn is a veritable chef. I do miss his cooking. I'd lie if I said I wasn't disappointed to see him go, but I'm also very excited about the blueberry pie idea, so I just blow him a kiss and admire the definition of his shoulders in his tight t-shirt as he walks out the door.

"So, you're legit happy with him, huh?" Jules asks, helping me pull the ingredients out of the cupboard. She examines the recipe card and starts measuring out the ingredients for the pie crust.

"So much that it scares me," I admit. I used to think of myself as an optimist, but apparently that was only when life really sucked. Now that things are brightening up and I'm in a good place, I find myself constantly bracing for the other shoe to fall. Life can't always be this good.

"You have so many problems. Happiness isn't scary. I hope you're seeing a therapist."

"Actually, yeah, I am. It has been helping." I'm learning how to recognize when I'm projecting my own anxiety onto Finn. I trust him with all of my heart and soul, and he's only ever lived up to my expectations. Minus a couple inevitable arguments that predictably ended in the bedroom with apologies and a lot of delightful nakedness.

"Keep working at it, baby sister. While it was really kind of our parents to make sure we inherited something from them, I don't think that either of us is obliged to keep all of this anxiety and shit. Damn it," Jules coughs as a cloud of flour rises from the dough.

"Maybe mix it a little slower?" I suggest in a tone that's usually reserved for toddlers.

She gives me the middle finger.

"Anyway, to go back to your question: yes I'm happy. I adore Finn."

"Would you say you *love* him?"

"Yeah."

"Really?" Her eyes widen. Apparently she was not expecting that. "Did you tell him?"

"Maybe. And maybe he's also said it back." I wince. "Did we rush that part?"

"Why are you asking me?" Jules spares a glance from working with the dough. She's going above and beyond on this project, because she's cut out tiny leaves from the dough scraps and has scored them with her knife to give the impression of veins. So fancy.

"Because you are old and wise?"

"Rune, calm yourself. The L word is between you and Finn. You don't have to compare yourself to anyone else's relationship and honestly, it doesn't matter what I think. You two are on your own timeline. Trust yourself and what you're experiencing."

I nod, mixing the brown sugar and cardamom with the freshly-cleaned blueberries. It's a recipe that Finn got from a friend—a writer friend that he promised to introduce me to some day—and it is absolutely amazing. "Yeah okay, you're right. I'm just jumpy. Finn's been absent lately, preoccupied and I know it's because of his book but...well, anxiety."

"How about we calm down, eat some pie, and then I'll make

myself scarce so you can *reconnect* with Finn," Jules says, giving air quotes. I think she's talking about sex.

"I would not object to that."

"Good. The bottom crust is ready. Time for the filling."

I sit back with my coffee and watch as Jules creates a visual masterpiece with the top crust, layering leaves made of dough with little dough circles meant to emulate blueberries. It looks like a Minnesota forest by the time she's finished. I'm impressed.

While the pie bakes, I set the table with a dark blue dining cloth and stemmed water glasses. It looks pretty fancy, if I do say so myself. And by the time Finn returns nearly an hour later, the cooling pie has also been added to the table as the edible centerpiece.

"Something smells fucking amazing in here," he says.

"Happy finish-your-book party, fellow writer," Jules says, handing him one of the stemmed glasses filled with a champagne bottle that we found in the cupboard. "May your work bring you new, wild amounts of wealth."

Finn gives a short laugh and taps his glass against hers. "Cheers to that." He holds out an arm and I nestle into his side. It's summer, but he still smells deliciously of wood smoke.

"Where did you get the blueberries from?" he asks, correctly guessing the contents of the pie.

"Well, there's this really special spot out in the woods, halfway down an enormous cliff," I say. "Freaking hoards of mosquitos everywhere, but the blueberries are amazing."

"Which Rune would know, seeing as how she ate more than she picked," Jules scoffs.

Finn looks down at me. "The place I showed you? The spot I used to pick with my grandpa?"

"Yeah. I hope you don't mind that I went there without you. I just thought it would be nice, since you've been working so hard and—"

The rest of my words are swallowed by his kiss. The words were not important anyway, not compared to the way he's currently cupping my ass with his hand, pressing my hips up against him. I shudder and tighten my own hold on his biceps. I haven't kissed him nearly enough lately.

I will never kiss him enough.

"How about I just take my pie out onto the patio. Give you two your moment," Jules says.

I barely hear her. I'm too distracted by his clever fingers, which are sliding under my shirt, finding the swell of my breast. His tongue sweeps into my mouth and all I can think of is ripping off those pants of his. He presses into me until my back meets the wall and I feel every inch of his glorious, hard body. I run my hands up the contours of his muscled back.

"I do not deserve you," he murmurs against my neck.

"Because of blueberry pie?" I can't help the laugh that escapes my lips.

A corner of his mouth turns up. "Yes. And because of your thoughtfulness, your dedication, and your love that I don't even deserve a fraction of. In fact—"

He hesitates, looking at me with darkened eyes and a fervor that always makes me breathless, that usually ends up with some of the raunchiest and most intimate sex I've ever had in my life. My body shivers in anticipation.

"Well, fuck it. I saw this going differently in my mind," Finn says. "But I can't seem to stick to the script. Life with you is far more beautiful than anything I could make up in my head."

"Debatable," I murmur, because I am absolutely head-over-heels in love with this man's mind and imagination.

"Regardless, I have something for you."

Curious, I watch as he draws something from his right pocket. It appears to be a paper torn from a book, folded in origami style so that it makes a tiny envelope. I'm a little disconcerted at how his hand shakes when he hands the envelope to me.

"Open it," he prompts.

Slowly, carefully, to avoid tearing the paper, I undo the flap of the envelope. I recognize the words on the page—it's from my favorite scene in the first *Crimson and Roses* book, where the female character holds a knife to the love interest. It's the scene where the two express their love for the first time...all of which is followed by a very iconic bedroom scene.

It takes a moment for me to realize what's nestled inside the folded envelope. And when I do, I just...stare.

"Finn?" My voice sounds a little scared.

And then my heart stops completely as he slides to one knee.

"I have a confession to make," he says. "For the last two days, I haven't done much writing in my book. I've been watching YouTube videos, trying to learn how to make that fucking envelope."

Another laugh escapes me. This one sounds more like a sob.

Gently, he takes the envelope from my hand. Gently, he withdraws the item from inside: a silver ring with a rough-cut stone that I'm fairly certain is a diamond. It's the most exquisite ring that I've ever seen: a trail of the tiniest golden leaves wrap around a plain silver band; a single golden flower opens up around the rough-cut stone.

"I've spent my life hoping to find someone like you, Rune Dubois. And I've spent my entire adulthood up until this point trying to recreate this dream on paper. The way your eyes light up with so much kindness and hope and beauty—the way the very essence of your soul sings to mine. But nothing could have prepared me for *you*. You far outshine anything my mind could possibly conceive of on its own. Every moment with you is a treasure, and every new piece of you that I discover is an answer to the deepest questions of my soul."

My eyes blur at his words—and at the complete, utter sincerity that I see reflected back in those blue eyes of his. I wipe away the silly tear that escapes down my cheek.

"Every morning for the past seven months, I've woken up with you at my side," he continues, a slight tremor in his voice. "And I was wondering if perhaps you might be amenable to waking up at my side for the next seven months...and every morning after. Indefinitely. As my wife."

I try to sniffle back more tears, but they fall anyway. I was not expecting this. Wishing, dreaming? Of course...but I certainly did not think that Finn would have taken the time to plan such a thing, not while he working so hard on his novel. And certainly not when I've already been such a distraction, albeit a distraction that he hasn't seemed to mind too much, all things considered.

"It's a beautiful ring," I whisper, brushing my fingertip against the sparkling stone.

"Do you...want it?" He lifts one brow and I realize I have not given him my answer.

"Yes, Finn. My answer is yes."

A fierce, exultant smile flashes across his face as he takes my left hand and slides the ring on. It glimmers against my skin. It is delicate and fae-like. Absolutely my style—and his.

"I can't believe you just—are we engaged?" I ask. This is unreal.

"You said yes. I believe that means you're mine." His mouth quirks, but it sounds like a question.

"I am yours," I affirm, dropping onto my own knees, gripping his hands in mine. "And you're mine."

"I'm all fucking yours," he vows, pressing a kiss to the back of my hands. It feels like a sacred moment, far more so than any hour spent on a wooden bench on a Sunday morning.

"Do I want to know what's going on?" Jules' dry voice breaks into our cocoon of romance.

I flash her my left hand.

"Did you fucking get *engaged* in the three minutes I was outside stuffing my face with blueberry pie?" Jules demands, outrage plastered across her face.

"Yeah, I guess so," I say, shrugging one shoulder. "But you haven't missed out on everything. We'll probably invite you to the wedding."

"Probably," Finn echoes, rising to his feet and pulling me with him. "But please feel free to make yourself comfortable. There are a few things I need to *discuss* with Rune for the next hour or so." He doesn't bother to hide the meaningful look he gives to my breasts.

"Gross," says Jules. But when I walk past her, she gives me a smile and a wink. *Nice work,* she mouths.

I return her smile and leave her to entertain herself in Finn's beautiful woodland home. There are so many things that I'm sure we're about to discuss...starting with how badly I want him. Now and for the rest of our lives.

Did you enjoy this book?

Honest reviews of my books help bring them to the attention of other readers. If you've enjoyed this book, I would be so grateful if you could spend just five minutes leaving a review (it can be as short as you like) on Goodreads, Amazon, Instagram, or wherever you like to leave reviews.

Thanks so very much.
  Xx Rowan Eira

❄

Keep reading for a sneak peek of the next installment in the Birch Lake Romance Series...

Maple Leaves & Lattes: Chapter One

Jules

"You look like a mildly unhinged Viking shaman."

"I'm totally taking that as a compliment." I lean my hip against the side of my car, watching my cousin Courtney pin a pale green shawl over her rag-like dress.

I don't typically wear makeup, but today I went all-in: heavy eyeshadow, runes painted across my face, and false lashes. I even bought a silvery blonde wig, which I already know will be horrifically uncomfortable in the unseasonably warm September temperatures. But it's a titanium blonde that I wouldn't ever dare try to replicate on my own dark brown hair. Not because I don't *want* to try, but because I would likely become obsessed with it and titanium hair is *expensive*. I'd rather save my money for other things… like buying a wig and full Viking attire for this year's Renaissance faire.

"I think she looks amazing." My sister Rune immediately leaps to my defense, glaring daggers at Courtney, who merely yawns.

"I obviously meant it as a compliment," Courtney says. "Not everyone wants to be a pink-winged fairy princess."

"Hey, Ella is not here to defend herself," Rune objects. I turn my head so she doesn't see my grin. The last time we brought Ella to one of these, she did, indeed, dress in a glittery pink outfit that could be seen a mile away. Maybe even farther.

Despite the fact that Rune and I have been fantasy lovers since before I can remember, it's been a few years since we went to a Renaissance faire together. But ever since the Faelight Fantasy Ball we went to this past New Year's Eve—well, let's just say it's a new obsession of ours to dress up and hang out with cool people.

Surprisingly, our serious, lawyerly cousin Courtney wanted to come with today, cosplaying as the character Valerie from *The Princess Bride*. It's pretty good and there's a tiny part of me that wishes I came up with the idea instead.

But my outfit is cool, too, I guess.

"Are we ready to head in the gate?" I ask, surveying our group.

Rune links arms with Finn, the engagement ring on her left hand flashing in the afternoon sun. Show off.

"Let's go," she says. "And remember to pace yourselves: we're staying until the bonfire and dancing."

"You pace yourself," I retort. "I already know that I'm perfectly capable of spending three hours at a Renaissance faire. Especially one that has seventeen varieties of mead."

Rune tosses a grin of delight over her shoulder.

"I heard you're moving up north," Courtney says, falling into step with me as we approach the tall wooden palisade fence that marks the entrance to the faire.

"The rumors are true," I confirm. "I just signed the papers yesterday. I'm now the proud owner of a little home just outside of Birch Lake, Minnesota."

"You obviously do not need to put up with my prying, but what changed?" she presses. "Last I heard, you were dead set on spending the winter on a work trip in the Nordics."

"That was before my boss suggested a sleepover. The adult kind."

"Oh, shit."

"And he didn't think that *No* was an acceptable answer." I give an involuntary shudder. That was not a great day.

"*Shit*. You ok?"

I shrug. "It all went down in the middle of social hour. He was drunk and there were witnesses. So just the usual creepiness."

Courtney's sympathetic look tells me that she's not at all fooled by my bravado. Harassment is scarring, no matter the circumstances.

"Anyway," I say with a flick of my hand, as if it will brush away the memory. "I have some money saved up from the little fae smut stories that I've been selling, which sometimes pays for gas—" I give a short laugh. I'm not quite at Finn's level of income from my writing. "—as well as the coffee shop."

Courtney's brows rise. "The coffee shop? You're working at Up North Coffee? I thought I heard through the grapevine that Barb was closing it down at the end of the summer?"

I nod. "The grapevine was correct. I believe Barb has officially made the move to Duluth to be closer to her grandkids."

"I'm impressed that you know all of this. So did someone else buy it?" Courtney guesses, her eyes sparking. "Who?"

"Someone did buy it," Rune calls from ahead of us, a delighted grin on her face.

I shake my head at Rune. "I bought. Yeah, well, I kind of bought it."

Courtney blinks and stops walking entirely. "Come again?"

I try to keep a straight face, but it's hard. "You are looking at the proud new owner of Up North Coffee, the one and only coffee shop in Birch Lake, Minnesota."

"Jules, what the *actual* fuck!" Courtney punches me in the arm. "You are not serious."

My smirk stretches into an all out grin. I have been secretly dying to drop the news—only Rune, Finn, and Aunt Mairi have been in the know up until now. It seemed premature to talk about it before all the papers were signed. "I am, indeed. Barb did, in fact, close it down—there's a whole crapload of stuff that has to be fixed and sorted through—but I'm hoping to have the coffee shop opened back up in November, for sure in time for the holidays." I am hoping this timeline gives me enough time to fully settle into my new house.

"You sly little Viking fox. So basically what you're telling me is that you're extra invested in this new move."

"Basically." I'm a shitload of money invested in this move, that's for sure.

Courtney slides her arm around mine. "In that case, I feel like I should buy you a drink to celebrate your new life as a hermit in the wilderness and the new owner of Birch Lake's most popular gathering place."

"I won't say no."

The moment we're through the gates, Courtney and I make a beeline to the drinks tent. It's absolutely packed. The scent of body odor mixes with oiled leather and smoke, and it takes some effort to jostle our way to the bar.

"I'm going to spill all over the place," Courtney complains, throwing a hand out to protect her drink as the crowd pushes us a few steps back.

"I think there's seating outside in the back, let's check there." I spin just as another patron steps away from the bar with a full glass of beer. There's a split second of panicked realization before I collide, very solidly, into his side.

"Excuse me," I exclaim, trying—and failing—to avoid the

mead that sloshes over the side of the glass, all over the front of his shirt. *Shit*. "I am *so* sorry."

His arm shoots out to steady me. "No, that's my bad. You okay?"

I startle slightly at the deep voice. The *attractive* deep voice. My eyes drag upwards, past muscled thighs, a belt of woven blue and yellow, a white tunic with Viking-style embroidery around the neckline. His outfit is on par, and I am very distracted by the detail for a long moment, until I notice the dark brown eyes, intent and staring back at me from a wildly good-looking face.

It's the kind of face that a girl is morally obliged to take a second and third look at.

My first coherent thought is that this is certainly, definitely the most handsome man I've ever seen in my life. His hair is dark chestnut brown; his eyes even darker in a deeply tanned face. He's got a strong, straight nose and a thin mouth that's half-twisted into a smile, tugging at the thick stubble on his face. There are black runes painted across the bridge of his nose, trailing across his strong cheekbones. I resist the urge to fiddle with the strands of my fake silver hair.

"You okay?" the Viking man repeats.

I give myself a mental shake. "Yes, sorry. I didn't see you until it was too late."

He glances over my head, then takes me by the elbow and shuffles me to the side, making room for a harried, red-faced waitress to scoot by with a full tray of beers.

"I really am sorry," I repeat, noting the dark stain on the front of his tunic that either came from his drink or mine. Possibly both.

He glances down dismissively. "It will dry. The bigger problem seems to be that you've lost a good amount of your drink. Here, let me get you another."

"I ran into you!" I object. "And I still have most of my mead." Or half, maybe. I spilled a lot.

"You really turning down a free drink?"

A few butterflies come to life in my stomach at the slight smile, the spark of warmth in his eyes.

"When you put it that way, I don't want to be rude." I smile back, lingering by his side until he hands me a new cup, filled to the brim. There's something vaguely familiar about the lines of his nose, the twinkle of his eyes, but I can't for the life of me figure out who he reminds me of. A distant memory, not sure from where or when. That's the problem with traveling so much: people come in and out of your life on a regular basis.

"Shall we?" He motions with his free hand towards the exit. It's much easier to walk with his tall frame blocking the crowd from trampling me.

I am thinking of something suitably clever to say, hoping that maybe he will stay and flirt for a while, but I only get as far as a mumbled repeat of my gratitude before he excuses himself.

"I wish I had time to stay, play the protector and ensure that your drink remains un-jostled, but alas: I am already behind schedule. Maybe I'll see you around." He winks and is gone.

The moment he's out of sight, Courtney emerges out of nowhere with a very interesting look on her face. "Who was that?"

"A stranger."

"A stranger," she repeats, incredulous. "You looked like you wanted to eat his face.."

"It's a nice face," I say simply, nudging her with my elbow as we follow the path to the square where the shops are set up. Rune and Finn are waiting for us by a sparkling fountain.

"Where did you disappear to?" Rune demands. "I needed your help deciding on a new necklace." She holds up a pearly, opaque crystal on a rose gold chain. "Finn had to come to the rescue."

"Jules stumbled upon some eye candy," Courtney announces.

I pinch her elbow. She jabs a finger into my ribs with a surprising amount of strength.

Rune practically melts with excitement. "Please tell me it was the dude with wings from the Faelight Fantasy Ball. I swear, if he reappears in your life, it is Fate literally telling you two to get married."

"It was not." I snort at her disappointed expression.

"This one was very easy on the eyes," Courtney continues with the barest hint of a smirk. I don't know why she's finding so much entertainment in all of this.

"You gonna write him into your next story?" Finn gives me the side eye.

"You know what, maybe I will," I retort back. But actually...I probably will. I'll write about those arms of his, if nothing else. Because I bet his thighs are equally strong and—well, *you* know. My heroine will thank me for it.

"Oh look, more tents. Let's go see what people are selling," I say to redirect everyone's attention away from me and the mostly insignificant encounter. It works...kind of.

There are crystals, jewelry, tooled leather backpacks, indie fantasy authors, and a wide array of other handmade, medieval-inspired goods. I want to buy it all, and start with a red toadstool tote bag that I use to stash it all in.

"You look like you're preparing to go on a quest," Courtney comments as I slide a pair of vibrant blue hand-knit mittens into my leather satchel with tiny toadstool mushrooms etched all over it.

"I can't stop."

"Do you want accountability or would you prefer that I merely smile indulgently at the fact you just paid eighty dollars for a crystal dragon statue?"

"Not sure yet. Ask me when I've spent another fifty, please."

"Fine, but remember to save some of that seemingly endless cash for food. Not to mention another stop at the next mead tent."

"Ugh, fine." I force myself to set down a hand-tooled leather belt, giving the booth owner an apologetic smile as Courtney drags me away.

We pack as much as we can into our day at the faire, all following the typical themed entertainments: axe throwing, horseback riding, and cheering on the jousting competitions. The sun is falling low in the sky when we make our way back to the tent full of adult beverages and medieval-themed food. Since we're staying the night at a hotel across the parking lot, it doesn't take a lot of convincing to partake in a round of shots before moving onto our mixed drinks of choice. My fingertips are numb and there's a slight stagger to Finn's step when we manage to find an open bench in the outdoor theatre where a trio of fire breathers are in the midst of doing some really complicated-looking tricks.

"I don't understand how they do that," Courtney says, eyes narrowed critically.

"Liquid fuel," Rune murmurs.

"They literally spit it out to get the plume of flame like that," I add.

"Why am I not surprised that both of you are familiar with how to do this?" Her eyes do not leave the fire breathers.

Mine don't, either. The two men are shirtless, their chiseled bodies glistening with sweat in a way that borders on the obscene. They both have muscles that I didn't even know could exist on a human being. The woman wears a leather wrapped crop top, her long black hair tied back in a braid that falls to her waist. They are perfectly synced with one another, alternating physical acrobatics with fire breathing feats.

The finale of the performance comes in the form of a man

(shirtless, of course), who's juggling freaking balls of fire. I'm so entranced with his skill—and the way his muscles glisten in the flickering light—that it takes far too long for me to realize who it is.

I lean into Rune. "That's the man I saw earlier. The guy juggling fire."

When she turns to me, it's with absolute heart eyes. "Oooh, he's something."

"Excuse me?" Finn says mildly.

"I'm gaping at Jules' new love interest, the fire juggler," Rune explains ridiculously.

I groan inwardly as Finn very obviously looks, then does a double take. "Impressive. Nice choice, Jules."

"You two can just stop."

"You gonna make a move?"

"I don't make moves," I inform him. "I indulge in momentary opportunities. Besides, I thought you wanted me to find my happily-ever-after with wing dude from the Faelight Fantasy Ball?" I raise a brow, referencing the man who I danced with all evening this past New Year's Eve at the bookish ball. He was a fabulous dancer and served as a very pleasant distraction for the evening, while Rune was busy getting romanced by Finn.

"Even I'm bored of bringing him up," Rune complains. "I wish you'd just gotten his phone number so I could properly check him out."

"Believe me, he was nothing compared to this one," I assure her, which may or may not be true, as I have only outward appearances to go off. I don't have a lot of interest in long term relationships—total opposite of Rune, who's dreamed of a cozy home with her true love her entire life—but I am one hundred percent for experiencing some facets of romance every now and again. The physical kind, if you catch my drift.

Despite the fact that evening is well underway, the temperature is still far too warm for comfort.

"You ready to dump that fake head of hair yet?" Courtney says on my other side, eyeing the sweat trickling down from beneath my wig.

"It's staying." I grit my teeth. "I'd look ridiculous if I had to carry it around in my arms."

"Not to mention your real hair is probably super flat at this point. Total turnoff for the Viking dude."

"I don't know, maybe he'd be into that kind of thing."

"You drinking any more tonight?"

"Probably one more." I lightly run my finger down my face. "I can still feel my nose." That's my gauge of sobriety: when my nose goes numb, I have to stop.

"That's so weird, but whatever."

The torches around the area are lit, and a trio of musicians start playing some medieval-sounding songs that are somehow both calming and incentivizing for us to dance.

"This feels strangely familiar." Rune looks up at Finn adoringly as she tugs on his hand.

"Except there's no doubt how the evening will end." He waggles his brows suggestively.

Courtney and I look at each other and gag.

"I need another shot to handle them." I'm already striding for the bar.

"Get me a water, would you? I just got an email from the firm...freaking new stack of paperwork might need some attention." Courtney stops at one of the benches, looking up from her phone with a grimace.

"Seriously? It's the weekend."

"We have a tight deadline. I don't really have a choice."

Well, that's lame. After getting her water, I take a large cup of mead to last me the rest of the evening.

Usually I'm the mother hen. The one who plans, monitors sobriety levels, makes sure everyone is accounted for. But we're all staying at the hotel across the parking lot—well within walking distance. Rune and Finn have each others' backs. Courtney looks like she's one email away from leaving altogether.

Which leaves me free to do as I please.

And when my eyes meet those of a certain well-dressed Viking, I know exactly how I want to spend the rest of my own evening. With one sip of mead for courage, I make my way over to the large oak tree, where he's standing.

www.ingramcontent.com/pod-product-compliance
Ingram Content Group UK Ltd.
Pitfield, Milton Keynes, MK11 3LW, UK
UKHW030837171224
452675UK00005B/565